EASY POUR

EASY POUR

Happy Reading!

Joel M. Roberts

Copyright © 2007 by Joel M. Roberts.

Library of Congress Control Number: 2007900684
ISBN: Hardcover 978-1-4257-5421-1
Softcover 978-1-4257-5420-4

All rights reserved. No part of this book may be reproduced or transmitted in any form or by any means, electronic or mechanical, including photocopying, recording, or by any information storage and retrieval system, without permission in writing from the copyright owner.

This is a work of fiction. Names, characters, places and incidents either are the product of the author's imagination or are used fictitiously, and any resemblance to any actual persons, living or dead, events, or locales is entirely coincidental.

This book was printed in the United States of America.

To order additional copies of this book, contact:
Xlibris Corporation
1-888-795-4274
www.Xlibris.com
Orders@Xlibris.com
28173

Dedication

For my parents—my first storytellers,
and my greatest source of inspiration as time went by

Introduction By The Author

I WROTE THE first paragraphs of what would become *Easy Pour* in the summer of 2002. It started out as a whimsical exercise to capture on paper something funny I had witnessed before it left me, but when five pages turned into twenty, I realized it was meant to be something more.

Six months later, I had a first draft. I took a deep breath, held it, went back to the first page, and dismantled it. Over the next four years, I did this no less than a dozen times. I guess I wanted to get the novel 'right'. In due time, however, I realized that every word I added or deleted put distance between me and the spirit of the original 2002 draft. So at the risk of losing it all, I decided to call it quits.

Sometimes you have to wait for the questions to pour out of you before can you stop, look inside, and see the answers.

August

Chapter One

I SHOULD LET the phone ring. Twenty bucks it's my dad, calling to bust my chops about sleeping in. He's the only person I know who gets up before the rooster has had a chance to sneak out the backdoor of the henhouse. I'm surprised he waited this long to call. The old man is losing his touch.

I toss the sheets aside and plop my feet on the floor. I hear the phone, but I don't remember where I left it. A few months ago I decided to get with the times and buy a cordless, and cordless phones are made to be lost.

There it is.

'Rise and shine!' a voice chimes, too cheery and high-pitched to be my father's.

'Hoo dis?'

'Paul.'

I can feel the sandbags hanging from my eyelids. 'Paul?'

'The Paul from last night,' the mystery voice clarifies.

'Oh right, *the fat cow*. So what does Moo-Moo want this morning?'

'Sorry if I woke you up.'

'No problem,' I snap sarcastically. 'I've been up for hours.'

I was having a fabulous dream. Steaming lust baths and slow-trickling, tickling waterfalls, gold coin towers, sparkling jewels and decorative statuettes. Servants standing by, all the flooding fornications of life dammed and pooled into my basin of desire. And Paul had to go and ruin it.

'Just wake up, huh?' Paul says, finally catching on. 'My bad.'

My bad. People think they can say and do whatever they want as long as they pretend to take responsibility for it.

'So what's wrong?' I ask, walking back to my bed. I sit down, the wood cracks the air, and the springs do their job.

'I'm fine.'

'Then what do you want?' I ask. I'm thinking maybe someone died. Maybe the police tossed Paul into jail, and he just used his one phone call on the one person who couldn't post bail for a hobo. Or maybe he awoke in a hotel room, handcuffed to a headboard. Poor kid had to use his tongue to dial a rotary phone. I bet he's swimming in a pool of Polaroids right now, freaking out at the sight of sex instruments scattered about on the floor.

'What are you doing?' Paul asks.

'Sleeping. What are you doing?'

'You first.'

'Huh?'

'Who's on first?'

'Paul, it's too early for the Abbott and Costello routine.'

'¿Que?'

'I'm hanging up if you don't put someone on the phone who speaks English.' My major was English.

'¿No habla Español?'

Ugh.

* * *

I'm back in bed, the covers pulled up to my chin. The heavy curtain pulled across the window is keeping out the light, leaving the apartment gray and vague. A shadow on the ceiling is bobbing up and down, revealing and obscuring and revealing a thin crack that zigzags a lightning pattern from my bed to the window wall. The air conditioner is rattling nuts-and-bolts and whipping up the bottom of the window curtain. My plant is swaying to the rhythm of the breeze. You water the thing, and its leaves turn yellow and brown and fall off. You don't water it, and its leaves turn yellow and brown and fall off. I've given up.

Paul and I agreed to meet up at his West 82 Street apartment, head to Central Park, and then grab some lunch. I hung up, ending the most retarded telephone call ever connected in the history of telecommunications. I pushed for 1 PM, but we settled on 12 PM, which is about two hours from now, meaning I should leave in about an hour because the subway has been a mess all week. A few nights ago I transferred to an express train at Grand Central to jet up to East 86 Street. I overshot my destination and found myself in Spanish Harlem, just a stone's throw away from the Bronx. I waited twenty minutes in the 125 Street Station before a downtown train arrived, only to space out and miss Grand Central on the pendulum swing back down the island. I got off and hit up the uptown track again, this time at Union Square. It took me almost an hour to go forty blocks. I could have walked that distance in less time.

The City subway system can be a nightmare if you don't know your way around. I love watching tourists in the subway stations, walking up and down platforms, running into MetroCard-only entrances, desperately looking for a way out. They are so clueless. They don't understand the concept of local and express trains, and they have no clue what to make of the different circles on subway maps. And forget about the signs that hang above the platforms and mark where certain trains stop during off-peak hours. Hell, it took me four years to realize that peak hour signs are a crock of shit.

The real problem, I think, is the layout of the subway stations. It is very easy to get lost in those labyrinths. Even Theseus would lose his way in them. I imagine he would put in a similar effort but also settle for defeat, sit down, have a smoke, and wait for the Minotaur to come and get him because, holy mother of mercy, the MTA decided a long time ago that it did not want its customers leaving. The City modeled its bigger stations like Fulton Street and Union Square after casinos, with signs pointing people in the direction of absolutely nowhere, ensuring the impossibility of escape. Walk down either station's stairs to a turnstile, swipe your MetroCard, walk down a ramp or another set of stairs, head straight for an indefinite amount of time, head up a set of stairs, swing around a corner and on to an overpass, drop back down a set of stairs, walk across a platform and back up a set of stairs, and you'll find yourself in the middle of Hades. You can't find an exit to save your life. Find a map and start staring. Retrace your steps, like the mouse after that piece of cheese on the side of a cereal box.

I almost feel sorry for tourists. *Almost.* As far as I'm concerned, learning the subway system is a rite of passage. You need to figure it out on your own. I did. The first couple of months I lived in the City, I rode half the length of Manhattan on a local train because I was afraid that I might accidentally jump on a connecting train and end up somewhere in Upstate New York. I suffered because I was slow to make a mistake. And making mistakes is a crucial part of learning how to get around the city. And like me, most people in the city can't afford a car in the City and *must* use public transportation. Insurance costs are steep, and you have to pay for parking because space on the street is an urban myth. Put insurance and parking together, and throw in the NYPD's annual parking ticket quota, and the bill will give a small studio a run for its money. You could taxi everywhere, but that can get very expensive very quickly.

I had a ride once. Back in high school. My father pointed to two tin cans parked in the lot of Rudy's Used Cars, and after some deliberation I went with the baby blue Cavalier over the shit-brown Cutlass, a decision entirely based on aesthetics. My dad fronted the cash for the bucket of bolts, and shortly thereafter I began my weekly installment payments.

The car you drove in high school made a very clear statement to the world: 'Take a good look, fuckers. This is how much my parents spoil my ass.' In my hometown of Billington, Massachusetts, rich parents threw platinum keys at their children and begged their forgiveness for never being home. Upper-middle class parents flirted with mortgage default to buy birthday rides that no seventeen year old should ever have. 'True' middle class parents might buy their children a used car, but if they were slippery like my father, they'd blackmail you with a square-shaped hat, a black apron, and grease-stained indignation fifteen to twenty hours a week. Last, and certainly least, low-income parents told their children that they were shit out of luck. Poor kids either rode bikes or yellow buses or jumped the tax bracket by making a friend with a car.

The exception to these socioeconomic vehicular rules was the BMW-driving John Peters, who successfully sued a miniature golf course for the negligent upkeep of its dogleg sixteenth green, which somehow gave way to his featherweight frame and broke his leg. But John's middle-class fortune was find-a-Honus-Wagner-baseball-card-in-your-radiator rare. Normally, it only took a few minutes in the student parking lot to separate out the young regal—who, by the way, only went to public school after they had flunked out of a dozen private schools—from the children whose parents slaved to keep up with the Joneses and the children whose parents laughed at the thought of making such a nitwit attempt.

Rich and poor get together on just two occasions in Billington, and if you happen to be an Atheist or an Agnostic, then you can strike church from the list. The survivor is the annual Fourth of July Parade, when kids will jump on candy thrown by local politicians riding floats like good soldiers falling on live grenades. After collecting the handouts, the children will get together to trade sweets, but their socially conscious parents always slap away their hands, reminding them, 'You know you shouldn't take candy from strangers!' *Psst, our kids seem to like each other. Send me a prospectus, and we'll talk on Monday.*

Now a car widower living in the City, I stand next to the richest of the rich and the poorest of the poor, holding the same stainless steel pole, balancing in the same buckling subway car. But that doesn't make the City a socialist society. You need only look at the other means by which people broadcast their capitalist purchasing power and help divide a land of eight million. Take a look at a man's shoes and the travel accessory he is carrying (briefcase, *Wall Street Journal*, box of Popeye's chicken) and maybe note his A to B stations, and you will quickly figure out whether he chose heat over electricity last month or whether he is sucking it up for the day because his Lexus is in the shop having tinted windows installed.

My arm hurts. I must have banged it last night. When, I don't remember. I had dinner in Soho, drinks at Smokey's, and a slice of pepperoni at a pizza joint with a 25-cent rodeo bull guarding the door. I don't remember hitting it at all. Maybe it's a sleep injury. Maybe I've taken up sleepwalking. How the deuce would I know?

I slip out of bed and make my way to the bathroom. I pick up a pair of pants, a few socks, and a V-neck shirt off the floor as I go. My apartment is a trailer park after a tornado touchdown, a highway behind a leaking retail truck, a dump.

I lived my freshman and sophomore years in NYU housing, the first year in a residential complex on Bleecker Street near most of the main school buildings and the second year in a high-rise located downtown in the Financial District. I had roommates, and they didn't care too much for my messiness. Nobody likes a roommate who turns communal living space into a personal laundry hamper. So after two years of moans and rants, I started looking for a place of my own. The summer after my sophomore year, I discovered an ad in the Village Voice for a COZY EAST VILLAGE STUDIO. I checked out the place less than an hour later. The broker was a fast-talking jackass with monstrous sideburns. 'The rent isn't negotiable,' the cock told me about a hundred times. I joked about being out of shape, telling him that the four flights of stairs leading up to the apartment might give me a heart attack. Not amused, the broker ended the chaffer by reducing the massive fee he commanded for taking three minutes out of his day to show me the place. We shook on it. We were both suckers.

My apartment is nothing special. It is definitely 'cozy'—NYC Apartment Ad speak for 'tiny'—but it has enough room for my rickety pine dresser, matching desk, and the small sofa chair I rescued off a sidewalk before a rainstorm. The location isn't great. The closest subway stop is Astor Place, which is on the local 6 line, so getting around is a major pain in the ass. I could have moved to Jersey or Long Island and saved some cash, but the commute would take forever and kill what little social life I have during the week. The local amenities are pretty good though. There are a lot of bars in the neighborhood, which makes walking home late at night drunk a cinch. Plus, there's a laundromat around the corner. It's dumpy and overrun with blue lint clumps that breadcrumb out the door, but it has a working change machine that spits out five quarters for every dollar that you feed it, and that's clutch. All and all, my over-sized closet has worked out quite well, so I renewed my lease a year ago, and it's up for renewal again in a week or so. I'm way too lazy to look for anything better or cheaper anyway.

I'm in the bathroom now, looking at myself in the mirror. I look tired. Drinking contests will do that to you. This mirror is filthy.

Guys can be neat, but they always dirty. I'm a guy, and I'm not neat, but I run a tight ship in the bathroom. Pimple juice streaks on the medicine cabinet mirror, crotch hairs curled upward ass-expectantly on the toilet bowl seat, dried globs of birdshit-looking toothpaste checkering the sink—it all grosses me out and into cleaning mode. Once a week I say a quick prayer, take a deep breath, and head into the holiest of holies to take care of holy hell business with a bowl scrubber, a jug of pine-scented ammonia, and a pair of latex gloves. When I'm done, I could eat off the floor. But that is the extent of my weekly cleaning routine. Most everything else runs on a monthly or quarterly cycle.

I leave the bathroom, head to the kitchen, pour myself a glass of OJ, and then sit in my fuzzy red chair. Black remote control in hand, glasses on, what's on the tube? *Click.*

Car commercial. Strike a deal with Saudi Arabia and keep Ford's vision alive. American cars are the worst on the market. *Click.* Cartoons. LOVE THEM. My first TV programs. Hours well spent in bunny pajamas with a bowl of Cheerios. I love the little ditty about car models predicted to grace the showrooms in the not-so-distant Twenty First Century. Cars spawn wings, fold up into travel briefcases, and go Red October. I like the older cartoons too, with their crude squiggles and poorly dubbed voice-overs. Those classics oozed hyper-nationalistic ideals and patriotic propaganda. They were meant to keep kids off of Communism. Of course, times have changed. Children are not so easily manipulated now. The little shavers need the subliminal shit—flash, flash, *KILL, KILL, KILL. KILL, KILL, KILL. KILL. KILL. KILL KILL. PEOPLE. KILL, KILL, KILL. KILL, KILL, KILL, KILL. KILL. KILL. KILL. KILL. EVERYONE.* Japanimation has it down pretty good. *Click.*

News. Great. Blah blah blah. Everyone is up in arms about the schizoids carving up their neighbors with steak knives. Everyone except me. I feel nothing in the morning. I guess my compassion warms as the day progresses. What's that? Ah, a late evening burglary gone awry. On such and such street in *da Bronx*. One person shot, said to be in critical condition. Eyewitnesses questioned, few leads. More information will be released once it is received. Stay tuned, we'll be right back. *Click.*

I grab the shirt that I picked up off the floor earlier, note the stench that I should have handled last night with Febreeze, and stuff it between my back and the chair. I could put it on, but right now my arms are unwilling to lift any higher than my shoulders, and that's a pre-requisite for putting it on. Back to the TV. Holy moly, this guy is wearing the biggest hourglasses that I have ever seen. It looks like someone painted a gigantic infinity symbol around his eyes. The preacher boy is talking about Corinthians. I always forget whether that book is in the Old Testament or New Testament. Old, I think. Flash the prayer hotline number on the screen. Call now and save your soul with a generous contribution. The man hasn't seen my checkbook. Fifty-six lousy cents in bank interest the last month. *Click.*

Back to cartoons. The Tasmanian Devil spins up the screen. A rumble of heavy bass starts in through the wall, and the ache in my head syncopates to match the thumping spondees. My neighbors must be up. The assholes in 4D blast their hi-fi, woofer-enhanced music sound system, and I can't do a damn thing about it. We share a wall, and the walls in this apartment are paper-thin. The racket seeps in through the wall by diffusion.

The Saturday morning hangover aside, I don't have a problem with people playing the radio loud. Hell, I play my radio loud. If you are preparing for a night on the town, I say crank it. And I'd rather hear anything than a duet between a squeaky bed and a wife crying middle-aged discontentment. But I have a problem with people blasting music to psych up for a fight.

My neighbors argue so loudly that the entire block becomes a spectator. They yell in sloppy Spanglish. If I figure out what the issues are, then I feel like I've accomplished something. Usually all I hear is guttural bursts from a pair of automatic weapons. They make Charlie Brown's teacher and the bumbling phony from that Dick Tracy movie sound like a pair of talented orators. The Spanish-to-English book helps a little. 'Food not on plate for Maurice with drugs and the police' is a start. But then the words get longer and louder, I can't keep up. Who is this guy Maurice? The pimp who beat the shit out of Holden Caulfield? Who threw the red shirt in with the whites? Huh?

Click. Click. Their quarrels are usually brief—ten or fifteen minutes, maybe—but they can raise the rafters. I've heard blood-curdling screams and hair-blowing roars. I've hear the sound of glass breaking. I've heard thunks and clunks. At times I feel guilty listening in like a voyeur, but then again this is my apartment. I shouldn't have to buy earplugs because my neighbors are a bunch of lunatics.

My OJ is done. Elmer Fudd's incorrigible stupidity has grown tiresome. I kill the television. I need a shower.

* * *

My orangutan arms droop to my feet, and my thighs bulge unnaturally to fit the implants inserted underneath the skin. I am a jungle bodybuilder. My knob has been reduced to a purple dot. I belong in a video with Puffy, or P. Diddy, or whatever the hell he goes by now.

I'm awake now, staring into the shower faucet head. I think I'm still drunk. My head is fluttering in and out like a flustered bat unable to get comfortable in a crowded belfry.

Left knob, right knob. Step left, step right. Green towel.

I walk out of the bathroom, grab my desk chair, and carry it over to the window. I step up, slide the curtain to one side. I crank the handle, opening the window on its characteristic tilt. I readjust my footing and take a quick peek outside. The window looks out to the ass of a building. Not much going on over there, not that there ever is. At night I sometimes catch a flicker of a light in a window, but I've never heard so much as a peep. The building may be abandoned for all I know, save one unwilling tenant, a firefly who lost his way during a yearly migration.

I step off the chair and walk to my desk. I take a thoughtful minute to pick out a CD, wanting something a bit rocking, and finally decide on a classic in *Let it Bleed*. I drop it into my boom box. My half toga comes undone, revealing my rusted pink machinery. PLAY. Sing it. YOU CAN'T, ALWAYS GET, WHAT YOU WANT. BUT IF YOU TRY SOMETIMES, YOU JUST MIGHT FIND, YOU JUST MIGHT FIND!

Chapter Two

TO GET TO Paul's place, do I take the L train to the 2, or do I hit up the 4 and then cross over at Grand Central?

Decisions Decisions Decisions. I've spent the greater part of my brief existence dissecting the pros and cons of each and every decision that I deem to be of the slightest shred of importance, but I still haven't found any rhyme or reason to the process. A decision can take a lifetime to make, or it can be made without batting an eye. It can involve brainwork that is pointed or arbitrary, scattered or collective, logical or emotional. But when all's said and done, a decision is basically a choice blindly dug out of a pocket and thrown up into the air to be tossed around by the wind.

When it comes to making decisions, every individual has a unique set of beliefs, motives, interests, and experiences from which decisions are constructed, deconstructed, and reconstructed—tools of evaluation, if you will. This huge collection of variables can make the process overwhelming. And to make matters worse, people are not mind readers. I can only speculate as to the manner in which words are strung together in the head of another. And when a decision is put to the explanatory melody of words, I can't help but suspect that the original composition has been lost somewhere in the synaptic exchange, rendering translation impossible; thus, when asked the question 'Why do something else?', too often I gong a 'I dunno' response and follow up with a question of my own: 'Why not?'

I think it has to do with familiarity. The familiar is comforting. It's easy. It makes sense. I see no reason to switch to real mayonnaise when I grew up on Miracle Whip and never had a problem with it. I blindly trust my barber. I'm sold on Charmin toilet paper.

And I think you have to include denial in there as well. People don't want to admit that they could be unhappy with the boring mediocrity of who they are, where they are, and what they have. Denial is a sweet ingestible that we all consume like a druggie would a narcotic, an Ithaca-bound sailor the fruit of a lotus flower, a junk food addict a bag of Double-Stuffed Oreos. We think that Denial will harmlessly pass through our systems, but we are wrong. With Denial's consumption comes a contamination, a virus that infects and reproduces. Before long the animal starts to eat away at us from the inside, shitting out byproducts of incorrigibility and indifference.

Take an extreme example: my father. When my Mom died, my Dad lost his spirit and his grip on the rational sequence of events. When he looked to Reason to explain my mom's passing and was shown an empty solution set, he decided that his own life was a confused equation. And by denying the natural order of her death and his continued life, my father effectively locked himself in a pitch-black cell with his past and present.

Although my father had no say in my mom's death, he did have a say in how he would live the rest of his life, and he chose to allow the past to live his life for him. A year past, and then another. Denial crippled my father's soul. His body followed suit, his right leg stopped cooperating with his left, and now my father walks with a limp. He refuses to seek medical attention from doctors. He calls them 'HMO ball jugglers'.

Maybe he's too old to change. I can't expect to know anything about that. I welcome change. The world changes, I might as well change too. *Step into a river, and you will begin to understand that change is forever.* It's not sexy, but it has punch. I found that proverb in a hundred-dollar anthology that an English professor forced me to buy. I've used the saying a number of times to rescue arguments weak on the merits. Unfortunately, I usually botch the word order and come out sounding like Dennis Miller on a good hair day.

Like any living and breathing river, I need to change. Circumstances demand it. I left a sleepy New England town and moved to the City that never sleeps for a reason. I got out of Billington because I had to. For me, living there was like watching grass grow for a cow. By graduation, I had consumed everything Billington, est. 1825, would dare hold out in its palm to me. And serving up one large supermarket, a coffee shop that ran out of its best doughnuts by 7 AM, two fast-food troughs, and a handful of mom-and-pop restaurants, the town didn't feed all that well. In due time the town turned parasitic, and I became the unwilling host. The town mutated into a ravenous fungus, growing on and replacing what was once ME, inc. 1980.

Moving out of Billington was a bold move by local standards. The town never lent itself to moving around much. Part of its charm resided in its never-changing, never-moving Puritan way of life. People moved there to raise families, and they never left. Their children might go away to college, get married, but they always returned to Billington to breed. They were like salmon. I called them 'The Townies'.

Jim Reynolds is a member of the newest generation of Townies. I sat next to him in Spanish. I have no idea why the senior was allowed to sit in with the same freshman students he brutalized between periods. I guess Jim needed the class to fulfill the school's foreign language requirement.

Jim was an angst-ridden teen, 'a troubled young man', the school guidance counselor likely said. A real dickhead, if you ask me. He was a post-modern bully, and by that I mean he wasn't too proud to revisit time-tested methods of kid torture—toilet-dunking, locker-stuffing, ear-clapping.

Busy with his own sense of hall monitor duty, Jim didn't have time to be a student. He spent most of Spanish class playing with his graphing calculator or picking his ear with a Number 2 pencil. He'd count down the Top Ten Jim Reynolds Plays of the Week, which were cut and pasted from footage of Friday night's football game. 'I told that motherfucker that I'd send him to the sidelines all fucked up, and that's just what happened,' he bragged to us one Monday morning. 'You should have seen me work on him,' he sneered. 'I sent him to the hospital with his teeth kicked in.'

I never missed a football game, so I knew that Jim was full of shit. The kid didn't have a speck of athletic talent. But big-sized linemen don't come around often in a small town, so the coaches spared Jim from the preseason cuts, threw him a helmet, and set him free every Friday night to run around like a dummy tackling moron.

Jim worked weekends and vacation breaks for his father, a heavy-set man with a poorly kept white beard and an obnoxious wardrobe of Hawaiian shirts. Jim Senior religiously attended Junior's football games, and I remember watching him stand by the sideline ropes with a monstrous camcorder in his hand, cursing what he always considered to be the worst officiating he had ever seen in his life. He owned a construction company that specialized in building concrete foundations, and his company spearheaded the construction of the Billington Elementary School's wing extension, which commenced right after I had left the prison for good. Every now and then I hear his name come up in conversation. I'm sure he still spends the day running his shitty company and supervising his dumb ass son. At night, I bet the two review tapes of Jim's football games.

My classmates feared Jim, so they would always nod and kiss his ass whenever he talked about how he was God's gift to high school football. I always wanted to make a crack, tell Jim to hold out on Texas A&M until a Firebird and a John Deere mower showed up on his front lawn, but I kept my mouth shut. Jim never thought twice about throwing a fist through the face of a wise guy.

Jim lived and died for the town's sporting events, fuck gossip, and thirty-pack parties. Jim was older and ran with a jock crowd, and on the account of him being a real bastard, I never talked to the kid. Fraternization would have suggested that the cock and I were friends anyway. Outside of the school's walls, I only ran into Jim at church.

My father had never been a religious man, but after my parents married, my dad became a devout Baptist on paper. He let my mom pick the church, and he let her pick the décor. When you walked from room to room in my house, my mom's religious 'decorations' worked like a Big Brother surveillance system, an interconnected eye that zoomed in and out of the occupant's transparent soul, watching 24-7, waiting for you to screw something up. I once pointed out this spooky Mona Lisa quality to my mom, but she responded by giving the voyeur a nickname—'Jesus Cam'. After she died, my dad took down The Lord's Prayer but insisted that I continue to make the weekly pilgrimage to church, perhaps thinking that I was better suited than he to carry on my mother's pious torch. Someone needs to be in with the Big Man, so my dad arranged to have the Whitmans swing by our house every Sunday morning at 9:30.

I would wake early, wiggle into an itchy TJ Max suit, clip on a tie, and look for my dress shoes. A loud horn would signal that the Whitmans had arrived, and I'd lumber out of the house with a Pop Tart and squish into the back seat with Kyle and Frankie. The ride to church was only ten minutes long, but it always seemed like the longest ten minutes of my life. I'm not sure what their parents feed them, but Kyle and Frankie terminally reeked most foul. One whiff of them, and I'd drop the Pop Tart in my lap, plug my nose with my tie, and sip air through my mouth like one of those kisser fishes. Thinking his sons' flatulence hilarious, Mr. Whitman would set the car into a deliberate swerve. With the vehicle washing the road and my seatbelt neighbors beefing the letters of the Alphabet, I must have had some sort of Superman stomach to keep those two, Pop Tart bites down in the second half of my digestive tract. Meanwhile, Mrs. Whitman—small, feeble, very much inconsequential—would never be of any help. She'd smile and keep conspiratorially quiet. She always brought baked beans to the church's semiannual potluck dinners. Obviously, she pulled out her Crock Pot more often than a few times a year to pork up her magical fruit.

Later in the day I would tell my Dad about the debacle. He always enjoyed a good bowel roast. 'Deal with it', he'd tell me. 'You have to learn how to breath your nose,' he'd explain, sounding a lot like that swimming instructor who almost drowned me in the town pool when I was six years old. I found his logic flawed, certainly hypocritical, because my father snored like crazy on his favorite chair. One night I even used my Fisher Price recorder to collect evidence. The following morning, I played him the tape. He accused me of tampering with the audio.

It was years before I took back my Sunday mornings. Admittedly, my delay in sedition was odd. Kids and religion mix like water and oil. But there was a reason for my inaction. I developed a crush on my

Sunday school teacher—a red-haired, community college honey with shimmering green eyes—and call me a dreamer, but I suspected that she had a thing for pizza-faced boys with short-term memories. She was always flapping those ungodly emeralds at me, helping me out whenever I got hung up around Ezekiel or the Second Thessalonians during my recitation of the sixty-six books. With her introduction into the church picture, I decided that the wet dream material was worth the temporary asphyxiation.

When we arrived at the church, Jim's family would already be there, sitting front and center in the cushioned pews, which were implicitly reserved for the elderly and the handicapped, just like the seats next to the sliding doors in these City subway cars. I'd spot Jim up front, picking his ear with a collection envelope he had folded into a point. I was always amazed that he had managed to get past the double oak doors without being immediately consumed by the flaming wrath of God. Hand me over The Book of Life and skip to the letter R. No 'Reynolds' there. Yank the gold lever and drop the heavenly napalm. Investigators arrive on the scene and sift through the wreckage. The rookie finds a burnt ear with an envelope lodged in its canal. And I'm off in the corner, giggling like a little school girl.

From my seat I'd watch parents greet friends with droopy hugs and limp handshakes. Their children would be scampering around the church like hamsters in a maze. Meanwhile, the pump organist would be blasting away a traditional hymn that never seemed to end—Wesley or Luther perhaps, but with the infectious-to-unnerving quality of McCartney's 'Hey Jude' or hokey camp songs that only work when a cabin sings them in a round.

During the service, I kept a close eye on Jim. He'd always appear genuinely disinterested in the proceedings. In between ear picks, he'd turn around in his seat and make obscene gestures at people. I couldn't help but wonder when God's hard love would make an appearance. The inaction upstairs troubled me. Why is God always leaving it up to his Earthly constituents to run ad hoc missions to set these fuckers straight? What about the chosen ones? What about Reverend Coles? If I were him, I would have stashed a handgun behind the lectern and taken aim at Jim after I had asked the congregation to bow its heads to pray.

When I was a senior in high school, Jim turned 21 and began attending O'Reilly's, The Townies' cross-denominational church. Occasionally, I would drift by the pub in my car and spot Reynolds sitting at a booth, drinking beer and talking to his Townie friends and naturally picking that God-forsaken ear. Something tells me that I'm cursed to remember him that way for the rest of my life: all bad, no good, just a bully, a jerk, a liar, a drunk, and a compulsive ear picker.

In some ways Jim became my personal cautionary tale. The idea of one day joining him at O'Reilly's frightened me, and this fear convinced me to extend my college search well beyond Billington's reach. I bombarded New York, North Carolina, and California with applications, picked up a safety in New Hampshire, and penciled in local UMass Amherst just to keep my father happy. Acceptance letters trickled in that spring from nearby state and private colleges, followed by a fluke nod from the University of North Carolina. Weeks later NYU humored me with an invitation, erasing my fear of spending the next four years as a powder blue 'Tar Heel'. When I showed my Dad my one-way bus ticket to New York, he raised a heavy eyebrow and squeezed my shoulder. 'Greenwich Village is not a charming ski village full of reindeer and trinket stores,' he told me, 'but I think you should pack your heavy coat anyway.'

Time may pass, but people like Jim Reynolds don't change with its passing because they are too damn sentimental when it comes to their traveling lanes. When I stepped foot into NYU's Office of Undergraduate Admissions on Washington Square North, I thought about Jim and all the other Billington schmucks I had left behind, and had a good laugh. But less than three months later, I skipped my last class before the Thanksgiving break, flagged a Greyhound bus speeding out of Penn Station, popped a couple of Dramamine, followed trusty Polaris north on Interstate 91 to Springfield, jumped out of its sketchy bus terminal and into the passenger seat of my father's Blazer, rumbled across the Billington town border and past

O'Reilly's on our way back to the house, and wouldn't you know it, Jim Reynolds hadn't moved an inch.

I guess my best friends Paul and Julian had a similar fear. A year after I left for NYU, Paul and Julian packed their things, kissed their mother Annie goodbye, and moved to the City.

Of course, with my East Village apartment located in the middle of nowhere, Paul might as well still live in freakin' Billington.

THE NEXT STOP WILL BE FORTY SECOND STREET!

Chapter Three

PAUL'S APARTMENT IS amazing: two huge bedrooms, a renovated bathroom, a modern kitchen with new appliances, a large common room drenched in sunlight, and a balcony that overlooks a convenience store with no lock on its door. I hate Paul for having this apartment. Right now, jealousy is my favorite sin. You get one.

Paul got lucky. At Colombia he met this guy, Tom, whose uncle owned a brownstone on West 82 Street. Several years ago, Tom's uncle entrusted a family friend to keep up the place after he decided to move to posh Westchester County. The trustee took the top floor of that building off the market and began leasing its four apartments to friends and family members at dirt-cheap rates. When Tom decided to attend Columbia, he simply took up residence in one of the apartments on West 82 Street.

Tom's roommate moved out of the apartment in July, leaving one of the bedrooms vacant. By that time, Paul had moved into residential mode because he was still without a home for the coming school year, which would be starting in just a few weeks. Luckily, he crossed paths with Tom at a party. A week later, Paul packed his things, rented a U-Haul, and moved thirty blocks south to the heart of City snobbery.

On Paul's nightstand is a picture frame—one of those free-standing, three-sided ones. The photo in the middle is a shot of Julian and me during last year's trip to Atlantic City. I came home with all my money that weekend, and I almost picked up a waitress from Caesar's Palace. It was a great trip. Breaking even at the blackjack table is a financial success, but a peck on the cheek is a sexual triumph.

We can't be more than ten years old in the picture on the left. All smiles from the boys.

When we were kids, Paul, Paul's brother Julian, and I did everything together. We were inseparable. We played the same games, watched the same television shows, consulted the same handbook of mischief. We were our very own subspecies. In the summer we would spend a lot of time behind their house, throwing rocks at squirrels, flicking ants into spider webs, and using jars to collect the tadpoles that swum around in the nearby stream. Sometimes we would get into the garage, find an empty aluminum can and dump anything and everything we could get our hands on into it, and then flood the backyard with the concoction. Our goal was to combat the growing expansion of year-round condos put up by Manifest-Destined ant colonies. We were sick fuckers that way, but at least we released our energy in a controlled environment. Better to kill a few ants at home then to show up with sawed-off shotguns and smoke grenades at school.

On the weekends, we'd ride our bikes down Main Street to Anthony's Corner Store and buy handfuls of Topps and Donruss baseball card packs. After exchanging doubles and hurling chunky gum wads at passing cars, we'd jump back on our bikes and connect a mile down the road to the dirt trail that outlined the Pincaugwait Reservoir. The tree cover broke up along the water at Silver Rock, where we would take turns jumping twenty-feet down into the water the town pumped out to thirsty Bostonians. When the designated lookout became spooked, we would jump back on our choppers and flee the scene before the cops could do anything cop-like about our illegal swimming activity.

Back at Paul and Julian's house, we would often host Nintendo RBI baseball game tournaments. For a long time Hilton Myers dominated with small ball and the St. Louis Cardinals, using the speed of Vince Coleman and Ozzie Smith to compensate for the team's serious lack of power hitting, save Jack Clark. In the spring of 1992, my Minnesota Twins triumphed when Kirby Puckett scooted a ninth-inning dribbler past Hilton's infielder, down along the third base line and to the left outfield wall. A computer glitch suddenly kicked in, and the baseball became stuck inside the outfield wall. As Hilton's outfielder ran helplessly in place next to the swallowed ball, three of my runners kept pace with the hustling Kirby and crossed home plate. Game, set, match. Head to the box score. Within seconds, system controllers and game cases were flying. Ten minutes later, Hilton's mother pounded down the basement stairs, wrestled the aluminum bat out of her son's hand, and dragged him upstairs by the ear, bringing to a close the Hilton Myers RBI Tournament Dynasty.

The photo on the right is a picture of Paul with my father's camcorder. We often borrowed it to film comedy sketches and movies. We called our production company 'Apple Lane Productions'. In one sketch, Julian played a shopping cart bum who accosted patrons in the supermarket parking lot by insisting that they accept our free handouts, which happened to be uncooked hamburger patties. I had one recurring character, 'Mr. McDick', who would walk up to the drive-thru window of McDonald's and harass the pimply kid wearing the headset.

In a separate frame on Paul's dresser is a black-and-white picture of Annie—Paul and Julian's mom—standing on the beach, holding up a pail and shovel.

My mom and Annie met each other when they were students at Amherst College and quickly became good friends. A year later, Annie graduated and moved to Boston. Two years later, my mom graduated, married my dad a few months later, and then they moved to Billington. Annie moved to the neighborhood four or five years later when Paul and Julian, like me, were getting old enough to start school. Annie and my mom rekindled their friendship, and Paul, Julian, and I started to spend a lot of time together. Annie regularly brought the three of us to the park and town pool, probably to make up for all the time my stay-at-home mom watched us everyday after school. Annie was a single, working mom—not an easy task, considering we lived in a His-and-Hers t-shirt community less than keen on having an unmarried 'whore' raise two 'bastard' children. I have no idea what happened to Paul and Julian's dad, and I'm pretty sure Paul and Julian don't know either, and I think Annie prefers to keep it that way.

My mom died the day I turned ten. A year later, to the day, my grandmother died. After that, I began taking the whole matter of blowing out candles very seriously. I stopped making wishes and started saying prayers. I didn't want to be responsible for systematically wiping out the whole fucking bloodline simply because I had to grow up.

Annie stepped in and took care of me. I guess she couldn't bear the thought of me facing the audience of childhood without a female figure waiting backstage, clapping on my lackluster school concerts. My father slowly gave way to Annie's growing presence in my life, stepping aside, lingering more in the shadows and perhaps preferring it that way. He adopted a hands-off, micromanager's approach to parenting. He'd return from work, interrupt Nickelodeon to ask me what I wanted for dinner, watch me watch the television a bit, squeeze my shoulder, and walk into the study adjacent to the TV room. Sitting in his black leather recliner, my father would reach over to set the needle on a record, and with a bottle of Jim Beam in hand, challenge the London Philharmonic to a couple of movements in double time. Needless to say, I ate a lot of peanut butter and fluff sandwiches when I was kid because they were easy to make.

Annie was an interesting surrogate mother. Like the better Disney movies, Annie could be both an adult and a child at the same time. She sat right up there with my father, Yogi Berra, Oscar Wilde, and Jesus of Nazareth in the running for the greatest human enigma of all time. 'You know, life and Monopoly are a lot alike', Annie once told me during a game of Monopoly that was not going my way. 'They last about the same amount of time, and both can make you angry for no good reason.' I didn't understand the whole of it, but I nodded my head and handed over Reading Railroad. In this way Annie had a power over me—a blind amenability, a prepackaged mixture of trust and ignorance. I left it to faith that Annie knew what she was talking about because I sure didn't.

Annie decided that her children were the artsy type, and her desire to produce the next da Vinci or Beethoven would take on curious forms. She'd have us dress up in these ridiculous outfits—old athletic jerseys, grass-stained baseball pants, and red firemen bump caps—and tell us to 'Take up arms!' That would be our verbal cue, our starting gun—'Take arms!' With that, we'd run around the house and hunt down our favorite Play Skool instruments. Before long, we'd be participating in yet another one of her silly musical extravaganzas.

It would begin with Paul, Julian, and I assembling at the base of the stairs leading to the bedrooms on the second floor. Marching in single file, we'd erupt into the living room, banging and blowing on our instruments, creating the most awful raucous you could imagine.

For years the living room, or 'Old Living Room', had this revolting, yellow-green wall-to-wall. The carpeting was of the thick, curly warehouse variety that instantly absorbed any sort of liquid spilled on it. Sometime in high school a man with a Swedish Chef mustache came to the house, knocked down a wall on the ground floor, and created the 'New Living Room'. At that point the living room became the 'Old Living Room' or the 'Guest Room', and Annie began using it to steer away guests from the ugly carpeting and our embarrassing improprieties.

Meandering past furniture, we'd leave the Old Living Room with the ugly carpeting and enter the dining room. Annie would be there, shouting, 'Left! Left! Left, Right, Left!', like a drill sergeant fucked up on a happy drug. Seconds later, we would burst into Paul and Julian's bedroom, the future site of the New Living Room, do an about-face, and then head back the way we came. This loop usually continued until one of us started a brawl by turning the back of someone's head into a makeshift percussion instrument.

I guess the chore of entertaining little ones year after year would make anyone start to think that the floors were made of lava. Annie had a buoyant sense of humor, eccentric but fun. I admired her for it. I always thought that one boy was all that *two* parents could possibly handle; nonetheless, Annie retained a stunning degree of patience when faced with the perils of our trifecta. She never lost her temper. But she was always firm with us. The love was gentle, but it was also hard. It made sense, now that I think of it. She worked, and still works, as a criminal psychologist, and she spends all day analyzing and counseling the so-called 'fuck-ups of the world'. I used to ask Annie what her job was, and she would simply reply, 'I work with adults your age.' At the time I didn't understand what she meant, but now I think I get why there was no clear dichotomy between Annie at work and Annie at home.

When we were old enough to pick up a razor, and when 'poop' became 'shit' and Kevin Simon swore he spotted Santa Claus in the parking lot of the town's only adult entertainment store, Annie started to talk more candidly about her profession. Her stories were often shocking, and always entertaining. She talked about drug remission and rebirth, domestic abuse, and demonic behavior. She talked about listening, digging below the surface of people, and listening some more. She told us that human behavior is about motivation and repetition. She talked about decoding codeless lives. She seemed perfect for the job. Annie always had a gift for knowing what people need to hear and when they need to hear it.

Annie was your friend first, your parent second. And this didn't change as we got older. When she heard the echoes of our underage drinking, Annie sought to contain them, not muffle them. She drove us to parties so that we wouldn't drive ourselves. She developed a pre-game lecture that wrapped with, 'Stay smart, stay in control, and stay together.' She met our friends' parents. One year she even hosted a post-prom party at her house. If she couldn't control our *what*, then she found a way to be a part of our *how*.

'Ahem!' I look up and see Paul peeking around the corner. 'I'm almost ready.'

'That was the longest shower ever,' I tell him.

'Can you grab the Frisbee?' He sticks out his arm and points. 'I think it's under the bed somewhere.'

'You get it.'

'I'm not exactly decent.' He holds out his towel.

'Just stay put.'

Paul laughs and disappears. I slide off the bed, fold back the blue comforter, and take a look in the space between the floor and box spring. A dust bunny rolls away from me like a tumbleweed. I spot the Frisbee, grab it and let go of the comforter. I stand up and hear something fall to the floor. I look down. A small green book, the size of a small photo album, stares up at me, waiting for an apology. I take it in my hand. It feels hard and gritty on my fingers, like fine sandpaper wrapped around a block of wood. I take a seat on the bed, shoot a look out to the bathroom, and turn to a page somewhere in the middle half of the book. The pages are white, the lines are blue, the ink black. I read:

> Bring the day
> Bring the night
> Bring the women
> Bring what might
> Be the last thing in the world that brings me to the place where I feel whole.

> This is me
> This is you
> This is what you see
> This is what you knew me to be
> Though I am not, though I feel it, sometimes.

'You ready?' I hear.

'Yeah,' I answer, slapping the book closed and quickly putting it on the nightstand.

'Find the Frisbee?' Paul asks, appearing in the doorway. His body sparkles in the natural light. Rays fan out like a solicitous peacock, radiant, God-like, all NBC sacrilege. I expect a hymn from choir singers. I wonder where they are. They must be stuck in traffic on the Cross Bronx Expressway.

'Right where you said it was,' I reply, picking it up off the comforter to show him.

'Cool.'

I give him a very deliberate look-over. 'Where are you going, a photo shoot?'

'Gotta look good,' he answers, holding up a black comb in his hand.

'Not on my account I hope.'

'Gotta look good for the world,' he elucidates, running the comb through his hair and sprouting a cowlick the size of a cornstalk. 'I used

a different conditioner today,' he explains. 'I needed something to give me a little more shine and volume, and I got that and a whollotah confidence.'
 'Whatever you say, Fabio.'
 'Your sass could use a little work today.'
 'So could your masculinity.'
 'Have you seen my keys by any chance?'
 'Nope.'
 Paul makes a quick pass of the room. He's so neat that he's disorganized. He arranges, rearranges, and rearranges, and then he can't remember where he put anything. He's like a squirrel. Stash a nut here, stash a nut there, find a nut nowhere.
 Paul looks at me, and my hands go belly-up. He falls into a Groucho Marx routine, palms up and flat on an invisible wall. 'Sorry man,' I tell him, 'but I think they're gone.'
 Paul grunts, falling out of character. He shakes his head and then leaves the room. 'Here they are!' I hear him say. 'I don't know what is wrong with me today. I couldn't find my wallet earlier.'
 'Must be your thieving troll again,' I joke.
 'Could be,' he answers, remerging. 'So, are you ready to go?'
 'Right behind you.' I grab the Frisbee and take one last look at the green book before following Paul out of the bedroom.

Chapter Four

A BASEBALL CRACKS the pavement, scoots behind a couple holding hands, and bounces against a plastic fence guarding a patch of dirt. A boy runs toward us, his arm stretched out high above his head, his hand devoured by a brown animal. The victim splits Paul and me, collects the ball in his glove, and hustles back to the grass.

'This is exactly what I'm talking about,' Paul says, directing his attention to the boy, who winds up, kicks, and delivers a low ball to his squatting catcher. 'People look out for themselves, not others.'

Paul looks back to me. I give my kudos. Only he could work a kid at play into an intellectual necropsy on the decaying corpse of City manners. Give that man an honorary degree in Recondite Learning and the scorn of the island.

We resume our walk. The August skies are clear, and the sun is beating down on us. Unlike the past couple of days, today is arguably pleasant, governed by a dry heat that is apparently filling in for its moist cousin. It's a good day to leave the lifeless company of an air conditioner and join Frisbee addicts, bicyclists, in-line skaters, sunbathers, stroller screamers, freeloaders, solicitors, lost tourists, book lovers, and failed products of the City's Little League farm system at the one cool spot in the outdoor City: The Park.

In theory, The Park is everything that the parched weary would want in an urban oasis: trees and grass, sky and water, and space. It is the moisturizing answer to the dehydrating elements of normal City life. Unfortunately, its medicinal qualities tend to attract billions of tourists, who mix horribly with the natives.

It's easy to rope off those who live in the City from those who are only in on a visit. Everything is faster for the locals. They always have a place to be, a person to meet, or an appointment to keep. Their lives are controlled by daily planners and Palm Pilots and the two hands that spin around on their wrists. Meanwhile, tourists drop their bags and jaws, suddenly aware that they are in for big, BIG trouble—no red lights, only greens and yellows, and the yellows are awfully green, per ease of order ROY G BIV. Confused and scared, the foreigners unnecessarily complicate the City's simple grid system and drop into an endless series of figure eights. The result is a hairy highway of City activity, where visiting slow pokes clog up the passing lane in front of native lead foots.

It's impossible to keep track of all the traffic, but you try anyhow. Even within the 'friendly' confines of The Park, you can't let down your guard, or at least you shouldn't. A smart City traveler grows mirrors on the side of his head. Drop your guard even for a moment, and someone will bump you, pickpocket you, or harass you with foot examination flyers or some other crap.

'Everyone thinks they are hot shit in this city,' Paul starts up again. 'City life encourages that kind of thinking.'

I nod. The city is filled with egocentrics, elitists, and self-appointed gods. It's a model anti-society society. Here, FUCK YOU, I'M A NEW YORKER is not just an attitude; it's a credo, and the only viable one out there. City folk live their lives on their own terms, keeping their pink-dyed heads of hair down while they walk, mindfully but reluctantly looking out for other people's toes. They rarely engage their neighbors or dry cleaners in conversation, just as their neighbors and dry cleaners rarely engage them in conversation. They have separate minds for matters, and they mind their own damn business.

The killer is, the system works. The City didn't become what it is today because people stop at turnstiles and revolving doors and wave a dozen people through.

'Is it a bad thing to live for yourself?' I ask, playing the Devil's advocate.

Paul squints out the light pouring in on our location. 'If we're talking about Homo Economicus living,' he points out scholarly.

Paul has a habit of using sixty-four thousand dollar words when he is making a point. It has nothing to do with intellectual superiority or pride or mental illness; the boy is just too freakin' smart. His vocabulary is thick with the words I once borrowed from a thesaurus to jazz up my school papers. Shelley exhumed the bodies of Nietzsche and Socrates, plucked the DNA from their flesh-stripped bones, added Annie's difficult and oft-misunderstood abstruseness, and engineered Paul in a test tube. Few minds rival the one trapped in Paul's skull. Very few.

'If people were perfectly rational,' Paul says, 'they would only help themselves. They wouldn't donate money to charities or pull people from burning buildings.' He starts his hands moving, which can only mean he's digging in for the long haul. 'True Homo Economicus believers make decisions solely based on how they themselves will be affected.'

'Selfish living,' I say, untying his esoteric knots.

Paul bobs his head and tells me that I am partially correct. I lengthen my stride to pull even with him.

'The problem is, we are social animals,' Paul explains, chugging along, 'and we can't subsist alone. We rely on other people.'

'OK, then a person who believes in Homo Eck-oh-nom—'

'*Economicus.*'

'This person still helps people if it improves his situation, right?'

'That's right,' Paul replies, waggling the Frisbee in his hand, 'but helping other people would be totally coincidental. It would be an accidental byproduct of self-interested behavior.'

'Why?'

'Because if the Homo Economicus model holds up, people always behave the same way. Experts get together, solve problems, and streamline the decision making process by making everything mathematical. They give us the facts necessary to make decisions and actions automatic. And the facts say, do what is best for you, not the other guy.'

'I see.'

'But this conflicts with human nature. Our intellect serves our emotions, not the other way around. We use our intellect to fulfill or deny these emotional demands. We are not simple mathematical creatures. We are driven by what we don't know, not what we do know.'

'We are driven by ignorance?' I ask, pushing along the discussion.

'Yes, in part,' Paul answers, 'but that's not the point. Self-interest carries with it social isolation, which is not only harmful to the soul but also to the wallet. Self-interest leads to self-regression *and* dehumanization.'

'But we still try to be what we're not,' I suggest.

'And maybe what we can't be,' he adds.

I grab the Frisbee in Paul's hand and take it away easily. The wuss doesn't put up much of a fight. 'I guess money isn't the most important thing in life,' I tell him.

'Try explaining that to the world,' Paul answers, clenching his jaw.

We walk in silence for a moment, pissed off at the world. I look up and see tops of residential buildings hanging over the tree line of Central Park West. The idea of living in a tower made of steel, glass, and brick never crossed my mind until I moved to the City, and even though I have lived here now for four years, the thought remains entirely repugnant.

To live in this City, you have to work, and work often, and this means you spend a lot of time indoors. You commute in congested subway boxcars or buses, work all day in some derivative of a high-rise building, whisk up and down on metal strings, and speed-walk three blocks to your office on concrete streets cracked more by air hammers than by nature. The workday ends well after six o'clock, and you race home to an apartment to fight off the justified attacks of a paper-trained pup. You throw your mail on a table, click on your TV, head to the kitchen, fill a dirty glass with water, and drown the plants sitting on your window sill. Of course few people buy 'real' plants in the City. They prefer pint-sized cacti, aloe growers, and bamboo shoots—knockoff plants that are easy to obtain and manage and, thus, are perfectly suited for self-involved New Yorkers with neither the time nor the inclination to care for anything else. Want a garden? Well, according to the local green thumbs, all you need is an asparagus-looking stalk, a hollow container, a few aquarium rocks, and *Presto!*, you have a backyard.

With more time on my hands lately, I've made an effort to get outdoors. Unfortunately, when you live in the City, the closest you come to nature is Central Park. Pretty fucking sad, I must say. It was meant to be an escape from the City, but herds of people have turned it into just another overcrowded neighborhood. Over the course of three centuries, this tiny island and its parks have grown to become the home of more than a million and a half people. Double that number between the hours of 9 AM and 5 PM, and it is easy to see why horizontal space is but a memory in this city and why rats, pigeons, and cockroaches must stick together to preserve their way of life.

A bird swoops past us and latches to a tree branch. The bird twitters happily and stretches out in the sunlight.

'Awesome day today,' I say, breaking our somber moods.

'It is,' Paul replies.

'Where are we headed?' I ask.

'How about The Lawn?'

I knew he'd say that. You can always find good action at The Lawn. It's sort of like the common room for the Park.

Paul steps to the side to avoid a woman zooming by us on a bicycle. A Yorkshire terrier pops its head out of the duffel bag stuffed in the bike's rear basket and starts barking at us. The little ones all have Napoleon Syndrome.

He reminds me of the mutt Paul, Julian, and I encountered at the bus stop one afternoon. We were maybe eight or nine at the time. The school bus pulled away, and there he was, barking at us as if he had been doing that all day long. I remember thinking it strange to see such a small dog out and about in Billington because locals take great pride in their practicality, and toy dogs are anything but practical. Those who actually owned poodles and other growth-stunted dogs kept them hidden in their houses. They didn't want their trophies smudged, and they didn't want their children eaten by Labrador Retrievers. City folk are just the opposite. They parade their neatly clipped doggies around town as if they were celebrities.

I checked the tangled mess for a collar, but I couldn't find an ID, so we continued walking to my house. The dog stayed right with us, or so Paul would later tell Annie when she returned home from work. Of course, he conveniently left out the part about how the spazz would have followed a Quaker Chewy granola bar over the side of a cliff.

Back home, Julian and I watched TV as Paul played outside with his new sidekick. Occasionally, I popped my head out the front door and watched the two fight over a shoelace or sleeve. When Annie returned home from work, the drama began. 'Mommy can't handle any more dogs,' she calmly explained to Paul. 'Frosty and Dallas are enough work as it is.' After a heated exchange, Paul ran inside my house, reappearing a minute later with a candy bar in his hand. He tried to lure the dog inside with it, but the pooch didn't have a sweet tooth and scampered off, crossing the street and vanishing into the woods. No hug, no goodbye. Better to hit the road than put up with this shit, the dog probably thought.

Paul and I continue to walk along the West Drive bicycle path, passing crowded tennis courts as we go. Farther back in the woods is the Jackie Onassis Reservoir. My ex-girlfriend ran on the dirt track there religiously, and sometimes I joined her to score brownie points. I could keep pace with her for awhile, but a cramp up around the second or third mile always killed my desire to continue, at which I point I would walk back to East 90 Street where we had started, sit on some stairs, and watch the activity along Museum Mile. After Heather finished her mini-marathon, she would come and find me, we'd head home, play patty-cake in the shower for a little bit, cook dinner, and then sit down at the kitchen table for the most uncomfortable half hour of the day.

Heather was a rabid anorexic. On many occasions I tried to help her by subtly testing her convictions. I slapped Skippy Peanut Butter on celery sticks and put them on her plate when she wasn't looking, but she ignored them and pick undressed ones out of the community plate. I slowly drenched a steak with A-1 sauce in front of her face, but she didn't bat an eye. One time I even suggested that we swing by the yellow double arch and pick up a McFlurry for dessert. Give into the temptation to release yourself from the temptation, I argued.

Experience it once, and then you can leave the experience behind you. But Heather didn't bite the Oscar Wilde aphorism and asked me to bring something back for her. She would eat it 'later'.

Despite my efforts, Heather never budged. And why would she? People who don't want to change are never willing to listen. And with Heather—she had the moxie of a druggie who had stumbled upon an extended speed high. In her eyes, when the world looked wafer thin, the world was right. But unlike a *real* drug addict, Heather was never sober, making it altogether impossible to run an effective intervention. I never caught Heather eating peanut butter or chocolate or fast food or anything unhealthy or anything in large quantities. I guess the chocolate fasting would have explained her voracious sex drive, but whatever, her life was hell, so Heather made mine hell, and that was no good. I can't stand people who think that you should suffer because they are suffering. That sort of thinking is sick and twisted.

Having survived Heather and her emaciated cobra pin moves, I feel pretty good about my infrequent aerobic extension outside the perimeter of a Sealy Posturpedic wrestling mat. I'm a fitness minimalist and proud of it. I drop by the gym once or twice a week to lift weights, but that's about it. And I could care less about my diet. My menu of beer and junk food hasn't changed in four years. And just for kicks, I started smoking my sophomore year of college. Ironically, I picked up my nicotine lust from my neat freak ex-roommates. Apparently, giant plumes of smoke, pot shavings and failed rolling papers make for clean, tidy living but not a sink full of dirty dishes. Who knew?

There are days when I sit in my fuzzy red chair, watching TV, gorging myself with Ben and Jerry's Chocolate Chip Cookie Dough, and imagine what I might look like if I could only motivate. I'm not fat, but it wouldn't hurt to lose a few pounds to loosen up my snug 34 pant waist. I thought about joining one of those City soccer leagues, and maybe one day I will, but until then I say bring on the pudge, my scruffy Green Mountain boys.

It is freakin' hot out today. I should have brought suntan lotion with me. I spent the last weekend of June holed up in my apartment, lubing myself with a humongous bottle of aloe gel and cursing my existence because I had cooked earlier that week on Coney Island. I took off my t-shirt the minute I stepped foot off the cool boardwalk on to the hot sand. A few corn dogs and beers later, I decided to lay down for a *siesta*. I awoke sometime later a fried cracker, lightly salted.

A short bridge takes us over the 85 Street transverse. Cars zoom in and out from underneath us, pushing air in and out of the tunnel, whipping up a roar that makes me wonder whether giant seashells are pressed against my ears. I can feel the heat rising up from below. Fingers of steam are rolling off the heads of the people jogging ahead of us.

'HOW'S THE JOB SEARCH GOING?' Paul asks, almost screaming it to me.

'NOT GOOD,' I answer. My response is a vulgar understatement, considering my job search has now entered the fourth month. I've dealt with inept staffing agency after inept staffing agency, posted my resume on dozens of websites, even dragged my ass out to two job fairs and a handful of informational sessions. All of this, and no dice.

'ANY INTERVIEWS?' Paul asks.

'I DID HAVE THIS ONE INTERVIEW—'

'What am I, *deaf?*' Paul asks, his voice returning to a normal conversational level. The drone of engine noise trails off as we leave the transverse behind us. He smirks. Jerk.

'I had an interview in Brooklyn last Tuesday,' I tell him in my best outdoor-indoor voice. 'It was for an assistant position in loans administration. A good one too.'

'Really?'

'If you like photocopying.'

'Sounds important.'

'I doubt you need a college degree to work the Xerox machine.'

'Sounds complicated.'

Paul is only serious when he wants to be. He's just like his brother.

'For some reason everyone seems to think they need a college graduate to do monkey work,' I tell him. 'Like a piece of paper somehow proves that I'm a somebody.'

Paul grabs my shoulders. 'Hey! Look at me!' He gives me a shake. 'Look at me! You *are* a somebody.'

'If I don't get the job, then I don't get the job,' I say, undoing his hold. 'The job wasn't anything to write home about.'

A man and a woman scream by us on bikes. These yuppy couples are all over the park. They live in apartments on Central Park West and collect six digits from their abysmal jobs. They can't stand each other, but the need to succeed keeps them together. Their sedulous efforts—bike rides, dinner dates with colleagues—keep their marriage intact, but barely. He's cheated twice and she's on the brink of philandering herself. A few months ago, they started talking about having children to spice up their cornmeal lives. His parents own a couple of Lightnings that sit in a Connecticut lake marina and collect dust. Her parents spend two months a year in North Carolina or Florida, hopping from one private golf course to the next, unable to spend their retirement nest fast enough. Mr. and Mrs. Manners show up once a year so that the six of them can survive together in the same lake house for the length of Labor Day Weekend.

'That sucks you haven't found anything yet,' Paul says empathically.

'I know,' I reply. 'I'm tired of living paycheck to paycheck.'

'The plight of the pauper.'

'Living on Fluffernutters and pasta from a box,' I add.

'It could be a lot worse,' Paul says, ever the optimist. 'My friend Jason took a job two months ago doing M&A work. He's working sixteen-hour days now. He absolutely hates it. He's always complaining that he has no life.'

I hear a powerful whistle. A white husky the size of a polar bear marches forward, dragging his overwhelmed owner. Physical comedy: the only breed of inter-species comedy.

We slow to a crawl. Paul looks down to his blinding-white sneakers. 'Maybe you should do something else,' he says.

'Like what?'

'You could apply for one of those teaching programs like AmeriCorps. Or you could join the PeaceCorps or Habitat for Humanity. You know, *build a house*.' He puts his thought into visual enactment, rounding out a pantomimed sawing motion with a *swish-swish*. 'Leave the Northeast for awhile,' he continues, 'travel the globe, live it up. You ever think about doing that?'

'Sometimes.'

Two women decked out in matching yellow t-shirts and black spandex shorts power-walk past us. 'Is there anything stopping you?' Paul asks. He comes to a stop, looks sideways, left then right. I follow his example and look for traffic. No answers there. Wait, this isn't a street.

'Besides cash?' I ask.

'Besides cash,' Paul answers, resuming the stride he had put on hiatus.

'No.'

'OK, so do something.'

'Like what?'

'I don't know!' He throws up his hands in surrender. 'Anything! Like you said, nothing is stopping you.'

'Nothing but you, *big boy*.'

Paul stops dead in his tracks.

'Oh stop it!' I jibe. I give him gold, and he cringes. 'You know you'd miss our late nights on the couch spooning,' I explain. I exercise my winking eye, and Paul laughs.

'But seriously,' he says, now walking again, 'a lot of college graduates put off work to do something else.'

'Is that so?' I ask.

'Absolutely,' he answers. 'Some travel, some volunteer. Some love school so much that go straight to grad school. Not that I would. God, four years is enough for me. Time to get on with it already.'

'You might think differently after you graduate,' I caution.

He looks at me funny, and he should. The warning is preposterous. I've only been out of school for three months, yet I'm talking like I've been out of school for years. And it's not like my life suddenly started sucking the moment I moved the tassel to the other side of my cap.

'Maybe we could switch for a semester?' Paul suggests. 'I'll work the tables, and you'll take my exams.'

'OK, but I want a cut of your tips.'

'Don't worry about finding a job,' he says. 'It will be OK.' Nodding, 'It's only a matter of time before the cheddar starts rolling in.'

'I hope so. I worked my ass off in school so that I won't be poor for the rest of my life.'

'Worked your ass off . . . ' Paul laughs. He can see me in a lecture hall with drool running down the side of my face.

'I did,' I say, waking up to the attack. 'And one of these days I'll have the money to buy those cheese barrels you're talking about.'

Paul laughs. Bud uh bum. I am hilarious today. 'You'll make money,' he says confidently. 'You have the name of a great school behind you, and that will go a long way in your job search.'

'You think?'

'Definitely.' He rubs his cheek with his hand. 'Everyone has heard of NYU.'

'I guess.'

'Worst case scenario, you could always just temp somewhere until you find something permanent.'

'Doing what?'

He shrugs his shoulders. 'Does it really matter?'

'You do that a lot, you know that?'

'What?'

'Oversimplify everything.'

'Is that so?'

'Yeah, it is.'

'Well, not everything has to be complicated. We have our whole lives to complicate things.'

'That's true.'

'But get it done before you shuffle off this mortal coil.'

Cynicism returns with a surprise guest: Morbidity. Alas, poor Yorick. Death is the great common denominator. We are all dying slowly. Some, like me, are dying from this heat. I really want to take off my shirt, but I'm sure to burn, and I'm pretty sure that no one wants to see the horror that lies beneath anyway. The demands of public decency weigh heavy on me right now. At times I wish I were one of those old, senile men who is too old to care about the opinions of others and too senile to know what he is doing. I yearn for the day that I can walk around in wool socks and leather strap sandals, hacking loogies and spitting them on the ground, scratching my hygiene-challenged ass, hollering at the impudent sky, and undressing in public at will. Beginning on that day, such behavior will be considered 'normal' by the world, or at least well within the character of an old, senile man.

If I survive today, maybe I will live to see that day.

* * *

Back I am from a sweet daydream where time passes quietly on its tiptoes. Maples, oaks, and unsure deciduous trees have given way to a smattering of pines. The skeletal outline of a baseball backstop comes into focus. We draw closer, and the metal cage grows gray flesh. Life is everywhere, even in the inorganic.

Curtains seem to pull back when the trees suddenly disappear and reveal The Great Lawn, a thumping urban beach community littered with towels, beach umbrellas, picnic baskets, travel bags, and, of course, people. All conceivable kinds of people. All ages, sizes, shapes, and colors are represented. The variety is immense. A return to Pangea. The City calls itself 'The Home for the World', a 'multiculturalist's playground', but in reality the megalopolis is nothing more than a group of strangers thrown together by Affirmative Action and a convoluted mixture of pseudo-nature, King Business, Disney collectible stores, and dollar peep shows. Necessity of urban separatist existence—nothing more, nothing less.

Sitting on a bench is a Michigan fan flubbing chords on a cheap startup guitar. I take it the guy is only a few weeks into his new hobby by the way he refuses to press down hard on the frets. I think to walk over to him and give him a few pointers. *Hurts like hell, but you have to build up the calluses on the tips of your fingers first. Stick with the C, the E Minor, and the D. Build up the strength in the muscles in your left hand before you take a crack at those tricky Clapton progressions.*

When I was a kid, Julian and Paul managed to one-up me in everything, leading me to abandon many pursuits and laugh off taking up others. The exception was music. That was my bag. I picked up the recorder in third grade and ran with it. In junior high school I dabbled with the saxophone, broke a few too many reeds to keep my money-conscious father quiet, and then moved through a number of brass instruments as the high school years ticked away. Once I had developed a fair degree of competency and saliva buildup in one set of spit valves, I moved on to another. My music teacher thought I might have had some vocal talent and convinced my father to sign me up for Chorus. I made an attempt to strengthen my pipes in the shower, but the bathroom had deceptively flattering acoustics, and a quick comparison of my winter concert solo to Simon's finale solo on the Chipmunks' Christmas Album promptly ended my run at teen superstardom. My freshman year in college, a Dylan-loving hippie by the name of 'Violet' seduced me with the four chords whirled together in 'Blowin' in the Wind' (A, C, D and G, I think), and ever since I've been plucking away at my 1970 Sunburst Hummingbird Westwood.

Paul and Julian didn't take to music like I did, so I developed a musical kinship with Annie, who is an amazing violinist. My father loved music too, but he was a classical and jazz loyalist who saw nothing exemplary about modern indie music or global generation movers like the British Invasion or Seattle's grunge movement. Whenever he saw me watching MTV or VH-1, the great pontificator would start in: 'I know for a fact that no good music was made in the 80's . . . Oh now look at that! Don't let me catch you trying to grow your hair long like that . . . They look like a bunch of women with all that makeup on their faces. It's disgusting. It's *emasculating*.'

My father had a point. My idols *did* wear mascara. But these same lipstick rockers snagged more ass after every show than the average man did in the course of his entire life, whether their junk looked big in leather pants or not. My father and I argued on the merits of this tradeoff regularly. He always presented a good argument, but I never floundered when defending the stud status of Vince Neil. Never.

The Park is hopping today. On the blacktop, power walkers and joggers are swinging their arms like hydraulic machinery, propelling their bodies forward. Pairs of skates and running shoes are passing me, their riders using me like a slalom flag. On the grass, people are playing catch with baseballs and tossing footballs. The energy level here is high. The day is all about aggression and energy expulsion.

Paul and I walk along the southern tip of the meadow to find people spread out on the grass. Some are lying out on blankets, attempting to tan; others are sitting cross-legged, reading books, ready to be plucked from the earth like vegetables. A troupe of ladies are parked on lawn chairs, knitting socks and sweaters for their grandchildren, cackling away and being old. Two women are bent over strollers, impressed with the fertility conquest of the other. A boy watches as his dad tries to get a kite off the grassy runway. The red flyer is a cheap, flimsy one—probably a five-dollar Duane Reade purchase. The man is losing patience with the lack of wind, but his son seems unconcerned, content to kill the time by running around in airplane corkscrews. A man dressed in a bright orange top is elbow-deep in a trash can. He pulls out a few items, tosses something into a garbage bag and drops the rest back into the cylinder. He seems oblivious to the world around him, and the people like me who are staring.

The ice cream vendor is making a fortune today.

* * *

Paul and I just finished talking about the Red Sox and Yankees pennant race and are now having a pointless debate about who should have been the last contestant to extinguish his torch on last season's *Survivor*. A kid had been watching us play catch for a few minutes, so we finally invited him to join us. After introductions, 'David' hurried over to an open spot next to a couple ogling and goggling on a blanket the color of their pale flesh. Paul took a few steps toward me and I slid a few feet to my right, effectively squeezing our imaginary isosceles into an imperfect right triangle.

Paul throws out the yellow Frisbee, and David chases it down like a Patriot on a Scud missile. David is an athletic guy, dark-haired and sun-bronzed, fitted in Abercrombie & Fitch garb and topped with a visor. He looks like every other guy I met in college. He mentions that he is a junior at Columbia. Paul, who will be starting his last year at the Morningside Heights campus in less than a week, takes interest and starts up the 'name game'. Paul brings his thesis proposal into the fray, and David counters with his internship. Somehow, a streaking incident in Low Plaza fits its way into the conversation. They are making me feel like an old-timer, a has-been.

College relationships are packaged into discrete windows of time based on circumstance and necessity. You befriend someone because he happens to live in your building, attend the same classes, study in the same groups or in the same library locations, or work out at the gym at the same time of day. Order exists, and your orbits conveniently intersect. But just when the Universe starts to make sense, a free radical enters the picture and throws it all into chaos. One semester you think that you are inseparable from a person: blood brothers, soul mates, friendship ring pals, whatever. The next semester, you learn that that person is nothing more than a passing electron. For this reason it is difficult, if not impossible, to foster relationships in college that extend beyond debauchery and fucking. You see a lot of faces, hear a lot of names, shake a lot of body parts, but that's about it.

I miss a toss from Paul and reach down to pick up the Frisbee. The grass smells like it has been recently cut. Radios are blasting away on separate frequencies, but no one seems to mind the discord of it one bit. Voices rise and fall. My eyes follow, mimicking the panning camera lens from that show *ER*. My senses are on overload. A bird squawks. I look up. The sky looks like it has been submerged in a bucket of baby boy blue paint. I can't tell if I am at the beginning or the end of the sky.

* * *

A slight breeze ripples the murky green pond. Farther off, a brown mallard dive-bombs into the water and skies to a slow drift, pulled by an invisible motorboat of momentum.

We said our goodbyes to David and are now walking away from The Lawn. Paul stops to tie his shoes, giving me a moment to look around. Over on a stone wall, a small black radio catches a signal from outer space and translates it into twangy music. Two women in gray, ground-sweeping dresses watch intently as an older man twists through a series of circle-step moves. His joints jerk haphazardly as he slowly works his hands into an extended V toward the endless sky, unintentionally mimicking a soldier statue that stands back a dozen feet with two swords crossed in a defiant X. The man's head tips back, exposing his sun-pruned face, which glows bright white in the strong overhead sun. The man drops his hands to his side. A grin stretches out his face, twisting his lips into a rich mix of coy and confidence. His eyes are glazy. The whole thing likens to the transcendental.

'Have you talked to Julian this weekend?' Paul asks.

'We got together last week for a couple of beers,' I answer, keeping my eyes on the man, who now appears to be singing to himself. 'We cut the night short because he said he wasn't feeling well. Why?'

'Oh nothing.' He stops to pick up a straw-woven hat. 'I talked to him on the phone a few nights ago,' Paul explains, handing over the hat to a woman and giving her a little nod. 'He caught me running out the door to class.'

Paul wants to graduate early, so he's been overloading his semesters and taking summer classes. Right now, he's taking on urban planning. According to Paul, it's a crash course on the evolution of City infrastructure—the expansion of commercial zoning to what is now Midtown, the art deco period, the construction race between the Empire State and Chrysler buildings, the organization of privatized rail lines, so and so forth. Classes, reading, and homework—not exactly what I would do with my summer, but Paul has the propensity to pair everything with intellectual pursuit. He's a neotic goof-off.

'Why, whazup with Julian?' I ask.

'He seemed down, that's all,' Paul answers. 'I think it's the whole Allison issue again.'

'Her again?'

'Yeah.'

Julian met Allison, a cute island native who started at Hunter College a year ago, at the restaurant where she waitresses. I met her a few weeks later when the four of us met up for burritos and a movie. By the end of the evening, I decided that I liked her. She was attractive and had a good sense of humor. She had a little princess in her, but I forgave that. She looked like good girlfriend material for Julian. And Paul agreed.

But things soon changed. Once Allison and Julian became an exclusive item, Allison began to show her true colors. She started arguments with Julian over the dumbest things. She wanted to know where he was at all times. Any rational guy would have dumped her ass in a heartbeat. But Julian enjoys the drama. He finds it amusing. Personally, I think he's a moron. The world is full of penis predators, and the city we live in is a feeding ground. Why throw yourself in a net during the best years of your life?

Not that I am one to speak on matters pertaining to meaningful relationships. Oh no. Not me. I prefer the pump-and-dump method.

I lost my virginity just days before my sixteenth birthday, in the woods behind some pinhead's house, without a jimmy and without a clue as to what I was doing. Despite my serious lack of grace, I decided that my two-minute performance was good enough to ensure future romps in the boom boom room, baring any irreversible damage to my wanker of course. But seconds after I had come, Tina went all crazy, telling me she wanted us to head over to her palace on Mulberry Drive to break the news to her parents. I freaked and took off running, my pants still down around my ankles. I nearly caught my tea bag in my zipper as I dressed myself in mid-flight.

I've been running ever since.

After that disaster, every women I've dated has been seriously fucked in the head. For six months I tolerated Meghan Kushner and her endless pill-popping and stamp-licking. After Meghan was Heather, the decrepit monkey skeleton who ran herself out of my heart and into a rehab program. And then there was Talia Epstein, easily the most spoiled rotten bitch I've ever met. Whenever she walked, I felt like throwing rose petals in front of her. I rode her and her Daddy's charge card ride for a few months, but I've always been a cash only guy, so it wasn't meant to last.

It's my own fault. I always pick the worst of the worst. My recruitment methods suck. I need to move out of the bars and clubs and into the churches, charity organizations, and book-of-the-month club meetings. I need to surround myself with *good* girls.

'I know Julian and Allison fight a lot,' Paul says, 'but I think something else is bothering him.' Slowly shaking his head, 'I think something's up and he's not talking about it. Like he's afraid to talk about it or something.'

'Afraid?' I crack. 'What does Julian have to be afraid of?'
'Something.'
'Like what?'
'Arachibutyrophobia?'
'Fear of spiders?'
Shaking his head, 'No, that's *arachnophobia.*'
'Fear of attractive spiders?'
'Fear of peanut butter sticking to the roof of your mouth.'
'What?'
'Could you imagine being a kid and eating nothing but jelly sandwiches?'
'That sounds like a dumb fear to have.'
'They get dumber.'
'Like?'
'Kakorrhaphiophobia.'
'You need to stop reading the dictionary.'
'Philophobia,' Paul says, the grin on his face straightening out.
'Huh?'
'The fear of laughter.'

September

Chapter Five

THIS LOBBY HAS what every other lobby in the City has: antiseptic white, wall-to-wall, fake plants, and a coffee table with *The Wall Street Journal*. The only interesting twist is the black leather couch. The cushions are firm and supportive, yet soft and yielding, morphing back behind my index finger. It's amazingly comfortable. Sharp-looking too.

I'm at the office of Feldman Associates, a downtown consulting firm and the capital of Corporate America today. My appointment was for one o'clock, and I made it to the building with plenty of time to spare, but I got held up at the front door. The security guards asked me for my ID and then started to drill me with questions. They asked me for my contact's information, the reason for my visit, the name of my clergy man's dog, all sorts of crazy shit. I guess they were hoping to extract the location of Osama Bin Laden from me and win that night for four with Rumsfield in the Lincoln Bedroom. Anyway, before I knew it, I was late and running for the elevators.

Today, I am begging for a job. I know it, and they know it. I'm the seller, and they are the buyer. And I'm selling junk: a flat resume fluffed up with pointless part-time jobs and a reminder of my massive college loan debt. I know that I shouldn't be here.

But I am, Spic and Spanned, Q-tipped and seasoned with designer cologne. Like a holiday present, I'm wrapped in blue and white and bound together with black cord. And from what I've heard, landing a job is all about looking good. It's about projecting confidence. Substance is a mirage. Blow smoke, if you have to. Lie. Tell them about your work on equilibrium theory—Chapter Seven, right after Nash. Tell them to buy you up, and fast. He who hesitates masturbates. They'll want to cut the plug and take the quarter of a point, but Hell, you make the CNN headlines, and they shouldn't move to sell until you return from wiping your ass in the bathroom. Tell them to get a grip, hold on, and Big Macro will drive Little Macro. Say something about 'consumption'. Talk about raising C in GNP. Throw out a Keynesian quote. Make one up. Tell them to put on a pot of coffee because you'll be spending the rest of the day pounding out supply and demand graphs for them. Blow that smoke.

The glass doors swing closed behind a blonde. The woman is a vision of sex—perfect breasts, an ass that won't quit, legs and legs and legs. Her body is mouth-watering. And her face—porcelain skin, cushiony lips, panther eyes. Sometimes the planets align perfectly.

The black skirt and red cardigan speak to the professional woman, but underneath all that is a happy school girl. I can tell. She starts jabbering away with the receptionist. I watch her run her hand along the rim of her hairline to curl golden strands over her ear. She starts to wiggle her black pump, her heel working like a fulcrum, swinging her foot back and forth like clockwork. The rest of her body synchronizes. Tighten and relax, tighten and relax, chant the movements of her magnificent buttocks. The shockwaves move up and down my body. I know what my one wish would be, but the genie would never find me a fit owner of the lamp. So I dream that we are together. I float in the impure carnality of her. I borrow material I like to work into late-night screenings, where my interactive props are a box of tissues, a bottle of coconut oil, and an overactive imagination. REWIND, PLAY. Perfection and I exchange knowing glances. We send the receptionist out on an impossible scavenger hunt, and then my lady hovers over to me like a bubble that has found its updraft. She transmogrifies back, bends over and fixes her lips to mine. She tastes of the sweet nectar of a peach plucked from an Elysian field. She bounces off me and springs down the hall. Garments fly. I am ready to erupt.

My hands are trembling, so I lay my resumé holder down on the coffee table. My eyes are bulging. I need someone to blink for me, be my collyrium. My princess laughs again. I want to lay naked with her on the floor, but she doesn't even know I exist. My presence doesn't raise an eyebrow, twitch a lip, or twist a hip. I'm short, forgettable looking. I have a ring of waist fat that only hideous girls find cute. I am a decent-looking guy, a guy who can score with decent-looking chicks. But this chick is not decent-looking. This woman is smoking.

My future wife starts to walk away. She hooks a right down a side hallway and drops out of sight. I blow a kiss. Goodbye, my love. Go ruin another stockpile.

I'm not here to get laid. I'm here to get a job. Focus. Go over the rules again. Keep eye contact, but don't stare. Will your sweat glands to dry up. Hands in your lap, sit up straight, feet flat on the floor. Ready, set, go. *Engage.* Ask questions. Act interested. Be enthusiastic, but don't overdo it. You don't want them to think you are desperate. Use examples, but don't ramble. Don't use six words when four will suffice. Keep the conversation moving. Be funny when you can, but don't act like a fucking clown. Keep it professional.

To my left is a conference room shaped like a giant shark tank. Inside are black leather chairs pushed underneath a long mahogany table. I can see the future. The corporate cronies are gathered, their hands busy on yellow writing pads like a flock of agitated seagulls. As I speak, they swallow my words whole and wash them down with sips from matching ceramic coffee mugs. My every bullet point, they acknowledge with twelve synchronized nods. My every joke, they honor with an equal number of laughs. I build to a crescendo and hold them for a fermata when I excuse myself to take a call from the Chairman of the SEC. Once our tee time is finalized, I return for the grand finale. Champagne corks pop, congratulatory handshakes and back slaps are exchanged. Perfection is pressed to my right side. I am King, and the world is my playground. Yes-man faces float above the table like hot air balloons, ready to take me on a trip through and beyond the cathedral windows to visit the architecture of my mind, a mind that knows how to build an investment empire.

'Hello?'

I look up. The receptionist is up out of her bunker. 'Sir, come with me please,' she says, motioning with her hand for me to come forward.

The day I began interviewing for a job, I became 'Sir'. I've noticed the change on the streets, in the stores and on the buses too. Sir, Sir, Sir. I'm living my life on a telephone with a customer representative.

I shake out of the couch and walk up to her.

'You can leave your coat in the closet,' the receptionist says, pointing to a closet built into the back wall behind her desk. I see white hangers dangling on a rail, ready to move in and take the prize.

'In there?' I ask.

'Yes. It will be fine in there.'

Yeah, right lady. That looks like a bank vault to me too. 'I'm OK,' I tell her.

'Would you like something to drink?'

'No, thank you,' I reply. I'm a liar. I want a Bombay Sapphire and tonic.

Mr. Edwards will see you now, the receptionist tells me. I nod my head and follow her out of the lobby. Her black-hosed legs scissor back and forth, splitting her hips and who knows what else. I step where she steps, turn when and where she turns. Natural light pours in from the building's glass façade. A halogen grill painted on the ceiling hums nosily. We make a right and pass cubicle walls arranged in the pattern of an ice cube tray. People are busy at their desks, typing, talking on phones. Plastic smashes plastic. Keyboards click, machines whirr away. Printers and fax machines spit out white. The whole place smells of Office Max.

'Here we are.' The receptionist comes to a stop at a door opposite a vacant cubicle. She adjusts the glasses on the hook of her nose and uses her free hand to rap a couple times on the door. Her hand is thick of blue veins. She grasps the handle, turns it, and swings the door open enough to fit her head into the room.

Life is a series of doors. Sometimes you have to knock. Sometimes you have to let yourself in. Other times you have to whine and scratch like a dog finished making water. It's all a guessing game. But here at Feldman, the receptionist handles all the doors.

OK Phil, I hear. I stretch out a smile. You whore yourself throughout the entire job that is life, but it is never more evident than at a job interview. I will shake Phil's hand, smile, and nod. I will chew on the crap that he feeds me, swallow, regurgitate, and throw it back up to him, and somehow I will make it all look pleasant. No, I will make inducement look like freaking genius.

'Please don't forget to remind me about that two o'clock lunch appointment.' The receptionist pulls out. 'Here you go,' she says, pushing the door open with her hand and waving me in with the other.

'Thanks,' I answer.

'You're welcome,' she answers, all peaches and cream.

A short, bald man in a gray suit greets me. I spot his hand and immediately understand where all the hair on his head went. I'm about to share a cordial *Planet of the Apes* introduction. We lock, and I am surprised by the half-man, half-ape's weak grip. Phil doesn't have a clue how to approach a handshake. He's paralyzed with uncertainty. He's worried about signals. Too strong, and he overcompensates for a small penis. Too weak, and he compromises his masculinity. I tighten up on my end, just a little, but Phil doesn't follow my lead. All I get is a flaccid ball of sweat.

Phil leaves my hand and walks around his desk, which is buried with crap. Books, paper, manila folders, pens and pencils, decorative doohickeys—I guess the City grew tired of all the complaint mail, scouted a site, signed the contract, loaded up the barges, and dumped the north side of Staten Island on Phil's desk.

'Did you make it to the office OK?' Phil asks.

'No problem at all,' I answer quickly. Prefunctory is the way of the professional.

'I'm glad to hear that,' Phil says. Clearly, Phil could care less about my navigational success. There is no inflection, no music in his voice. He is all about the HR deadpan. Have a seat, he tells me. He finds his own seat and drops into it. I examine my options: two blue chairs, identical. I go with the one closest to the door. I put my resumé holder on the floor and then shift my focus back to Phil. His eyes are dark and indiscernible; his cherub face, pale and smooth like a baby's butt. My guess is, Phil is in his mid-forties, single, and totally in love with his job.

'Is it getting windy out there?' Phil asks, now out of his monotone.

'Yeah, it's a little windy,' I answer. I'm tempted to suggest he ask Mary Poppins, but I'll resist the wise ass in me.

Phil is staring at the top of my head. Maybe he wants some of my hair. That's fine, I can spare it. I wanted to get it cut yesterday, but Gino takes off Mondays, and day-old cuts never look right anyway. I had hoped the extra gel would keep the fro under control, but I guess I shouldn't have put my faith in cheap toiletries. I thought to visit the little boy's room earlier to throw a little water on the mullet, but I wasn't about to ask the receptionist to point me in the right direction. I don't like people knowing when I'm going potty. I find it very uncomfortable, especially when you know you are about to shake hands. No one needs an excuse to visualize me tinkling and trickling finishing drops on my hand.

'I asked because the sky is getting dark,' Phil muses. The comment is dumb, considering he doesn't have a window in his office. 'I'll be surprised if it doesn't rain,' he adds.

I nod my head idiotically. I haven't heard a thing about the weather, but Phil doesn't need to know that. 'I heard there may be thunderstorms too,' I add.

Phil nods his head, taking to my pants-on-fire comments like a dog with Alzheimer's to an electric fence. *Phil Edwards*. What a name. Sounds like a fucking meteorologist. *Don't go anywhere. Phil will have your four-day forecast as soon as he's done banging his new intern in the dressing room.*

'Maybe it will hold off until later tonight,' Phil says, full of hope.

'I hope so,' I answer truthfully. 'I didn't bring an umbrella.'

Phil thinks that is funny. He has a laugh that sounds like a hyena. 'The storms come racing in from the west,' he explains, 'and whip off the Hudson. The wind can't go through the buildings, so it has to go through you.'

People like Phil think they are local weather experts because they work or live in the area. Mr. Callahan, a retired military man who lives down the street from my house back in Billington, believes a temperamental jet stream circles his property. Last year, the First Lieutenant walked over to my house cradling a zucchini, and he started bitching about El Nino. I never heard so much profanity come from a man's mouth. I walked away when he started predicting when the first frost of the year would affect his harvest. Mr. Callahan loves talking about the weather, but he *adores* talking about his garden. Years ago, he wrote a book entitled *Making the Most of Your Garden Space*. I think it went on to sell about seven copies, one of which is now sitting on a bookcase in my father's study, collecting dust.

I do some more nodding. I hate pretending that I care.

'I guess that's why they call it "Wall Street",' Phil says. He looks at me. 'What do you think?' His eyes, nose and mouth connect into a question mark. I shrug my shoulders. 'I think it is,' Phil says, bolstering with confidence. Phil is the butt-baring interviewer, and I am the ass-kissing interviewee. That's how it is, and more brown-nosing dribble from me is good. I need to win him over by making him feel like the smartest person in the world.

'I heard you went to NYU,' Phil says. I nod. 'Are you a New York native?'

'No, I grew up in Massachusetts.' The announcement is delicious.

'Really!' Phil explodes. 'I lived there too! Out in the Berkshires for a year. Right before I decided to come to Feldman in, oh—' tapping his lips with a finger. '—it must have been about five years ago. Is it peak foliage up there yet?'

'I'm not sure,' I answer.

To Phil and most of the world, New England is nothing more than a picturesque diorama of dying leaves. Two months a year, jigsaw puzzle makers and foliage aficionados book up our B&Bs, poke at our pale clam chowder, snap their cameras, and leave. These annual trespassers could care less about what transpires in New England the other ten months. They probably prefer not to know.

'I miss that area.' Phil stares into space. 'Well,' returning, 'where did you go to school? Oh right. *NYU*. We've been over that. Great program they have at NYU. Very competitive.'

Great. I got a total pecker interviewing me.

'My youngest son might go there. He could if he wanted to.'

The proud father takes a breather. My patience is razor thin for these types, but I am a GOD at disguising it. 'Is he a senior?' I ask him.

'A sophomore,' Phil corrects me. 'He's still got a couple of years to go, but his mother thinks we should start looking sooner rather than later. And there's no arguing with that woman.' He rolls his eyes.

I can't believe Phil is married. *With children*—shit, I wouldn't have guessed that in a million years. He says 'his mother' and not 'my wife', which can only mean that Phil hasn't had sex with Mrs. Phil for quite some time.

'But what do I know? Location, academic reputation . . .' Phil flips up his hand and writes something on his invisible chalkboard. 'She's the school counselor. She can have it. I'm clueless. Bamboozled.'

Bamboozled?

'If he doesn't go to NYU,' Phil continues, still yapping, 'he'll probably end up at Princeton, which is where my oldest son is. Maybe he'll play basketball too, like his older brother. His mother seems to think he'll get a full scholarship if he does.'

I really want to meet Phil's wife. I'm starting to think she might be a dominatrix. I bet her wardrobe is packed with lots of leather and steel. On the weekends she lets Phil roam around in a dog pen to investigate the rears of other corporate knob jobs. I can only imagine what twisted fucking things she dreams up while Phil is down on all fours, sniffing away.

'I brought him to the city a couple of months ago to check out a few schools,' he tells me, 'and he really like it. Did you like it? Of course you did.'

Phil loves his life. Someone please take me out to the back and shoot me.

'They have a heck of a theater department at NYU,' Phil continues. 'A lot of famous actors started there.'

'I've heard,' I reply. He nods. I bet he's thinking of The Julliard School.

'Anyway, let's talk business.' Phil looks down at his desk. 'I know that I have your resumé here somewhere.' He rustles a few papers.

'I have an extra copy if you need it,' I tell him. I start for my portfolio, but Phil waves me off. I know I have it, he tells me, and he resumes his search, adding narration. 'Maybe it's in a drawer. Maybe I left it with her . . .' He thumbs through a foot-high stack of paper, then looks on the other side of his computer monitor, which is decorated with yellow memo stickies, giving it the appearance of a poorly executed paper-maché project. Phil crosses back to the middle of his desk, his hairy hands still moving furiously. He has no idea where my resumé is.

Don't forget to bring extra copies of your resumé, my headhunter told me about sixteen thousand times. One day, I am going to destroy my resumé with a book of matches and a bottle of lighter fluid. It will be a small, intimate ceremony. I'll invite my closest friends, say a few words, and then fire it up. Maybe I'll have some finger food and cocktails as well.

'Here it is!' Phil exclaims. He holds the sheet up over his head like a baseball player would a ball to show the official he had held on to make the catch. 'I knew I had it!'

Of course I celebrate wildly. My hands come together explosively, my feet stomp uncontrollably, my mouth rolls off my face, but I keep it all bottled up inside. I sit up straight in my blue chair and fold my hands.

Phil puts on a pair of gold-rimmed reading glasses and starts reading. He clenches his jaw, like he's nursing a toothache or something. A quick look around the office. Aside from the mess on Phil's desk, the office is bland and boring. Pressed up against the corner of the wall is a gray filing cabinet with three drawers. Resting on top are a few cardboard boxes shaped like the ones manufacturers use to package VCRs. Directly behind Phil's shoulder is a black frame hanging on the wall. Squished inside is a piece of white parchment bordered with gold foil. **FELDMAN ASSOCIATES** reads across the top in big, black letters. Below the company name is a few lines of calligraphy which I take to be a mission statement of sorts. The words *excellence*, *client*, and *needs* jump out at me like dinosaurs from stereograms. Ducking the frame is a standard end table—pine, four legs. A lone picture frame sits on top of it, propped up on a sharp angle. In it is a photo of a woman dressed in a white ski suit. Dark sunglasses hide her eyes. Her long, fire-red hair hangs past her shoulders to her waist. She looks too old to be Phil's daughter, if he even has one, and definitely too young to be his loopy wife. Maybe Phil's niece. Maybe she came with frame.

'So tell me.' Phil leaves the resumé on the desk and removes his glasses. 'Why did you pick your major? Your major—' He looks back at the sheet and taps it. 'English and History, it says here. That's interesting. Why history?'

'I've always liked history,' I answer.

'Why is that?' Phil leans in. I smell stale coffee. Phil must drink triple espressos.

'History brings the past into the present for us,' I begin, sounding way too rehearsed, like a professor reading straight from the textbook on the first day of class. 'It covers everything from culture and art, to government and business. It brings everything together. And it gives us some indication of what the future will bring.'

'Those who forget the past are destined to repeat it,' Phil says. 'That's why the past and the present are the same.'

I have no idea what that's supposed to mean. Phil sits back in his chair and feeds on his words and lower lip. I continue. 'I think it's important to know about the past because the past is full of cycles—'

'Oh I agree,' Phil interjects. 'History *is* cyclical. But I think it's because people forget what they did in the past.'

He pauses and smiles. I almost want to give him a standing O. A minute ago I wanted to give up on this conversation, but now he's starting to sound like an educated man.

'We may forget about events from time to time,' I tell Phil, 'but I would argue that it isn't because people forget their mistakes. I don't think people are going to forget September 11 or the Holocaust.'

'9-11 was the work of crazy people.'

'What I mean is, I think people look to the past for answers,' I clarify.

Phil tilts his head halfway to his shoulder to explore me from a different angle. 'How's that?'

'Well, in business, for example,' I begin, 'analysts are always interpreting data to shed light on what the future may hold for a company or a market. In a sense, the past is the only tool analysts have to make sense of today's data before tomorrow is upon them.'

I'm a genius for working in a business analogy. I'm set to call it a day. But Phil isn't done with me. His ears are pricked, hanging on to my last sentence as if there were a dangling modifier to rectify. Everything about him urges me to continue. So I do.

'People are tied to the past whether they like it or not. We repeat the past because the past seems correct, or at the very least, good enough. And we keep repeating the past until we accidentally come across something better.'

'Interesting.' Phil tucks his lips into a purple gumball. 'That's a very conservative way of looking at the world.'

'Well,' I butt in, trying to cauterize the wound I just ripped open, 'by that I didn't mean—'

'A safe take on the world,' he says, twisting the knife.

'But—'

'But I know where you're going with this.' It is the gauze I require. 'I think we can live with each other on this,' Phil decides. His fist jumps into the air, and he clinks his imaginary mug with mine. We drink in our bogus camaraderie. He looks at me admiringly. He's starting to creep me out.

'It's important to think big,' I press on, 'and I'm a goal-oriented person. So I know how to set goals and follow through on them.' I pause for a moment. I stole that last bit straight from the mouth of my college adviser. Plagiarism is the game, and right now I'm winning. I've got this big pushover right where I want him. I found my window, and now it's time to take the house. Time to scoop up the poker chips at this berry patch and head my mechanic butt home.

I take a breath, and continue. 'I want to learn as much as I can, and I want to make a contribution and make a lasting impression wherever I go. Hopefully, that will be here at Feldman.'

'That sounds good,' Phil says, clapping his hands together, apparently satisfied. He knows it can't be said better than that. 'I like what I'm hearing here.' He leans in. 'I think it would be good to have your kind around.'

Great. I'm filling a quota. I'm reversed Affirmative Action in action. All of a sudden I want to run out of here as quickly as possible. But Phil absolutely loves me right now. He wants me as his right-hand man. And with power and position comes the opportunity for treachery, *coup d'etat*.

'We need real team players here,' Phil marches on, proudly falling back to his HR manual, 'and we need people who are always heading for the finish line. Here at Feldman, clients are royalty. They are the reason that we sit behind these desks everyday. They put bread and water on our kitchen tables. They are our—' with his hairy index finger extended, '—number one. Nothing is more important than our clients' needs. Nothing.' He clears his throat and then leans in real close. A conspiracy close. So close you can smell the grinds brewing trouble on his tongue. 'You know why Feldman is successful?' he asks, his eyes getting big.

I have no fucking idea. 'Teamwork?' I answer. I don't know why I bother speaking.

Phil sits back in his chair and points to the mission statement that I had been examining earlier. 'Feldman is successful because we never fail,' he explains. 'We do everything it takes to be the best, and this is understood throughout the entire company, from top to bottom.' He lets me soak it in. 'But let me ask you something else,' he continues, scooting up in his chair, 'and please be honest . . .

Why do you want to work here?'

Chapter Six

ELLEN STEINBACK AND I met at NYU. I was a junior at the time. She was a sophomore transfer, a trust fund baby from Iowa, and a total bitch. She liked me for some reason.

For two years I resisted her advances. It wasn't always easy. There were nights she'd pull me aside in a bar or pull me into the bedroom at a party, and dribble her glassy-eye intentions. A lot of people thought Ellen was hot. The pressure to mate was immense.

But I stood my ground. Ellen and I were both English majors and were in many of the same classes. If I fucked and fled her on the weekend, I would be fucked and stuck on Monday morning. I constantly reminded myself of that fact, and the fact that professors can smell trouble in the den. Fight with your fellow cubs, and Mom will use the Socratic Method to suck you into a conversation on the poetic angst of Plath. And the last thing I needed was Ellen and Sylvia tag-teaming me in an unwelcome threesome.

But then graduation day came. I slept through the second half of commencement exercises, woke up and realized I was in Washington Square Park, alive, so I celebrated by throwing off my cap, putting down a fifth of Citron Absolut, and hunting down Ellen. I had been on a devastating drought at the time, and I figured it was about time to water my sex-thirsty crops with a little T and A. I siphoned through secondary criteria—namely, quality of character and foreseeable future liability—and retained one and only one requirement: Is she worthy of a poke?

After a night of mediocre sex, we parted ways, and I didn't expect to hear from Ellen ever again. I don't recall negotiating a post-sale service contract, but I guess the contract was implied. So now once a week Ellen goes out, gets smashed, pushes down her emotional coil, dials my number, I pick up, listen to the blah blah blah and reply with the appropriate blah blah blah.

'I know you said that we are over,' she says, using all the regular material, 'but I really need to talk to you.'

'We never started,' I correct her.

'It's really important.'

'What could be so important at this hour?' I ask. I should stop asking questions. I'm only prolonging the conversation.

'You sound tired. Maybe I should go.'

Ellen thinks I was born yesterday. She is teasing me, showing me an escape to this engagement. It's a trick. If I hung up right now, then I'd be an insensitive prick. I need to wait until she slips into full Ellen mode. I need her to deserve whatever I end up dishing out later.

'You called me, so what's going on?' I ask.

'You sure it's OK?'

She seems unconvinced by my wishy-washy pass at sincerity. Am I that obvious?

'I said it was fine,' I reply sharply.

I'm not fine. My air conditioner is acting up again, and my apartment is a sauna. To make matters worse, I accidentally spilled rubbing alcohol on my bathroom floor earlier. I sopped up the mess with a bunch of napkins and closed the bathroom door, hoping to contain the noxious fumes, but my quarantine was too late. I opened the window to air out the apartment, and the blower on the air conditioner laughed and shut off completely. A few minutes later, the chemicals on the floor gathered into a vaporous cloud of putrid stink. I closed the window, and five minutes later the blower guffawed back to life.

I would rather die of heat exhaustion than asphyxiation, so the window is open again. Considering every molecule of water in my body has seeped out of me, I'm amazed that I have managed to stave off death this long. But the end is near. The signs are telling. My general motor skills have been reduced to conserve power. My brain is no longer a stronghold. I feel dizzy. I bet this is exactly what it feels like to be high on whippets.

'I know it's late,' Ellen continues to ramble on, 'and I know we talked about me calling you with problems and stuff, but I'm really upset and I don't know who else to talk to.'

'Why don't you just tell me what's going on?' I say. I sound like that Movie Phone guy.

'You sure it's fine?' Ellen asks.

I'm so tired of this balancing act. I have to be diplomatic but assertive, distant but receptive. I have to play the good guy card, but I can't be too nice to her, otherwise Ellen will think that I want to be with her.

'Are you still there?'

'Yes.'

Her present ubiquity is the price of my past iniquity. I blew it, so now I have to talk to her. I want to empty my lungs, but that would do no good. No one would hear me. I'm soundproofed. I'm bound to a Munch canvas.

'You sure?' she asks.

'Damn it Ellen, do I have to spell the word *yes* for you?!' I am a patronizing jerk, but I swear it's like pulling teeth with this girl. No, not the actual pulling—the *waiting* for the pulling.

'Well, it's just, you know—'

'WHAT!' I explode.

Great, here come the sniffles. I knew this would happen. Feelings are fragile like champagne glass, and Ellen's feelings sit on the hood of a car with lousy shocks. Now I can't hang up because I made her cry. Nice work, dip shit.

'Talk to me,' I say.

'Promise you won't yell at me?'

'Yes,' I reply. I'm so good at lying, it's disturbing.

'Say it.'

'What?'

'Say, "I promise."'

'I'm not doing that.' She wants validation for her craziness. Fat chance.

'I won't believe you if you don't say it,' Ellen insists.

'Ellen, don't act so *childish*.'

I worry about parts of speech. Children can throw around names and labels and live to see another day, but it's a totally different story with adults. You can use the words *child* and *childish* fairly interchangeable, but not all word combinations work that nicely. You call a woman a 'bitch', and you might as well sign your death warrant. But if you tell her that she is 'acting bitchy', then you might escape with only a few cuts and bruises.

'Say you promise.'

'Fine. I promise.'

'I'm pregnant.'

'What?'

'I'm pregnant.'

'Pregnant? Are you sure? You took a test?'

'No.'

'You didn't take a test?'

'No.'

'Ellen, it's either pink or blue, plus or minus, baby or no baby. You can't just guess.'

'I wanted to tell you first.'

I should be off the phone by now, but I made her cry and now she's pregnant. I am a MORON.

'Why are you telling me this?' I ask her.

'What do you mean?'

What do you mean, she asks. 'Ellen, we had sex months ago,' I explain, 'and we used condoms.'

She tells me that it has been three months. Whatever. Like that matters. Sperm might be long distance swimmers, but they don't like to take their sweet ass time.

'I can't be the father, Ellen,' I tell her. 'You don't just skip a month like that. Even I know that, and I'm a guy.'

A pretty smart guy too, one who knows the basics of the menstrual cycle. She's whimpering again, but I don't care. This is all wrong, oh so terribly wrong, and I know it, and she knows it, and I'm not going to put up with this shit.

'I need to see you,' she says.

'This is not happening.'

'I can't do this over the phone. Can I come over?'

'I have to go. The battery on my phone is about to die.' Please let the phone die.

'Just for a little bit?' She is all about begging. 'Please?'

'Ellen.'

'PLEASE!'

'ALRIGHT!' *Click.*

Did I suddenly make a jump into The Twilight Zone? Bizarro World? I am hating science fiction right now.

Me, a father? That's the dumbest thing I've ever heard. Not that I *couldn't* be a father. My Navy Seals learned how to swim upstream a long time ago. My elementary school health teacher brought me up to speed on the anatomy of the male and female body. Willie goes in, shakes around, and out comes William, Will, Wilma, Wally, Walter, baby. The very real consequences of gonad samba. I don't need someone to draw me a diagram.

Yes, the tools are all there and functional, I assure you. Not used enough, but operational nonetheless. I'm fit as a fiddle. I could fertilize a nation if I wanted to. And Ellen's got hips, which means it wouldn't take much. Damn her and her child-bearing hips. Now I have to sit here and sweat like an innocent man on his last hour of death row. That's me on Court TV for sure. I'm holding on to that fifty-fifty shot of receiving a miracle call from the governor.

* * *

A knock on the door. Showtime.

'It's unlocked.'

The door swings opens. Ellen stands in the doorway, dressed in a pair of hot pink warm-up pants and a white, short-sleeved shirt. The words **LIVE IT** stretch across her chest in silver glitter. Her hair is tied back in a ponytail and looks much darker than its true, straw blonde shade.

Ellen steps on to the tiled floor and closes the door behind her. She sweeps away a tuft of hair. She looks like shit. Her face is pale, her eyes are coffee-stained. She either skipped the makeup or cried it all off.

'Hi,' she says, sweet and pathetic at the same time. Like I am supposed to be all gushy and sympathetic right now. 'Do you have something to drink?' she asks me, brushing past me.

'What do you want?' I ask. I guess I'm playing host now.

'Tea would be nice.' She finds my bed, walks over and dumps herself on it.

'I'm burning up in here, and you want tea?'

'Don't you have any iced tea?'

'I might have some Lipton bags, but it's going to be hot.'

'Don't you have ice?'

'Yeah, but—'

'You've never brewed tea and then put it in a glass with ice?'

'That sounds disgusting.'

'It's iced tea. *Iced* tea. How do you think they do it in a restaurant?'

'They use that machine.'

'What machine?'

'The machine that makes iced tea.'

'You don't know what you're talking about.'

'You want the tea or not?'

'I do it all the time.'

'OK, it's your funeral.'

I walk to the kitchen and find a box of tea in a cabinet. 'I have green tea,' I yell. I had no idea I had this stuff. I don't even drink tea.

'That would be nice,' I hear.

Uh-huh. Let's see how nice it is with spit floating in it. 'It will be a minute,' I tell her, working up the phlegm in my throat.

My freezer has four ice cubes. I pop them out of their barracks. My microwave dings, and I drop the cubes into the red cauldron. They spin in the liquid, distort into funky ovals and then disappear.

I walk around the corner, Crate & Barrel mug in hand. 'Thanks,' Ellen says, reaching up with her hands the way a baby begs to be picked up by a parent. I return to the kitchen, shovel two scoops of lemonade mix into a glass and fill it with cold water. A quick twirl with a teaspoon, and then I walk out of the alcove, around the corner. I try my glass. The tart liquid pinches my throat and feels good.

'Do you have a cigarette?'

I point to my desk.

'Lighter?'

'On the desk. There should be an ashtray over there too.' She gets up, locates all three. 'Just be careful,' I tell her. 'I don't want this place going up like a Roman candle.'

'What?'

'Nevermind.'

Ellen takes a sip from her mug, pretends she likes what she tastes, and clears some space on my desk for her mug. She stretches a cigarette from the white Marlboro Lights box and uses the lighter to work a few sparks into a long flame of blue. I watch her singe the tip of the cigarette, take a drag, and then blow out a big cloud.

'What is all this crap about me being the father of your kid?' I ask her. Our weekly session has begun, and I'm ready to end it before Conan comes on the tube.

'Take it easy.'

'Fuck that, Ellen. You can't call me and start talking about babies, especially when you didn't take a pregnancy test.'

Mumbling over the rim of her mug, 'I'm not taking the test.'

'What are you talking about?'

Ellen rests the mug on the desk. 'I'm not taking the test. I don't need to.' She looks down and finds the zipper splicing the side of her pant leg.

'Why is that?' I ask.

'Because I already know,' she answers dryly. Zip, unzip. Zip, unzip.

'Oh you do, do ya? How?'

'I know because I know.' Ellen take another puff, then dabs the cigarette in the silver ashtray until the smoke disappears.

'I don't get it.'

'I'm not surprised.' Ellen backtracks to the bed, sits, folds her legs underneath her butt, and starts on the zipper again.

'Ellen, would you just tell me what the hell is going on?'

She looks up.

'What?'

'I lied.'

'What?!'

'I'm not pregnant, and Jesus, I'm definitely not pregnant with your kid.'

'Are you fucking kidding me?'

'Do I look like I'm kidding?'

She uncrosses her legs and drops them to the floor.

'What's the matter with you?'

'It was just a joke. Jesus, don't get all crazy.' She reaches out her hand to take mine.

'I will not relax!' I fire, taking a giant step back.

'I wanted to talk to you, so I made up a story. It worked, didn't it?'

'You have some real fucking issues, let me tell you.'

'Yeah, I know.'

'It's time for you to leave.'

'Before I go, ya wanna fuck?'

'Are you kidding me?'

'Why not?'

'Leave, Ellen.'

'Why?'

I start for the door.

'I was just kidding.'

'I'm not!' I spin around and see Ellen on her feet, walking toward me. 'Get the fuck out!' I holler, swinging the door open.

'Relax, drama queen. I'm going.' She reaches for my cigarettes, pulls one out of the box, and heads to the door.

'Out!'

'I'm going.'

'Fucking right you are!'

October

Chapter Seven

DREAM A DREAM of white. Watch the sanguine liquid begin to fill invisible tubes. Swing around and follow one root branch. Synaptically web in and out as the spidery pattern grows around you, moving up, left, down, right, and vertical to the horizontal and reverse. You return to the white. You feel the sensation of legs crisscrossing, but nothing passes you and you pass nothing, so you may as well just stand there motionless for the experience would be altogether identical. Your feet begin to feel like balloons. Something rises up and fills your head, or where your head should be. A block of white expands and contracts, taking on breath and a yellow halo that darkens with the shadowy effects of misapplied gloss. Your arms should be in front of you. You look there for comfort, but you see only the white. Your hand closes upon itself. You are entirely limbless. A phantom, a hologram. Only white. All white. Bleached and unblemished. Perfectly free of imperfection. All other senses shut down, and you hear nothing, smell nothing, feel to the touch nothing. Abject terror suddenly fills you. You turn, and a blue swell races toward you. Despair collides and immediately erases the white. Swallowed and electrified, you are. Poncho paralysis, the glory toaster-found, overflowing bathtub. Tumbling, turned up and around and over you. Screaming soundlessly, you must be. You, I, rapidly. The heat is intense. Then, all is quelled like an invisible hose to a fire. White. Switch to black. A beating now. Valves open and close. Aorta, ventricle. Your heart slows to match the beat. You feel it within you. Count the beats. One, two, three. Count the beats. One, two, three.

* * *

I'm up, awake but groggy. I didn't sleep a wink last night, and the pains of post-partum alcohol depression are hitting me like a circling freight train. I wonder what would have happened had I awoke in a hospital, hooked up to a machine. End it now, I would have told the nurse. Check the COMPASSIONATE HOMICIDE box on the waiver form.

I'm gorging on delightful roughage, Velcroed to my fuzzy red chair, not going anywhere anytime soon. I stretch, and my tendons crack. *Click*.

Good morning everyone! It's half past the hour, a comfortable fifty-five degrees here in Midtown. Ray Wu is on hand in the studio, ready with the day's weather forecast. He'll give you the entire scoop on what you should expect out there today. But first, Matthew O'Leary is here with a rundown on all of last night's sports action and scores. Matthew? Thank you, Molly. Ladies and gentlemen, after last night's come-from-behind 4 to 3 win in Seattle, the Yankees are one win away from returning to the World Series. Behind Roger Clemens' two-run, four-hit, seven-inning pitching effort, a pair of solo shots by Bernie Williams including the game winner in the eighth inning, and a 1-2-3 ninth by Mariano Rivera for the save, the Yankees are now in a position to wrap up the series at Yankee Stadium here in New—*Click*.

Fucking traitor. Just once I'd like to hear about the Yankees losing a game. But how can you argue against a certainty? I'd have to go back in time and rewrite the past. I'd have to go back and change the outcome of Game Seven to match Pudge Fisk's earlier shot to left over the Green Monster. And with that, I'd do what they've been trying to do for over eighty years: lift The Curse of the Bambino, dethrone The Sultan of Swat, fell The Colossus of Clout. Lure The Babe back home, away from the cradle of the world's richest sports franchise. How likely is that? Fuck that, you fat fuck. 1918 and still proud.

Year-round I suffer through New York baseball, New York football, New York this, New York that. I've thought about calling up Time Warner and voicing my complaints. I'd rather watch international curling on FOX Sports World or bass fishing on ESPN 2 than watch these New York teams.

It's time to make a few changes around here, and we might as well start off with the fall football schedule. I missed yet another Patriots game yesterday, thanks to New York local broadcasting rights. On Sundays, it's nothing but Jets and Giants football, all played in New Jersey. The City tries to confuse the world by cutting off the 'City' in its teams' names, but I'm not buying it. I started calling the New York Jets the 'New Jersey Jets' and the New York Giants the 'New Jersey Giants'. The people here hate that. *Click.*

I'm hooked on TV—the bromidic goofs perpetuated on sitcoms, the farfetched plot twists conjured on medical dramas, the lame commercials. I am on the morning clock now, handling the early news, but I assure you that the viewing will continue later today. I leave and return to the television screen like fat on Oprah Winfrey's body.

If there is someone else on the planet who loves to watch television as much as I do, it would have to be my father. He reads the TV Guide as often as my mother used to read her Daily Bread. He's a connoisseur of sorts. When we watch TV together, my father talks non-stop about dialogue, plots, production sets, lighting technique, and most everything else TV.

Law firm commercial. My Dad *detests* commercials. He critiques them like a ticket-holder with no concept of suspension of disbelief would a fantasy film. 'That doesn't make any sense!' he once exclaimed while watching a coffee commercial. 'Why would anyone walk all the way home just to have a cup of coffee? Can you explain that to me?' He looked back over to me for an answer, apparently forgetting that I hadn't written the commercial. 'If the coffee's so good, then why doesn't he bring it to work with him?'

Whenever I brave a comment, I try to keep it concise.

'Dad, I think it's a metaphor.'

'Metaphor my ass!' he growled. He looked back at the man savoring the steam floating away from his mug. 'It's not like the coffee is going to taste any different if he's drinking it at the office instead of at a restaurant,' he argued, his hand now shaking, 'or down the street at Billington Donuts, or at his house. Is the water so different at his house? I don't think so! I could make a much better commercial.'

My father always thinks that he can make, create, or build something bigger, better, or more efficient than the other guy. Shopping for furniture is a great example:

'You want this desk? Are you serious? Look at the size of these screws. Look! If you pulled out this drawer too quickly, the stupid thing would fall right off. I can build you a much better desk. Maybe we'll use pine, possibly poplar. Come on, let's go. We'll drop by Home Depot on the way home.'

On clothes:

'*Boxers*? Walk around, and your balls slip out and start flapping in the wind like a wind chime. Congratulations, you're a porn star. Where's your shame? Hanes—now *that* is some good underwear. Here. Let me show you a pair of mine.'

Pop. What a comedian.

I empty the cereal bowl and set it off to the side. I reach for a pillow, fold it in half, and tuck it under my head. Finished with its pick-me-up coffee, the sun has its butt in gear, penetrating through my one beige curtain and casting a golden glow over the studio. It switches to black mode, catches up to fallout material, and reveals secret airborne fliers. Pasta sauce commercial. Chunky, not the runny kind. Flip to the Weather Channel. Here we go. According to these guys, the day will be a warm one—mid-seventies, mostly sunny, no precipitation expected. Next door, Maurice has nothing to say. *Nada.* 4D is a tomb. *Una tumba.* I walk over to the window, my desk chair in hand. I pull back the curtain, and the light is blinding. I look down to the ground below and imagine a vibrant street scene. My eyes skip from a parked red convertible—a small one, maybe a Miata, unattended and topless—to a shopper thumping and shaking melons, to a street sign and an empty window that sparkles more than the others, to a busted fire hydrant gushing water in one of those coming-of-age crime movies.

It is a perfect day to be out and about, taking in all the elements, *living,* but I will only be a spectator to its perfection today. Such is the life of an employed man. There is no justice or fairness in the world. Only work.

Work.

Shit!

Chapter Eight

'ARE YOU OK?' Ted asks.

'Yeah,' I answer.

'YOU SURE?' His dark eyes crinkle. 'THAT LOOKED LIKE A NASTY SPILL.'

'I'm fine,' I tell him, 'but I think the chair is broken,' holding a piece of chair in each hand.

Ted's empathy shrivels up his face. He looks constipated. 'YOU SHOULD HAVE THAT LOOKED AT,' he says, pointing at the scrap metal in my hands.

No shit, Sherlock. A nice guy, that Ted, but a little heavy on the imbecile. He's a giant of a man, towering well over six feet tall and reaching a potentially fatal weight of four hundred pounds. The company's dress code calls for business casual, but Ted always shows up to the office in battle gear, wearing a full suit with a jacket whose sleeves ride high on his arms. Ted wears the same black pinstripes everyday, but few probably notice this because he runs a weekly cycle of underlying combinations, dark blue and gray collared shirts and paisley patterned ties.

'I THINK YOU SHOULD CALL OFFICE HELP,' Ted suggests. 'THEY'RE THE ONES YOU SHOULD CALL. DO IT. CALL THEM. THEY'LL HELP YOU.'

Ted is a guy who speaks exactly like he writes and writes exactly like he speaks: rambling, pointless, and entirely histrionic. He has this very annoying habit of writing all of his emails in CAPITAL LETTERS. Conventional email lingo explains CAPS usage to be a deliberate attempt to add extra emphasis to a message, but Ted's CAPS LOCK is permanently snapped down into his keyboard, and this essentially kills any urgency that might be hidden within anything he sends you electronically. Ted makes no distinction between what is of particular importance and what just *is*, and this is exactly how Ted conducts himself in person. What he lacks in reason, Ted makes up in volume. Call it 'Audio Brutalism'. The world is hard of hearing whenever Ted speaks.

'YOU KNOW THE NUMBER?' Ted asks me. He looks at the palm of his hand as if he had written the number on it.

'I think it's—'

'EXTENSION 677. GIVE THEM A CALL. YOU CAN'T BE WORKING WITH A BROKEN CHAIR. YOU COULD FALL DOWN AND BREAK YOUR NECK. NO SIR-RE BOB. NOT SAFE AT ALL. LET'S CALL RIGHT NOW AND SQUARE THIS AWAY. WHERE IS THAT PHONE?'

Ted spots the black Nortel telephone on my desk. I turn to go after it and inadvertently block his path. We exchange uncomfortable glances. We both seem to realize that Ted's ass couldn't fit through the Gibraltar strait. 'That's OK,' I tell him. 'I've already called.'

'YOU DID?'

Cross my heart, hope to die, stick a skewer in fat guy. Three calls in the past four days. I even sent an email to help@feldman.com and pleaded for a company reevaluation of its ergonomic ledger. Of course emails are one-sided and, thus, offer little assurance of sender delivery and recipient confirmation. For all I know they all drop out of my Sent Box, down a chute, and into a furnace.

I have no idea who runs employee motivation experiments in any of these department cages. If I did, I would bug that person until a Hågnet Signét found its rightful place underneath my fanny. But no one cares about the new, no-name, know-nothing guy in the office anyway. People like me—the bottom of the totem pole dwellers—have to fend for themselves. So after a couple of days of HR inaction, I tried to fix the chair myself, wrapping a football field of Scotch tape around the metal rod holding the chair's cushion to the top of the swivel pod. On the trial test, the chair held for a few minutes, earning my trust and full body weight before it fell to pieces and sent me backwards on to the floor. I had little confidence that my belt-and-suspenders approach would work on the second attempt; nonetheless, I felt compelled to give it the ol' college try. For the second run, more clear tape and an up-and-over weave pattern proved to be slightly more effective, holding together the catapult just short of 72 hours.

Ted is looking at my pigsty of a desk. 'WHATCHA WORKING ON THERE?' he asks, giving my cube wall a tap and setting it into a dangerous sway.

I'm in the middle of a hand of computer Hearts, but Ted doesn't need to know that. 'Just catching up on some email,' I answer.

Ted dips his head in to take a closer look, extending his neck like a giraffe would to reach the last leaves on a high branch. He then backs out and gives me a cockeyed look, like he is missing something. Firing is a daily possibility, but I'm not sure that Ted *could* fire me. Six weeks on the job, and I still have no idea who my actual boss is. I report to four people—'senior group analysts,' as Feldman likes to call them. It's been aggravating. Saying OK to this 'Boss' and that 'Boss' and this 'Boss' and the other 'Boss', day in and day out—I feel like a damn taxi cab driver.

Let me introduce you to the scatterbrained, *Where are we on this? Oh! That's not for you!* Lewis Gardner, who is always sniffing. I think he might have a coke habit. There is Jack Ranch—yes, like the salad dressing—who suffers from a gastric disorder that sends anyone within a mile radius of his unlocked jaws running for his life. And then there is Phyllis DiAngelo, the fragile flower of the floor. One morning I tinkered with office amenity and complimented Phyllis on her appearance, saying she looked nice in a dress or something to that effect, and she gave me a look like I had broken up her Wonderland tea party. The woman fell to pieces.

Finally, there is TED, the only 'boss' who has dared dropped the managerial whip with me. Two weeks ago, he invited me for drinks after work. I expected a short round of vodka tonics, but it turned into a three-hour conquest of a full bottle of Belvedere. The whole evening, Ted told these awful jokes and blasted his colleagues. He even went after his boss, poking fun at his hairy earplugs. I couldn't believe what I was hearing. I acknowledged his one-liners by nodding, but I said very little. The whole thing could have been a Feldman sting operation, so I behaved myself. I kept my mouth shut and drank heavily to drown out the holy fucking uncomfortable. Ted stayed right with me on the sauce, tossing back rocks glasses and chasing them with bar olives. I think Ted ate enough olives to shit out the Cadillac his wife bought him for Christmas. We finally parted, I went home, and a new nightmare began the following morning when I had to sit in with Ted on a nine o'clock conference call.

These are the winners I work with.

'HOLD ON A SECOND,' Ted says. The beast of burden trudges off, and I go to work fixing my chair.

Welcome to a typical workday at Feldman, my personal Hell. I'll skip the first two hours of the day because I'm half awake, half in a coma, and I don't think that counts. Right around eleven o'clock I begin with the PIDDLE PIDDLE PIDDLE, deleting voicemails, writing memos in haiku, and cursing central air. I wade through paper, stare at computer pixels, and wait for Francis to drop my cubicle to tell me that, 'We're heading out for Mexican. You hear that? Brrhritos!' I'm the poor guy on the floor, so I wave off the jalapeno-popping freak, reminding him that I bring my own lunch to work.

Lunch is always the highlight of the day for me. Last Friday was the best. I was working on my economy-budget ham sandwich, choking it down the folds of my esophagus with water from the Poland Spring bottle I've reused for the past month, when mustard leaked through the bread and Pollock-dripped on my pants. I grabbed a napkin off Carol's desk and tried to undo the art the best I could, but I only made the mess worse. I grabbed a notebook, held it up to my midsection, and started out into the hall. I spotted a herd of people coming toward me, so I ducked into a copy machine room, waited a minute to let the stampede pass, and then resumed my journey to the men's bathroom, a long and dangerous one because it is on the other side of the building.

Once there, I quickly got to work, soaking my pants with a wet paper towel, dabbing with a dry one, soaking again with the wet. The whole time I nervously watched the door, praying that someone wouldn't walk in. I kept the expletives to a minimum because I knew that the rest of the office would come running as if reacting to the company-wide email FREE DONUTS IN THE MEN'S RESTROOM. The system seemed to be working, so I picked up the pace. Big mistake. The wet towel ripped and left shriveled paper flecks on my pant leg. I tried to brush them off, but they wouldn't un-stick themselves. When I finally finished, the area between my navel and knees could easily have been condemned by The National Board of Health and Welfare upon determination of general nastiness. I left the bathroom and returned quickly to my desk. I didn't move for the next half hour. I used a manila folder to fan my crotch.

The rest of my days are no better. I battle boredom by browsing the Internet, playing with my stapler, coloring in the O's in documents and patting the dust off my keyboard with a Scotched finger. When I'm sick of that, I dream up contests and set my own betting lines. I keep track of the time as I wait to hear one of the following statements: 'When you have a few minutes, can you handle this?' or 'Do you know what the status is on this?' or 'Do you know if it's supposed to rain tonight?'

I also work on my Microsoft Word processing skills, particularly on my speed and general spelling aptitude, typing the alphabet forwards and backwards as quickly as possible or constructing one nonsensical phrase in which every word contains the letter V. *I've investigated every conceivable activity over seventy-seven visits*—how many times can I type the word *tortilla* in a minute? tortilla, tortilla—and only at the sixty-second mark do I stop to note how wonderful my left pointer finger feels as it goes back and forth from the letter T to the letter R, and how completely smooth and balanced the downward transition is from the letter I to the letter L, whose tee-tee repetition is drilled in musically by the ring finger on my strong hand. My right hand. My mouse hand.

Ted is back, looking out the window at Lord knows what. He turns back to me, taps the cube wall again. Clearly, he wants to knock it down and crush me. 'I WENT AHEAD AND PUT IN A REQUEST FOR A NEW CHAIR FOR YOU,' he tells me.

'I hope it wasn't too much trouble,' I say graciously.

'NO TROUBLE AT ALL! WHY WOULD IT BE ANY TROUBLE?'

I sort of shrug. Despite his annoying tendency to pop-in whenever he feels like it, Ted is a decent guy. At least he pretends to try. A few times a day Ted comes by my cube, talks sirloin steak preparation or argues his case for building a football stadium for the Jets in New York. I nod politely and smile. He means well. He might just come through for me on this whole chair business.

Ted is glowing like a stick of plutonium. He is in a great mood today, which is good for everyone. He's a yeller, and when he's mad that snake jaw of his unhinges and drops down, and his mouth grows to about three times its normal size. One day he's going to swallow a colleague whole. I'm sure he has the appetite for it.

Ted clears his throat. 'LET ME KNOW HOW THE CHAIR SITUATION ENDS UP.'

'OK.'

'DO YOU NEED ANYTHING ELSE?'

'I don't think so.'

'LET ME KNOW IF YOU DO.'

'I will, thanks.'

Ted starts to walk away but then turns back abruptly, probably creating a mega-tsunami underneath his coat jacket. 'I ALMOST FORGOT!' he bellows. 'WE HAVE A MEETING AT TWO O'CLOCK. FINISH UP WHAT YOU'RE DOING,' he instructs, 'AND MAKE COPIES OF THAT 10Q I GAVE YOU YESTERDAY. WE ARE COUNTING ON YOU TO HAVE THEM READY BY TWO.'

'10Q?' I complete the thought aloud, the end of it rolling off my tongue before I can close my trap.

'THE 10Q REPORT,' he repeats. 'THE QUARTERLY.'

Gosh, even the office idiots find a way to make me look like an incompetent loser. Every document has a corresponding number, letter combination, or some cutesy, thoroughly unprofessional name like 'piggy slip', which I think is the house nickname for a timesheet. A week in, I decided that I needed a system to keep track of everything, so

I started writing document names and their slang on a piece of paper, which I later tacked to the north wall of my fortress. Unfortunately, the list fell off its mooring and became lost in a moat of office carnage.

I really need to start a new list. I've come to realize that my position demands proficiency in three, and only three, tasks: making gopher runs to Starbucks, babysitting the copy machine, and maintaining a running list of code names for documents that mean nothing to me beyond their pet names. I've proven myself quite capable of negotiating the 700 different versions of the cafe latte, but I always manage to jam the copy machine just as a group of colleagues decides to form a line behind me. Two out of three will do. Maybe not one out of three, but certainly two out of three.

'*Oh, the 10Q,*' I answer, trying to sound like I knew what Ted was talking about all along. I write **10Q** and **10 COPIES** on a yellow stickie and throw a big circle around them. Now to ask a question to make him feel better. 'The 10Q report on gold paper, right?'

'THAT'S RIGHT,' Ted says. 'THE 10Q GOES ON GOLD PAPER.'

An excellent recovery, if I say so myself. One more circle around the chicken scratch.

'YOU'RE AS GOOD AS, AS GOOD AS . . . WHAT'S THE WORD I'M LOOKING FOR?'

There's a four-letter word that comes to mind, and it would fit perfectly right now.

'GOLD!' Ted explodes, unable to wait any longer. 'GOLD!'

Triple Word Score for my boy over here. 'I'll have the copies ready by then,' I promise him.

'GREAT!'

Ted, you corny bastard, I'm ready for you to leave. Lead him out with your eyes.

'OK, I GUESS YOU ARE ALL SET. UNTIL THEN . . .'

'Until then,' I repeat, answering his queer wave with one of my own.

'BYE!'

Full rudder to port, the barge turns and disappears out to sea. Ben shoots the moon. Bastard.

Chapter Nine

A WOMAN IS jumping back and forth between a notepad and a thick textbook. She looks up and misses my stare. Puffy cheeks squeeze in big eyes, which sit back deep in dark sockets. She has that tired, working look.

She prefers to browse the petite departments, much to the eye's dismay. Her tight tank top punctuates her cellulite-dimpled arms and works with a suffocating cut of pepper stone denim to squeeze out a fold of white flesh whenever she leans back to examine her work from afar. Her hair, so big and unnaturally colored that I'll call it '80's red ultramarine-violet', throws her body grotesquely out of balance. A thick chain of gold drapes around her neck, held up at the bottom by a chest stuffed with round pillows.

A new woman, her face painted white with theatrical tragedy, tugs on the arm of the woman sitting on the bench. After a moment, the student concedes, tucks the notepad between the book's pages, collects her black bag, and follows her eager escort to the lobby's exit.

I've been people-watching on account of the length of this line. I never do well with lines. The minute I join a line, I turn into an old man. My back and feet start to ache, my stomach closes in on itself, my brain rushes to lock in on a focus, my limbs falter, and my eyes dry up and beg to be scratched out.

I do a lot of waiting these days. Waiting to pay for groceries. Waiting for movie tickets. Waiting for my coffee to be made drinkable with lots of sugar. Waiting to be paid. Waiting to be seen by the doctor. Waiting to be told that I'm not wanted. Waiting for the cashier. Waiting for this weather to leave, or at least the wind to subside. Waiting for the new guy to arrive. Waiting for the page to turn. Waiting through commercials. Waiting for my change to be counted, and recounted. Waiting for the rain to fall again. Waiting for a document to half-print, then jam. Waiting for the door to open. Waiting for me to shut up. Waiting for the corn to pop. Waiting to tie my shoelaces. Waiting for the ink to run out. Waiting for him to say I have nothing to worry about. Waiting for a free dryer. Waiting for directions. Waiting for him to move out of my way. Waiting to wave hello, and say goodbye. Waiting for the cold to hit my naked body. Waiting for the bottle to end, or the bottle to end me. Waiting for the lights to die down. Waiting to cross the street. Waiting to see the sun again. Waiting for the right time, place, and person. Waiting for a guitar string to break. Waiting to know if I like it. Just a lot of waiting.

Chapter Ten

I'VE SEEN THIS a million times—the three of us sitting around a table, engaged in a never-ending debate full of scrappy metaphorical dogma and misemployed philosophy. The roles are well defined. Julian accuses Paul of disjointed argumentation, Paul accuses Julian of insular thinking, and I sit off to the neutral Swiss side, twiddling my thumbs. Occasionally, I step in and point out that an opinion is just that, an *opinion*, but they could care less. They won't stop until they achieve apotheosis. It's fun, for awhile.

'You believe that our actions cannot be controlled.'

'That's not true.'

'It is true. You say you have no accountability for your actions because you *can't* be accountable.'

'How's that?'

'You don't take responsibility for anything.'

'What?'

'It's like the puppet and his master—'

'Oh God.'

'We'll get to him, but hear me out first. You have the Puppet player, the silent operator hidden from the audience, and then you have the actual puppet, ironically called the "Puppet master," who moves only when someone takes a hold of its strings. You're the Puppet master.'

'You knockin' puppets?'

'What?'

'If you had a hand up your ass, you'd probably put on a show too.'

'Are we having the same conversation here?'

'Puppets, ass play—'

'No, idiot. The puppets with strings. *Marionettes.*'

'Oh.'

'I guess the other works too, but let's just stick with the marionette example for now.'

'Let's.'

'When it's time to take responsibility for your actions, you remind every paying customer that you are just an unwilling participant in some traveling sideshow. You play the role of the innocent Puppet master.'

'I feel a reference to God and his hold on the world coming.'

'Where did you think I was going with this?'

'OK, fine. If you believe that there's an all-powerful god, a god you call the "Puppet player," then you're forced to conclude that we are all Puppet masters—*God's* Puppet masters, you and me, and every person walking the Earth. Am I right?'

'No, that's where free will comes into the picture. We get to make decisions. And our decisions affect other people. Your decision to, say, *romance a man*, not only affects you, but it affects me, as we share the same last name.'

'I hate you.'

'An unfortunate symbiosis, but a very real symbiosis that we both have to live with.'

'So am I the Puppet player?'

'No, that doesn't work either. We get to pull the strings, but we also dance the dance.'

'So we're both?'

'No, and that's the point.'

'At last, we have arrived at the point.'

'There are no strings. They are constructs. In reality, the puppet acts independently.'

'Then what's the deal with the Puppet player?'

'You see the Puppet master move, and you assume that there is someone behind the scenes, pulling the strings. But if you focus just on the stage, you never see the Puppet player.'

'You see him when the show is over—'

'Exactly. When the Puppet master dies or—' hand quotes, '—*finishes its performance*, the Puppet player is revealed. You're not supposed to consider them together at the same time. So think about it. Maybe the puppet attaches itself to string to make it look like he's under someone else's power. Is that so hard to believe? Don't you think it's possible that the Puppet player is just a figment of the imagination?'

'Now you're questioning the existence of God.'

'Not necessarily. Maybe he's out there in the audience, watching from the balcony.'

'What about religion and ethics?'

'What about them?'

'Don't you think it's odd that there are so many people in the world who share the same idea of right and wrong? How can it be a coincidence—how can you say that a glass is half empty when you have never seen a full glass, or even an empty glass?'

'Because half of the glass is full of water.'

'You could argue that it isn't.'

'Half empty?'

'It's not a play on words.'

'Then what?'

'Without objectivity, every person could have an equally different and valid argument for what is right.'

'OK, every person is right.'

'Then the world is based on subjectivity, and that sounds like chaos to me.'

'The world *is* chaos.'

'But that leaves one huge problem.'

'What's that?'

'How does the puppet move by itself? It has to be given life from somewhere. Life can't materialize from nothing.'

'My memory is a little fuzzy around origin. But I'll be lucid for the end, and I think that's what life is for. To prepare for the end.'

'Or what faith is for.'

'Whatever you prefer.'

'That's convenient.'

'So is blaming tequila shots on your choice of conquest tonight.'

'I hate you.'

'Can we order here?' I interrupt. 'I'm starving.'

It's almost three in the morning. Julian and Paul share a big yawn. My nose is bugging me. It started right about the time we walked into this diner on Ninth Avenue, on the corner of twelve or thereabouts. We settled on BLU NIGHT DINER because it was open. The light pouring out the front pulled us in like a tractor beam. At the entrance, I looked up at the sign's letters, examined the clumsily arranged oranges and blues and thought about abandoned movie theaters. Just as I was about to walk in, a loud noise spun me around. A motorcycle screamed around the corner, weaved around potholes, and disappeared down the block. The brick warehouse across the street looked haunted. Something about the whole thing reminded me of home.

'Decided what to have?'

Our waitress, a portly woman with extraordinarily high hair, manages a weak smile as she pulls a long pencil out from behind her ear. From my vantage point, she might stand five foot six, but her Eighties hairdo easily adds another four or five inches. Her forehead wrinkles a moment, sucking in a puffy yet attractive face. *Lily*, I read. The letters on her nametag are black and monstrous. **LILY.**

'I guess I'll go first,' Julian says. 'Burger and fries for me.'

'How do you want it cooked?' Lily asks.

'Medium,' he answers. 'And I'll have a Coke.'

Lily and I make eye contact. I wonder how long was I looking at her chest. 'Burger and fries for me too,' I tell her. 'Medium rare.'

'That it?' She looks down as if suddenly compelled to pray. She must have caught me staring. Great, now she thinks I'm some sort of pervert who needs my soul saved.

'Coffee,' I tell her. 'And one of those coffee rolls I saw on top of that display case.'

She looks at Paul. 'What can I get you, hon?'

'I'll go with the western omelet with Swiss cheese, no onions,' Paul says, speaking from behind a raised menu. Paul, a notoriously picky eater, is always very specific when he orders food. 'The home fries,' he continues, 'white toast . . . ' looking up, 'and a Coke too, please, but no ice in it.'

'I'll be back with your orders.' She grabs the menus from our hands, tucks them underneath her arm, and trudges off.

'So what do you think?' Julian asks me.

'About what?'

He jiggles his nonexistent titties.

'You're a bastard.'

He laughs. I move away from the topic of Lily's rack of lamb and take in my surroundings. The diner has a Yankee gift shop feel to it. The walls are covered with war propaganda posters, needle stitch art, and essays written on yellowed parchment. Up at the door is a glass display case packed with pastries and layered cakes. Fake plants shoot out of oak barrels. A large aquarium tank fits the back wall, and the bloated goldfish inside are fluttering around and making fat faces. On each table is a small metal basket that neatly holds a pair of salt and pepper shakers, short stacks of sugar and sugar substitute packets, a swan-necked milk pourer, and an Easy Pour ketchup bottle with a wide mouth.

You can't accurately predict the quality of diner food by looking at signs, or menus, or decorations. But there are certain things that might tip you one way or the other. For example, every table in this joint has its own bottle of ketchup, which is unusual because diner owners are typically too stingy for that sort of extravagance. I'd like to think that the token bottle of ketchup spares this diner from a shithole Zagat review.

The place is certainly lively. Across from us, a group of college students are playing a non-drinking version of quarters with water glasses. Two attractive women sitting to our left are giggling at a man sitting alone at a corner window table. The man, dressed in a red and black checked hunter's cap and gray rain slicker, is running nasal samples through a series of taste tests. Yum yum, eat up, the service is slow here. Up at the cash register, a short woman with curls thick enough to snare a bird in mid-flight is busy shelling out dessert dishes to the waitstaff, emptying coffee filters, and handling customer checks. She's a firecracker. You can tell.

I turn to Julian. 'Why couldn't you tell it was a man?' I ask him.

I missed Julian's run-in with a man-chick at the bar we just left, and I only caught bits and pieces of it as we walked here. Apparently, the 'funniest thing ever', as Paul put it, transpired as I was stuffing all the mints and cigarettes I could fit in my pockets before the bathroom attendant kicked me out. When I returned to the party, Paul was laughing hysterically. Unfortunately, the object of Julian's affection had already disappeared.

'He looked like a chick,' Julian explains, a whiny desperation filling his voice. 'He had long hair, and I swear I saw breasts.'

The bar had all the features common for drinking dens stretching from Tribeca to Hell's Kitchen—high ceilings, exposed piping, grimy concrete floors, and poor lighting. The window frames were boarded, painted. Night or day—you couldn't tell when you were inside. The main floor housed a long, narrow bar off to the right of the doors and an open floor in the back which served as the dance floor. A DJ, squished in a balcony overhanging a pit of overdressed and hardly dressed hottie wannabes, spun hip-hop tracks without interruption. Less than a half hour in, we pushed our way through the crowd. Down the stairs we went, passing those trying to return to the dance party, those squeezing PV muscles as they waited in line for the bathrooms, and those like us looking for a change of scenery. We ended up congregating at the downstairs bar, where Julian met his little friend.

'It was crowded,' Julian continues, 'and the guy's head was turned away from me. I didn't get a good look at his face.'

'I noticed it right away,' Paul responds dickishly.

A slight tremor ripples through the place, flexing and crunching its joints. A dump truck passes by the window front. The couple sitting at a table up there doesn't seem to notice. The woman is busy glaring at the rowdies. Her acquaintance, a Mediterranean-tanned man with greased jet black hair, looks more interested in keeping his tie out of his scrambled eggs.

'So? What did you say?' I ask Julian.

'What?'

'Talk to me, I'm dying over here.'

'I just asked her—him, if he would like a drink.' He turns his head with the sound of glass breaking. A coin rolls over toward us. 'I hear Rum and Coke, so I turn to the bartender—'

'A beauty,' Paul interrupts.

'—and order two. When I got them, I turned back around, and he's talking to this blonde girl—'

'A real girl,' Paul adds. 'One without a penis.'

Julian ignores the comment, 'I hand him a glass, and I think he said "thank you". I'm not sure. The bar was mad loud.'

The woman at the register is giving it to the busboy, yelling and waving her arms. The Medusa locks on her head appear ready to strike.

Julian drinks from his water glass and continues. 'I couldn't hear anything. He probably said "F-U" for all I know. Then Paul elbows me, I drop my drink—'

'You dropped your drink?'

'Thanks a lot for that too,' Julian says, now glowering at Paul. 'You made me look like a total ass.'

'You did that yourself,' Paul fires back.

'Whatever,' Julian replies, taking a sip of clear stuff. 'It was totally uncalled for.'

'Landed right on his foot,' Paul says, nudging me. 'Priceless.'

Lily is nowhere to be found, and my stomach has begun to voice its displeasure. A man has to eat. 'So then what happened?' I ask Julian.

'Oh, OK. So get this. We both kneel down to pick up the glass, and that's when I notice the little bump on his throat. The, ah, whatchamacallit?'

'The Adam's apple?'

'That's it.' Julian thanks me with a point. 'But other than that, the guy totally looked like a chick. I mean, it could have gone either way. Anyway, I just stood there, staring at him. I didn't know what to say.'

'Will you be my buh buh buh girlfriend?' Paul stutters.

'Ha ha, very funny.' Julian waves him off and continues, 'The guy must have realized that I had made a mistake because he had this strange smile on his face, like he had figured it out before I did.' He looks up. 'The food's here.'

Finally. Lily puts a plate in front of me, and I go right for the fries.

'I'm serious about this,' Julian says, intent on making his point before touching his plate. 'It's amazing what a facial expression can do, or even a simple gesture. The other day for example, I was at one of those fancy delis uptown, waiting in line, and there's a lady behind me, holding a dog in one hand, and she's obviously in a rush because she's hollering away about how her guests will be arriving at any minute. Well, everyone starts staring at this woman—'

'What were you doing there?' Paul interrupts, taking a bite of his toast.

Julian shrugs. 'Buying a Gatorade or something, I don't remember. But I'm there and committed, so I'm waiting it out. Well, all of a sudden this kid comes up to the woman with a card in his hand, and let me tell you, does her story suddenly change. She starts kissing the kid on the cheek, the tears well up in her eyes—all over a stupid library card she had dropped. But I guess that's all it takes sometimes. A simple act of kindness.'

Julian picks the lettuce and tomatoes off his burger and then heads for the ketchup bottle. I have another fry and watch Paul dissect his omelet with a fork. Julian finishes with the ketchup, I grab it and douse my burger. The diner is outrageously loud now, making conversation a shouting match. My thoughts move to the events of the night: the bar, the beer bottles resting on the shoulders of wall-mounted porcelain gods, the fun of androgyny.

The boy in the deli is a hero in this world, a world most people enter and exit alone. Most people, most of the time, walk by and keep their hands to themselves, dispensing recycled courtesies and automated pity looks from an impersonal distance. They hate themselves for doing it and hate others for allowing it. But once in awhile, someone like the boy breaks out of the funk, stops, and extends a hand. If the woman reaches out and takes it, then she in turn gives that boy a glimpse of the most desperate desires of her heart. That's how the exchange works. If the hand isn't extended or she chooses not to take it, then she remains whole and unshared. That happens a lot because the boy's hand scares away most people. It reminds them of their own unwillingness to put out a limb. But deep down inside I think all people want to take that hand. It keeps them in touch with their own humanity.

My burger is fat and juicy, bleeding, the way I like it. The coffee roll doesn't fare so well. One bite, and I decide that the insipid mess would be better off back on the counter. The mismatched couple get up to leave. I'm not surprised. Incompatibility can never sit still for more than a few minutes, especially on these hard-as-a-rock booth cushions. Lily wanders our way with the check. I ask for more water. Lily leaves, and I duck down and quickly pick up a couple of quarters off the floor. On to the table they go. There you are, Lily. Job well done.

* * *

The thick, tepid October night smells of a recent cow massacre. I hail a taxi and get in. Paul caught a taxi uptown a few minutes ago, and Julian wanted to walk home, so I'm on my own.

'Eleventh and First, please.'

'Got it.'

The cab pulls away, and the BLU NIGHT DINER sign slowly disappears.

I can't wait to get home. My head hurts, and a taxi door is no substitute for a fluffy pillow.

The taxi cab zips through an intersection, trying to outrun time. I listen intently. Sometimes, when you are speeding through life, even in a taxi, the ironies start hitting you. Splat, splat, like insects on the windshield. You stop and listen, and for a moment you can hear the melody of contradiction tapping itself on the windshield.

'Howz yore night?' I hear. I look to the front and see a white cowboy hat. A glassy eye looks at me through the rearview mirror. Beyond its Windexed surface, a question waits for my answer.

'Not bad,' I answer. 'You?'

'Just great,' drawls ID 7Q58. I catch half of a smile, crooked and superb John Wayne.

'Warm night, huh?'

'Shur-es. Mind?' A blue flash slices up the dark night. A harmonica. Curious.

'Not at all,' I answer.

A bluesman? A country crooner? Nope. Much to my chagrin, a Whitney Houston fan.

* * *

The cab pulls away. My block is quiet and dark, not a pitch-black dark, but dark for the City.

I walk to my building, unlock the outside door, and yank it open. Clumped on the floor is a pair of dark blue jeans and a pumpkin-colored sweatshirt. Hidden underneath is a man, fast asleep.

I clear my clear throat. No reaction. I rap one time on the door. Nothing. The poor guy must have got hammered, stumbled his way back to the building, realized he didn't have his keys with him, and passed out waiting for someone to rescue him. Fortuna had turned against him. I can hear Ignatius on a tirade.

I guess I could shake the man out of his slumber, prop the door open for him, or call the Finest to wake him up at gunpoint. But I prefer option D. I step over him, unlock the door, and close the door quietly behind me.

Pleasant dreams, ya drunk.

November

Chapter Eleven

I DON'T KNOW why I kept my NYU papers, but I'm glad that I did. Nothing cracks me up more than reading something that I've written.

My junior year of college, I took a creative writing seminar. Loved it. The first day of the semester, the Philosophy slash English professor walked into the room, went to the white board, snapped the cap off a dry erase marker, and wrote:

> **In this class you will write what you feel,
> or I will fail you.**

I trust that guy with my life.

No page limit. Write about the ethical nature of making decisions. Good versus Evil, Wrong versus Right. Base your piece around a unique experience. Feel it, and then write it. Do not hold back. Philosophical, historical, and literary references are encouraged. Topical humor is fine, but in small doses. Make it good because this is your last paper for me.

* * *

The world is full of hate, the hating, the hater and the hated. Every child has an older brother, a bully, a teacher, a vegetable, a bathtub, an attic, or a cellar that he or she hates, but you find the hate in all of nature, in all of the world, everywhere really, in most everything. Take, for example, dogs. Each and every dog has a live-in cat or daily mailman or weekly garbage truck that it absolutely hates. Heck, there may even be a dog that hates *you*. You may not know why the dog hates you, or the cat, or the mailman, or the garbage truck, but the *whys* of life are never all that transparent.

Unable to settle on a definitive *why*, you might have decided that the dog actually needed to hate whatever it was it hated, as if the very existence of the dog was contingent upon the continued existence of its nemesis. You may have decided that the dog without an adversary would do nothing but take naps, have a lap here and there of its water bowl, lick its balls, pee on tree trunks and fire hydrants, and beg for food. Without an enemy, the dog would be without purpose and personality, completely worthless to its security-conscious owner, not unlike a superhero would be to a Flanders society comprised of a bunch of "okeley-dokeley" goody two shoes.

Leaf through the pages of an ecology book, and you'll read that the needier of two conjoined organisms is the "parasite" and the more needed one of the two is the "host." Every dog needs a host; however, staying true to the definition of the word *host* and avoiding reflexive folly, the host neither needs the dog nor any other parasite to live. A cat, or a mailman, or a garbage truck would manage just fine without a dog on its paws, heels or bumper. In fact, all the merrier they would be without having to deal with the barking and the pouncing, the urinating and the biting. Likewise, a villain does not need a hero counterpart as such to exist. Villains like Lex Luther need *victims*, not flying justice clowns dressed in blue leotards dropping in on the scene to foil their diabolical deeds.

But a superhero certainly helps to give that villain credibility. Inversely, it's no secret that Mr. Kent would lose Superhero status in a heartbeat if Lex decided one day to throw in the towel. So in reality, it is by and through a need-and-needed relationship that the evil baldy becomes both host and parasite, both hater and hated, and the good greaser becomes both host and parasite, both hater and hated.

To be hated is to be understood for hating, and to hate is to accept the receipt of hate. The natural order of things relies upon the continuation of revolving hate. At all times you, me, the dog, the cat, the mailman, the garbage truck, the superhero, and the villain are all, individually, the hater *and* the hated.

Most people would agree that hate stems from the bad of the world. But when is good *good* and bad *bad*? Could good be bad and bad good? When is black *black* and white *white*, other than on a black-and-white cookie? They say that everything that comes around goes around, so how can you tell when you are going forward, doing *good*, and when you are going backward, doing *bad*? If you start at a unique position on a circular track and begin moving, sooner or later you will find yourself back at the point of origin. It's a merry-go-round. Walk forward, and you might as well walk backward too.

Back in the bedlam of the third grade, I sent my archenemy and 'hated'—a boy by the name of "Ronald Stubbs"—to the hospital emergency room. I didn't really *make* that decision. It sort of just happened, coming to freaky fruition like the multiplication table trick with the number 9. It was an event of dumb chance. I'm tempted here to use the more comfortable *luck* in place of *chance*, but I balk at such reckless substitution because I suspect that if I were to use the word *luck*, I would set a dangerous precedent that could not be retracted. One *luck* would turn into ten, which would turn into a hundred, and eventually we'd have an epidemic of stuttering diction on our hands. The word *luck* would cease to mean anything specific. I would lose credibility and be blamed for starting a global war of semantics, and the world would crumble into a fine dust and be blown out into the great cosmic cloud. So yes, I will not use the word *luck*, for it would only buy me membership to the club of the safely uncommitted, where it is OK to slide dizzily back and forth attributing the laws of statistical probability to select events and blaming superstitious fortune on others.

As "chance" would have it, I went to elementary school with an asshole named "Ronald Stubbs" who needed to be taught a lesson, and I was the one to administer it. One day during lunch, Ronald P.A. broadcasted a comment about my lunch box—a yellow Sesame Street lunch box with a picture of Big Bird on the front—to a ridicule-hungry mob of sugared-out third and fourth graders. He managed to balance himself on a metal chair, and then he began flailing his arms up and down and squawking like a damn fool. I almost died when Ronald simulated the release of his bowels on the table. I shouted back the usual insults—"Fat Ronnie" and "Ronnie Rolo"—but Ronald went on unbridled, working his effort into a cafeteria-wide chant of "Big Bird Turd! Big Bird Turd!" For days I had that grating mantra running in my head like a hamster befuddled by an exercise wheel.

That fat bastard stole my pudding snack cup too, I think. Ronald was a wily fucker. Everyone knew that he had a reputation for replacing desserts with bananas and other undesirable items whenever you turned your back to him. On occasions too frequent to dismiss as mere coincidence, the lunches of certain uncool students would disappear into thin air shortly before lunch period. I think my teacher, Ms. Perkins, knew that Ronald was somehow involved; nonetheless, she'd always play it cool, never vocalizing the possibility that a criminal could be walking among us. She'd throw up her hands and saying something like, "I guess your lunch was thrown out by accident. We'll just have to fix that." And then she'd reach for the string roped around her neck, pull out the gold key to her top secret desk drawer, and by almost magical means materialize the exact amount of lunch money needed to quell the looming hysteria.

Now that I think about it again and recall how upset I was, I'm positive that Ronald treated my lunchbox to a five-fingered discount. Ronald was an opportunist. He knew how to strike, and where to strike. He found your weakness, grabbed a bat, and went to work on your family jewels like a pair of miniature piñatas. Pudding was my favorite dessert, and Ronald seemed to know this as he smiled and let a brown, syrupy substance dribble out of his mouth. But honestly, had he taken the Swiss Miss or not, it probably wouldn't have mattered. He had brought the spark, and the public humiliation that he had kindled was enough to fan the flames flickering out of my ears into a raging bonfire.

The pandemonium caught the attention of the teacher on mess hall duty, who happened to be Mrs. Whitehall, my humorless music teacher who never seemed to like me much after my stirring, but slightly inaccurate rendition of "Oh, Beautiful!" at a class recital some months prior. Dutifully, she roared out a monster rebuke to Ronald and demanded that he sit back down in his chair. With the source of the mischief discovered and extinguished, Mrs. Whitehall then turned away from Ronald, whipped off her horn-rimmed glasses, and frightened the mob into a controlled riot. As I was about to propose to her on the spot, Mrs. Whitehall suddenly looked at me, shook a piano-crippled finger in the air, and warned me to stay out of trouble. "I'll be watching you," she told me.

She was a witch, *literally*. Halloween was the one day of the year when Mrs. Whitehall woke up in the morning, peered into her closet, and picked out her outfit correctly. She would don the black cloak, the hat that drooped to one side of her head, and she'd carry an old broom in her hand wherever she went and use it to point out misdeeds. All day long she would stay in perfect character, twitching her green-wart nose and flashing an incomplete set of pointy teeth at her terrified Hanzels and Gretels as she explained the difference between a quarter note and an eighth note. She was an absolute fright. I had nightmares about her—gory, damaging nightmares. The memory of her still gives me the willies. She was evil. Oh yes, thirty hours a week of evil. To this day I still tell my friends that I used to flick off Mrs. Satan.

Mrs. Whitehall hated me, but she hated *all* children. She was an equal opportunity child hater. I guess that's why she taught music at a public elementary school.

In a slowly quieting cafeteria I sat there in my chair, a frozen corpse. I wanted to disappear. Having finally returned to his chair, Ronald gawked at me from across the table, contorting his face like a ball of flesh-colored Play-Doh and egging me on for a reaction. I wanted to grab my lunchbox and unload a helping of PBS whoop ass on the back of his head, but I kept my cool. I didn't want to give him the satisfaction.

It didn't take long for me to realize what had to be done. Retaliation was in order. It would need to be swift and decisive, and it would have to come soon because timing was of the essence. Nine-year-old politics vacillated quickly, and I risked losing credibility in the eyes of my fellow classmates if I sat on my hands too long. Ronald had turned me into the laughing stock of the chocolate milk drinking community, and I had every intention to make him pay through the nose for it.

I spent the rest of the day planning my revenge. I considered my options: replacing Ronnie's lunch box with a bag of dog feces, planting thumbtacks on his chair, gluing together the pages of his textbooks. One by one I added and crossed them off with a green highlighter. Before the ring of the last bell, I had a winner. The *what* in place, I shifted my focus to the *when*, and eventually decided to strike when Ronald would be at his most vulnerable state: Recess.

The following day came, the rain tapered off early and the morning gave way to the noon. Ms. Perkins announced that indoor entertainment of 7Up and the like would be an unnecessary evil. I looked out the window and rejoiced. The day was mine to have.

I watched Ronald as he followed the line heading out of the classroom. Ronald was a canker of a human being. The kid had beady eyes, a bulbous marshmallow nose, a tangled mess of ruddy brown hair, and big ears that sort of melted over at the tops. And he was fat, oh so very fat. I know that having a little extra blubber when you are young is perfectly healthy, but Ronald took it well beyond the point of normal candy bar tubbiness. The kid had gigantic chunks of flesh slopped on his body in places that seemed to break down human mechanics and make movement impossible, and no shirt from his mother's department store of choice could have disguised this. I'm talking Pillsbury Dough fat now. He had the look of a boy whose mother had begun the spoiling at conception, gorging him, expanding him into a fat, zygote balloon. The feeding continued. Ronald always had a mess on his shirt—doughnut powder, chocolate milk, anything he could get his hands on.

Like many of his deplorable peers, Ronald relied on a handful of assets to compensate for a slew of liabilities. His principal strengths were a foul mouth, an on-the-fly ability to customize insults to the individual, and his massive size. This powerful combination made him a formidable opponent for any kid who dared meet him on the battlefield of life.

And how could they not fear Ronald? He could sit on his classmates and end them. He was a Blue with the teeth of a Great White, and with whaling reserved for the resilient Eskimos (and periodically taken up as hobby by drunk oil tanker captains), my dream of one day melting down Ronald Stubbs into a lifetime supply of tea-light candles remained just that—a dream. With an excellent handle on penetrative rhetoric and a growing arsenal of physical offensive weapons including a men's size-seven foot, Stubbs subverted the notion that a safe haven actually existed for lunchbox-carrying targets like me. I bet money that Ronald is now studied at bully training institutions around the globe. The case for his textbook immortalization is strong, for it is *the Ronald Stubbs* who successfully unraveled the fallacy that words, unlike sticks and stones, will never hurt you.

I cannot adequately express how much I hated him. My words almost fail me.

He was just a fat, dirty, whiny boy that no one liked.

I had my wits about me to enter the line five or six students behind Ronald, close enough to keep him in view the entire walk out of the building but far enough away to avoid detection. Ms. Perkins liked a good straight line, and we liked her; thus, we normally obliged with what would have been perceived to be an unreasonable command had it been ordered by any other teacher. And be it that Ronald was the size of two other students pushed together at the hip, picking Stubbs out of the infantry line was as easy as looking at a snake's belly and locating the prey it had just swallowed.

As the class made its way down the hallway, I kept tabs on Ronald, watching him laugh away like a doltish clown, picturing him with one of those beanie hats on that giant watermelon head of his. I walked behind Charlie, a quiet kid who had the unfortunate distinction of being the class smelly kid. Whenever he walked, Charlie would sort of bounce side-to-side and yank on a monstrous, hand-me-down flannel shirt. He liked to sing these songs with no clear lyrics, show off his T-Rex impression, and talk about his adventures with his best friend Pucky, who I think was invisible. I don't think Charlie had many friends on account of his offensive odor and peculiar behavior, but it didn't seem to matter much to him. Charlie was one of those strange boys who was content to be left alone in his own world.

I swallowed quick gulps of air as I walked behind Charlie, who had a thing for choo-choo train whistles at the time. When the teacher stopped the vanguard of the platoon to let the tailing stragglers catch up to the rest, Charlie turned around and looked up with laser blue eyes. I waited for him to say something, but he only buzzed some sort of incoherent nonsense and sent a delightful string of spit in my direction. After wiping his perpetually runny nose on a snot-frosted sleeve, Charlie turned back around and became the locomotive that could again.

The walking and choo-choo choo-ing and booger-smearing continued as we made our way to the playground. The autumn air, still saturated with the moisture trapped between the gray clouds overhead and the black mud on the ground, smelled of revenge. Puddles kept me sliding left and right like Mr. Frogger. I kept my distance. Any suspicion on Ronald's part would have been catastrophic to Operation Make Ronnie Rolo Pay For Being Such A Mean Fat Bastard. I had the element of birthday surprise going for me, and I wasn't about to blow out the candles early, creating a victory smoke that would set off the fire alarm and blow my wish out the window. I knew that running into Ronald prematurely would have thrown my concentration or even weakened my resolve, so wisely I went transparent, became a ghost, stayed out of sight.

As the class approached the gate, I begin to inch my way to Ronald, cutting in front of Smelly Charlie and several other students in the process. At the honeycomb-style fence, I felt the pack swell forward as the front of the line debouched out on to the playground. I quickly moved behind Ronald, to the point where I could have reached out, grabbed him, thrown him to the ground and ended it right then and there. The thought crossed my mind, but I had neither the nerve nor raw strength to attempt such an audacious feat. A wedgie would have been a more feasible act of vengeance, but I wasn't going anywhere near Ronald's ass.

A few seconds expired, and with the discipline of the platoon beginning to falter, I sensed that in a heartbeat Ronald would be out of my reach and gone forever. With that, I struck. In perfect stride I extended my right leg forward and hooked my foot around Ronald's ankle. I felt a quick tug, then a release. In a flash Ronald fell to the ground. Almost immediately, he began to scream all bloody hell at the top of his lungs. A second later, Ronald rolled over on his stomach, beaching himself like a confused humpback.

I could see the headlines, hear the crowds lining up for the victory parade. Ronald had finally come to the end of his uncontested reign of terror, met on the battlefield by someone who knew how to wield a green Converse All-Star sneaker. Soundly defeated, Ronald ceased to be our Hitler, the one who had owned the fear of all those too frightened to resist him. His blitzkrieg Gelb conquests and brutish Kristellnacht victories fell to the side and into the past. His military might broke, and his propaganda machine crumbled to ruin. With his Barbarossa stalled, my Overlord kicked into high gear.

But when Ronald fell to the ground, the impact shook the galactic playground, opening up an ulterior gap in the Universe, and people began to gravitate to him like all matter does to a black hole. Teachers, students, even a man jogging by the playground with his German Shepard were sucked into the collapsed body of gas, sweat, and baby fat. Ms. Perkins witnessed the commotion, bolted into the school building, and called for an ambulance. The touch-feely Suzie Rowlands tattled on me to Mr. Marlow, who later rounded out the Axis of Evil by bringing news of my violent outburst to the principal. Ronald, of course, skipped the nurse's office—a death-smelling asylum for the incontinent and bullied—and headed straight to the hospital in a siren-blasting speedster fit for a president. I just stood there like a chump, holding on to a receipt that evidenced my purchase of Ronald Stubbs' bump into glorified martyrdom.

After hearing the coached testimony of prosecution-appointed witnesses, Principal Walters had no choice but to put a call into my mother. Naturally, my mother blew a gasket. Her anger turned into disappointment, then guilt. She enrolled herself and my dad in a weekly parenting class held at the community development center not far from town hall. A few weeks later, they became child psychology experts and set aside Pasta Night Tuesday to discuss 360-Degree Communication and Child Anger Management. I stuck to my guns, but my parents dismissed my defense as fallible, deciding that I had flipped out in a childish rage and staged a violent plea for attention, brought on in no small part by their parental neglect. The idiots at the center must have done a number on them.

Adults forget that children survive childhood by fighting back against bullies. You can't let fat bastards pick you apart in the cafeteria. You can't allow them to spread scuttlebutt about surgery you had to correct a hermaphroditic condition at birth. Popularity means a lot to the cool kids, but it means absolutely *everything* to the uncool kids.

And surprise of surprise, I was not a cool kid. I was a hobbledehoy, a biological anomaly, what the horrified geneticists down at the lab called "a cruel joke of nature." I had a mother-subsidized crop of unevenly shorn hair, a deathly pale complexion and a pair of invisible blond eyebrows to match. I looked as though I had been handed over to an aspiring butcher, marinated overnight in a pool of bleach, and then gnawed on by a pair of starved Rottweilers. I also had a skinny body that refused to grow into the two, humongous incisors sticking out of my mouth. This pair of jumbo-sized Chiclets—supposedly, a byproduct of my mistaking my fingers for a Popsicle when I was a toddler—gave me an intolerable lisp. This lisp, coupled with an ear-piercing voice of a dwarf mouse continually kicked in the balls, gave me cartoon status, something in the likes of a cross between Rocky and Sylvester the Cat.

My speech impediment earned me a spot on a "special" team comprised of a half-dozen linguistic retards who were subjected to the weekly humiliation of being rounded up and herded down the school's hallways like cattle. One at a time we were dragged into the windowless 101 room, held down to a chair by sheer terror, and tongue-slaughtered by a woman known only to us as "Angry Agnes." During my interrogations, the choleric bitch would snap at me like a threatened turtle, poking her head out into my face to click corrective syllables off her tongue.

My Boston accent didn't help. The local throat bubo infected my vaccine-less diction, symptomatically eliminating my R's and crudely extending my A's. With the words I scrapped together with the remainder of the alphabet, I protested my detainment to Angry Agnes, insisting that I didn't belong in speech classes and that I spoke just fine. Of course the sneaky battle-ax always tricked me into saying something that exposed my weakness for words borrowed from the less than kind parts of the alphabet. Having duped a child, she'd laugh with smug satisfaction and then launch into another diatribe about how I should keep quiet because unlike her I wasn't paid to have an opinion on the subtleties of the English language.

I expected to muster some sympathy at home, but my tears did little to convince my parents that speech classes were degrading. They failed to recognize that elementary school is a tough crowd, full of unwavering critics and aspiring journalists with slanderous punch lines and libelous headlines. I made the attempt to be heard, to be understood, to be embraced. I yelled and cried, stomped and pouted, but my parents shook their heads and made it clear to me that "Cafpah the Friendly Ghost" would never make any friends if he couldn't pronounce his own name properly.

My little stunt with Ronald cost me a trip to the Principal's office for a parent-teacher conference. I voiced my moral outrage at the meeting, but my words fell on deaf ears. When you are young, you have no voice in the daily debate over what's good and what's bad, and you can expect every adult that you know to remind you of just that. With my eyes fixed on my clasped hands, I listened to Principal Walters explain that two weeks of recess on the fence, a 500 word essay entitled "Treating Others with Respect," a written apology to Ronald, and a part-time job clacking together erasers was a "fair" punishment for my behavior.

When I realized that I could say and do nothing to influence the future course of events, I gave up and served my punishments. I decided that it was collateral damage for a successful strike. Present Humanity called The Act "Callous Vindictiveness," but Future Humanity would call The Act "Heroic Duty Performed." I no longer cared what these people thought. In my mind, I was a fucking hero.

The world caught me red-handed, so I wrote:

Dear Ronald,

I'm sorry for tripping you. It was a very mean thing to do. I will never do it again. I promise. I hope that you get better soon. I hope that we can be friends again.

Deeds are only pinned with a good, bad, or just plain rotten tail when someone brings up the word *ethics* or Ms. Perkins points to "The Rules For The Classroom" chalked up on the board. Adults don't punish fairly and objectively; they are subjective disciplinarians, grazers of misguided truth and justice, and children are their poorly groomed fodder. Don't bother looking for the words *kid, child*, or *Young General George Washington* in The Bill of Rights because you won't find them. Columbia District living, ass-spanking without representation. Honorable rebellion? Hah! Thoreau never talked about *adolescent* civil disobedience. You're a kid, so you do what you're told.

But the smart kids fight back, quietly. They turn the page over and write in small letters:

jello man ronald

Turns out, Ronald didn't exactly come out on top either. The next day he dragged his lame ass into school on crutches, looking like a defeated cripple and my newly dubbed bitch. Fellow student Timmy Finmore asked to sign his cast, Ronald obliged, and Timmy penned a hilarious obscenity. As Ronnie hobbled after the little trickster, I realized that every bad surprise has a good twin somewhere in the Universe, and if you wait long enough, they find each other, the good offsets the bad, and everything turns out OK. If I had known that earlier, then I would have started tripping jerks like Ronald the minute I realized what those two things growing out from underneath my wee-wee were.

My Ronnie Rolo story sits packed away in a closet, reemerging every now and again to remind me how to smile. It is a fabulous tale of retribution. Dicks like Ronald deserve what they get.

The story explains the fate of religion in my life. That day on the playground, Ronald Stubbs got the best of me, and no angels from on high or below did a damn thing about it. As my Earthly sentence was read, I felt alone, utterly alone. My whole confidence in religion flew out the window. Everything I was told in church was a lie.

My only reason to be at church was to keep an eye on the ushers. I never trusted those guys. I always envisioned them sitting around in their password-secured room after church service, counting their weekly spoils, blowing rings from Cuban cigars and swishing around cognac in giant snifters. I figured that there had to be at least six or seven ushers in cahoots, dishing out a scam that would have made Savings and Loan conspirators cream their pants. Of course I never had any real evidence to prove that they were thieves, but having a lack of information demanded that certain questions be asked. And since I was the only one asking the right questions, I couldn't help but let the imagination run wild. They smiled, took our envelopes, I formulated conspiracy theories of the JFK assassination kind, and this was one of them.

Clued into their subterfuge, I often considered palming the envelope and dropping in a placebo, using a bit of sleight of hand to pull off the deception. I thought to make a trip to Gethsemane to press the oil of anguish into sacrificial lamb's blood. I thought about taking a stand, achieving martyrdom. But the whole matter of sainthood a la Larry Underwood or Whitney Horgan had a way of sucking me out of the body of Paul and blowing me back into the body of Saul whenever it was time to stone Stephen. I never followed through on my plan to undermine the ushers' work because I didn't have the balls to attempt it. I was afraid that the men in black would retaliate, and I was petrified that my parents would catch me in the act and not understand why I had to steal their money to do the Lord's work.

I also feared religious consequences. As a Baptist, one follows the implicit rule that punition should be handed out immediately. Baptists expedite the humiliation of apology, the bottom redecorating, the guilt trip. At least that's how the Northern Baptists like to do it, the same folk who clap their hands to the music only if the grape juice making its way around the room spent a bit too much time fermenting on the shelf.

On the other side of the street, my Catholic counterparts appeared to have it pretty good. They slept in on Sunday mornings and caught services in the evenings. Their church hosted bi-annual carnivals, and members of the "right" denomination received free ticket vouchers for rides, booth games, and refreshments. Teenagers took a crash course to salvation, a class that could be repeated if necessary to bump up their mean G-O-D scores to a passable level. At times I couldn't help but think that I would have preferred fifty Hail Mary's and an altar boy contract extension to the torture that I suffered as amends for The

Act, or "sin," as my mom put it. These days, older and wiser, and with my multimedia head now filled with stories of pre—and post-mass shenanigans by priests—I vehemently quash such a foolish tradeoff.

I never knew what to think of the bronze medalist Methodists. Their church was tucked in the woods near the reservoir and away from the rest of human civilization. I don't recall knowing or even meeting a Methodist. They must have home-schooled their children.

So I was a Baptist, and that's how life was—mostly without explanation. I'm sure that God has a good reason for giving us legs to trip people, brains to contemplate vengeance, and flabby butts to absorb the blows of the corrective hand, but don't ask me what I think. I don't have a clue, and he has yet to respond to my query on the matter. I just have to trust that the powers to be knew what they were doing. Or maybe I can trust that a few of those offering envelopes fell through the cracks, passing through the ushers' tightly cupped hands and catching a ride with Elijah up to The Man Upstairs, and that's the reason why I was never struck down by lightning when I tripped fat, disgusting brats or did anything else of the impish sort.

Religion has failed to answer my questions, so I've severed ties. I still consider myself to be spiritual, but my new calling is humanism. And this serves as the epilogue to my Ronald Stubbs story.

Bullies like Ronald are dangerous to society because they paralyze people with fear. And paralysis dehumanizes people by taking away their ability to make decisions.

We never like to be told what to do, what to say, where to go, and how to act, and I'm not just speaking as a citizen of a nation that recognizes democracy as its preferred form of structured anarchy. I'm speaking on behalf of the entire world community. All humans beg for the right to make decisions. It is not only undemocratic to impose your will on another, it's *inhumane*.

Humans have long pushed for financial betterment and in the process have evolved entirely too fast for the rest of the world. Our ancestors were root-and-berry gatherers, then nomadic hunters, then subsistent farmers. They slowed down because they became tired and greedy and wanted more stuff, and soon they invented intercoms and cars and food additives. Today, we sit in our seventeen-per-highway-mile gas guzzlers, sucking on delicious carbon monoxide fumes, and debate between the double bacon cheeseburger and the chicken fillet. We love making decisions; thus, we create more havoc so that we can remedy it by making more decisions. The moment you close out an outstanding matter by making a choice, another matter automatically spins into that vacated space and demands your attention. It never ends. This orbicular reality hangs over the head of humanity like a baby's toy mobile.

Our avarice has run its course. Now we have too many decisions to make on a regular basis, too many options to exercise. There is no longer enough of everything to please everyone, and that is precisely why NASA was created: to examine the possibility of returning to our pre-primordial homes back in the black womb of space.

Maybe the need to make decisions is coded in our genes. History appears to welcome such a postulate. Choice has existed since the genesis of human DNA. Back in the Garden of Eden, two souls decided what fruit to eat and what fruit not to eat. We see it is an easy decision, almost a "non-decision", but this is only because we read it in a book. We scream at the top of our lungs, "Pick B! Pick B!". We renounce the lies of the Serpent, but the contestants still pick the wrong answer to the world's easiest question. As readers, we fall silent to the ears of the past, including the ears of the two corpses that decided our lives for us even before we had begun to breath amniotic fluid. And then what? One minute we are living in divine bliss, butt-naked, without a meddlesome care or worry; the next minute we are earning a meager living spit-shining the shoes of a corporate executive, over-tipping the Chinese food delivery boy because we can't break through the language barrier, and driving an ass-numbing car through a snowstorm on our way to the drugstore to pick up pills designed to quiet the wife's morning sickness cramps. With a single piece of fruit, two screw-ups eliminated human limitation and made life hard for billions to follow. Rule made, rule broken. Human Choice became whole.

Now, we pick careers and unsightly hair out of our foreheads. We think about saving the environment, volunteering in nursing homes, and returning the wallet to the man who dropped it in the subway station. We hold together marriages, hold the hands of our children walking across the street, and hold on to the hope that our car brakes will work as we descend steep hills. We juggle relatives' homes during the holidays. We juggle the torches of mind, body, and soul. Our decisions may not bring upon The Fall of Man, but they are still significant because they are sliced from the same beef of Eden cattle.

When you are young, there is a certain appeal to making naughty choices, particularly when you are confident that you can pull them off and go scot-free. You test the bottomless cookie jar, and if you succeed, you go back to it and keep going back to it until you are caught.

Dropping Ronald like third grade recess was a choice bent on vigilante justice, a choice to step outside of my jurisdiction to right a wrong. I was young, foolish, and pumped full of delusions of grandeur. I had lost touch with reliable realism and picked up risky romanticism for a companion. I looked forward to a happy ending, to the closing of a Shakespearean comedy when each and every cast member on the playbill is rewarded justly and fairly. Unfortunately, such poetic order is the work of fiction, a piece of idyllic rubbish.

If it looks too good to be true, then it's probably make-believe— follow this rule of thumb, and you will always be able to differentiate between what is real and what is not real. And that's the rule, and the rule hasn't changed with time. Look at television. Look at cartoons. A mouse repeatedly outwits and maims a cat twenty times its size, and no one has the good sense to hit MUTE and exclaim, "Gimme a break! Look at the size of that cat!" Look at movies. I keep *Dirty Harry* blasting so that no one will hear me yelling, "Clint's old, and chicks still love him! What is that?" As much as I would like to believe in childhood fantasy, I know that I live in a world of harsh truths, and in this world the lawless cowboy has the men, *not* the women, all over him—in a prison shower room, to boot.

Everyday is a day that we make decisions—small and big, important and insignificant, voluntary and involuntary. So many colors and flavors, just like a good ice cream parlor. We wake up in the morning, throw ourselves in the shower, throw on clothes, and throw ourselves out the door to head to school or to work or to wherever we should have been ten minutes ago. In each of these fleeting moments of routine, a demand for unique decisiveness exists, yet somehow we don't seem to notice it. We are AFS to automated action and reaction behavior. As to the control panel of our mindless existences, we know how to operate only one of its levers, and it moves us up and down, up and down. An asshole jumps off his end, drops us hard on our butts, and you and I are too stupid to know that climbing back on the seesaw may not be such a good idea.

Absolute Fucking Slaves.

We can try not to make decisions, but we're slaves to the decision making process as much as we are to the actual decisions we make, even more so one might argue. Sure, we could superglue ourselves to chairs, fix our heads in vises, and stare aimlessly into space, or we could climb into a containment chamber with Han Solo and pump it full of frozen carbonate, but we would still be acting for the sake of inactivity, which in itself is a decision. Do or do not—either way, Yoda advises that a decision must be made.

That's what life is and has to be: a long series of decisions. I've made a host of decisions in my life, most of them I would label neither "good" nor "bad" because, after all, decisions are merely actions accompanied by consequences. That thing I did to Ronald—was it a good decision? I don't know. Who am I to decide what constitutes a good decision? You make one, move forward, and wait to see how the world defines it. I am Lex Luther, I am Clark Kent. I am both.

Chapter Twelve

OUT OF THE subway station I take a quick left and follow the black arrows pointing the way to the museum. Rain is falling, and a strong wind is gathering the drops into pencils and whipping them sideways into my face. I walk around a corner along a temporary divider. I stop to look between blue-painted panels. Stacks of dirt are collecting the sky's tears and channeling them into black circles on the ground. No one is around. I guess they put construction on hold for the day due to the bad weather.

Rising above me is the Brooklyn Museum of Art, an impressive structure dropped on the tip of Prospect Park and sidelined by botanical gardens. The museum, Parthenon-looking with massive concrete columns that stand in its grand front entrance, could well have been picked up by Aeolus on Poseidon's orders and flown across the Atlantic.

I decided to take the day off. I couldn't use a vacation or personal day because I haven't accrued the time yet, so I came down with one of those twenty-four hour flus and called in sick. A truancy officer would call it 'playing hooky', but I call it 'taking a mental health day'.

The blacktop path wraps me to the right of the building and to the back. I walk through a parking lot, trudging through mash potato puddles as I go, all the way to the main visitor doors. I come to a stop and negotiate around a massive puddle caused by a plugged sewer drain. Raindrops explode up and out of the puddle, defying gravity to meet their friends in the air. It is pouring now.

I enter through the doors and into a dark lobby. On my way to the ticket booth, I part a large group of children. I look back and watch them mold back together, their moves coordinated like a school of fish. I buy a ticket, try to make charming talk with the hottie at the counter, fail miserably, grab a floor plan, and run off to the African art gallery with my tail between my legs.

Read the handout. *While most of the City's museums were busy the past century collecting European and American art treasures, the BMA focused its efforts on acquiring mostly Asian and African art.*

The word *educational* comes to mind. That's Pee Wee's secret word of the day: *educational.* Today's topic: 'How Not To Be So White'.

I really like this museum. It wells a soft inner passivity, an almost meek and acquiescent acceptance of purpose that ripples through flesh and bone, cushioning the pressing demands of the more educated and, thus, more critical guests. The exhibit halls are generously wide and tall, and the collections tend to be earthy and subdued as opposed to gaudy and loud. The museum rarely becomes crowded, even on the weekends, and I like that.

A black panel, six feet high and three feet across, nailed on the wall and protected by Plexiglas. Behind the panel are Ethiopian crosses made of silver, iron, wood, and copper. My attention is drawn to one particular cross, intricately detailed and symmetrically tight. I mentally trace the border of the cross, working my way slowly to the middle, where a smaller cross appears. As I move back out, a square infinity pattern flutters into bird beak shapes that point inward and outward from the central focal point of the bigger cross. I skip from the core to the individually etched sections of the artifact and step forward so that my face nearly kisses the glass. Variations in the metal bubble up into mountains, sink into valleys, and run off into rivers that spill into pools.

I roll around the corner and nearly bulldoze a kid. We do an impromptu left-right-left dance before deciding to follow British traffic laws. Into another room I go, this one packed with ritual masks, figurines, and decorative door slabs. I stop to look at a Terra-cotta head chiseled from a brownish-red block of sandstone. The item is tiny, small enough to hold in the palm of my hand. Almond eyes. Lids, no balls, no pupils. A pair of smooth lips are interrupted by a large chip on one side of the face. Grooved striations run vertically up at a slight angle, maintaining a remarkable straightness and even spacing as they curl along the cheekbones, up to the hairline and to the back of the cranium. A curator or historian dates it between the Eleventh and Fourteenth Centuries. According to the summary description, the head was likely striped to connote ritual scarification of an important social figure, perhaps a king.

The world loves to assign meaning to art and life, post-completion and post-facto. We have to have a reason for everything. Why is the head scarred? Why does a wound scar? Why am I terrible in sports? Why did I flunk that Poly-Si exam my freshman year? Why does the pizza delivery guy hate me? We define everything to make sense of the world. The Why Virus lives in our body, moving from limb to limb as if it were just another component of our blood, like plasma or platelets. Spin life in a common sense centrifuge, and you'll see the Why Virus separate out from what little remains. The bugger runs our brains and our lives.

And then they get all vague and throw in *between such and such centuries*. It is a new millennium, and the United States Military can shoot a rocket into the window of a house yet no one can figure out how long that container of pork lo mein has been sitting in the back of my refrigerator. One day someone excavated this 700 or 800 or 1,000 year-old object, stuck it in a corner of a room or the bottom of a storage chest and forgot about it. Sometime later he accidentally stumbled upon it, passed it to a person who passed it to another person who then sold it to the highest bidder who then donated it to this very museum, and now here I am looking at it, asked to accept that such and such grooves mean this and that.

These days, archaeologists and anthropologists have to go for shock value, so they formulate theories and statements solely intended to pull the rug of accepted human knowledge right from under our feet. Nothing is sacred. And these troublemakers succeed because the people standing on the rug are complete pushovers who salivate over the emitted smells of specious, Pop science delivery. They are no better than the idiots who stand outside MTV headquarters in Times Square on a cold and rainy day, holding I LOVE YOU CARSON! signs and screaming in unison, 'I love awful music!'

I retreat up the stairs to the Asian Art galleries. Off the last step, I spy burly Indian sculptures of granite and black schist playing chess on the floor. I approach the board. They all look so grave and unfunny, yet at the same time nonchalant and comical.

I have a great affinity for this floor. In this part of the museum, I feel as though I am traveling beyond myself, displaced from the floor on which I walk and removed from the boundaries of my senses, floating downstream on a raft of catharsis, exploring the waterways of mind and soul. I close my eyes, and suddenly my home in time and place is a million miles away, hardly qualifying as a warm spot in my memory.

Voices echo hauntingly through the hall, picking up and losing volume as they bounce playfully off the walls. One of the granite Buddha sculptures stands quietly, eyes cast down, hand extended out from the chest, palm open. I want to reach out and take the hand, and step into a perfect existence. I want to feel what it was that compelled men so many years ago to create. 'Look what you've done!' my father booms to me in memory, reverberating through all the years to find me here and now, reminding me of that day he caught me flooding the cellar to make way for a future ice-skating rink. 'You are what you make, and you've made a mess.' Of course, by my father's rationale, I should have ended up a hockey player. But a bit too blasphemous I think—skating on water and such. Ask any of the boys sailing the Sea of Galilee toward the shores of Gennesaret, and they would agree with me.

I walk around a corner and enter the Japanese section. The room throws me into a world of distressing possibility. Everything about this Emma-o damns me to the eternal fire: its red eyes, ripped eyebrows, flared nostrils, and sharp teeth. This soul killer has no knowledge of its gentler Buddhist versions. It triggers thoughts of violence in my head, an instant recall of history texts that chronicle the bloody fight for and against the imperialism that swept the Pacific during the World Wars. I have Pearl Harbor and high school and Mr. Barry's simulated aircraft carrier landing in my head as I move away to a collection of Chinese decorative bowls and three-legged, copper wine vessels.

I hear a door slam closed. It is a special access door, one that hides the world from the behind-the-scenes people who hunch under desk lamps and, with air brushes in hand, battle the elements paradoxically responsible for decay, beautification, and historical entitlement.

I take a seat on a bench and have a breather. A long outlay of ink and absence of ink becomes my world. Three screen panels. A mother sits and watches her children play. Behind them, bottomless mountains sneak a peek at the rest of Creation. Black, gnarly trees dig deep into the panels, mangling the silk, twisting and waving in out of the foreground and loosely tying in the landscape with the human figures. The interaction between humans and nature—a theme visited by artists from all walks of life, their strolls nearly complete and just begun.

But the more I look, the more the dwellers appear outside the world of ink and silk, floating very near its natural current but not in it. I read the description card. The elder is a *father*, not a mother, and the screen painting is a pentimento, a reworked piece of art that shows off many of the ideas that the artist dabbled with early in the creative process.

Funny that I bitch and moan about others defining art, and then I go and hypocritically paint my thoughts of meaning all over this museum. Not ha ha funny, but *ironic* funny, so much as to keep me here looking and thinking, thinking about being far away from the intellectual slumber of Feldman and Phyllis Angelo's panic attacks, away from my cramped apartment and The Wall and a life that is entirely restless.

The museum is very quiet now. All I hear is white noise from the fan blowing from the opposite end of the hall. I tuck my hands into the front pocket of my blue, hooded sweatshirt and curl the museum floor plan around my cell phone. I walk into a different room and instantly recognize Avalokitesvera—the most popular Chinese bodhisattva, the granddaddy of Chinese bodhisattvas. Buddha and future Buddha is everywhere today. He looks especially tired today. Waiting for ascension out of this temporal world is no easy task. His perseverance is remarkable. One day he will. One day.

I find the elevator and take it down to the lobby floor. My ticket mistress has punched out for the day. I hold the door open for two ladies and then step outside to find a November sky that is no longer an ominous gray but a murderous black. I throw my hood on and begin my walk back to the subway station. The wind is howling, the rain is still falling, so I pick up my pace, working into a jog. I feel my feet leave the pavement. If I run fast enough, maybe I'll be able to outrun the wrath.

Chapter Thirteen

THE MICROPHONE CRACKLES. My lopsided chair crooks left, away from the stage and toward the door. It wants out too.

'Cruelty is a game that people play with other people. A one-sided game. It is calculated and thought out. There is life, and there is death, and there is cruelty, and it lies somewhere between the two. Not purgatory. In purgatory there is learning, and hope. There is hope. Dreams are based on hope, but the cruel do not believe in hope. They believe in suffering. Mercy is unknown to the cruel. Undefined. Not in the vocabulary of the cruel.'

'That was all that was written. I turned the page—first time quickly, second time slowly. I expected fresh words to appear on the page, having decided that the words chose to remain hidden from me so that I would hunger them more. The words chilled my inner core. My breath left me for a moment. The wind quieted. The calamity passed below to the cars, which screeched and roared in horror, one last time. There was only silence. A dreadful silence. It grew to a silence more silent than . . . but my ears could hear no more of it. My body failed. My senses, once acute and vibrant, dulled. The light around me grew strong and then flickered just once before vanishing. Blackness passed itself around.'

Applause.

* * *

Where is the train?

I turn around and look at a support beam on the platform. Wrapped around it is a photo of a red-haired girl dressed in a black apron. Encircling her eyes is an enormous pair of goggles designed to protect her eyes from an atomic explosion. There's a big smile on the girl's face. In handwritten black are the following words:

Lola, know it or not, has a posse

Above the paper, written in black marker on a metal light fixture, is a melancholy tribute to a lost love. Eulogy, requiem, benediction—praise be Urban Art, everyone wants to be a Basquiat. A genius makes music with white buckets and a silver sauce pan. Latin feel. One of those beats I punch out of my Casio keyboard during Moby moments.

The weirdest shit you find in City subway stations, and every station is like every street block—frustratingly unique. Some of the best music in the City comes out of the subway station here in Union Square. Some of the worst hails from Penn Station. One night I was waiting for a train in the latter, and I listened to a woman in a polyester jumpsuit tra-la-la on her electronic piano for twenty minutes. I wanted to throw myself on the third rail.

The City of New York: the best and worst of everything.

I follow a rat as it weaves in and between rail ties. The urban squirrel stops at a crushed Pringles tube and investigates the smell of Idaho. Warning wind. The 6 train arrives, here to pick up where the L left off. Silver rolls on in, b-buh b-buh b-buh, and screeches like a giant fingernail to a giant chalkboard, ripping through eardrum past malleus, incus, and stapes and turning my brains to soup.

Julian, Paul, Allison and I step on. *Do not hold doors. Do not lean on doors.* NEXT STOP IS—*Budweiser, Budweiser, Budweiser, Budweiser, Budweiser.* Eyes and eyes. Eyes open, closed, tired and wired. Everywhere there are eyes.

* * *

Spring Street will be up and hopping shortly, but for the time being remains hush-hush for a Saturday night, and Dyna is no exception. All will likely stay this way until eleven or eleven thirty, which is about the time when people and brouhaha tend to filter into a place like this. Dyna's patrons are scattered in booths to the right and flank of the L-shaped bar and are exceptionally well behaved. The exception is the three gentlemen pounding the bar, yelling at the muted tele. College basketball, Duke and someone else, twenty-something to twenty-something, first half, who cares.

Allison and Julian settle into a semi-circular booth near the entrance door and Paul heads to the back, looking for a place to piss. I move to the bar, just to the right of Armani, Versace, and Valentino. I lean in to study my choices. Tasteless crude in the well, two shelves of hi-test on the back counter, and better stuff promoted on a shelf screwed into the brick wall. Beer on tap—beautiful. Beer it is. The bartender makes eye contact with me, puts down a glass, and quickly moves to a sink to give two other glasses a dunking before standing them face down on a counter. Finally, he makes his way to me. He has no desire to serve me. His face is pulled back and twisted into hard ass by a ponytail.

I order four pints of watered-down light, toss a twenty and a couple of singles on to the counter for a tip. He noticeably scowls from behind the tap. I am the niggardly customer. I deserve to be tied to the bar, drubbed with lime rinds, and subjected to a round of fountain gun fury up every orifice. You'll be leaving now, his eyes say.

Back to my comrades I go with two pints. I drop them off and return to the bar for the other two. The bartender retreats to the other end to wipe down the bar with a white rag. I scoop up the remaining glasses and return to the table. 'Lovely party we have going here,' I inform my companions.

'Dead,' Julian answers clairvoyantly. He leans back and puts his arms up and over the backrest, showing off his gigantic wingspan.

My joke is weak, but so is the scene. Thank god for booze and tunes. So far I've heard Hendrix, Aerosmith and G'N'R—a nice mix. I set the beers on the table, sit, and look back across the floor to give the bartender more of my hate. He doesn't seem to notice, having returned to his plunge-plunge-hold in and above the bar sink, which I noticed earlier has no soapsuds floating in it.

Allison turns to Julian. 'I thought you said this place had dancing?' she asks. Her words have a resonating whine, half cute and ninety percent annoying.

'It's still early,' Julian answers. 'People will show up.' He reassures her with a smile. Allison takes a sip of her beer and then nudges Julian's armpit with her head. Julian gets the hint, drops down an arm, wraps it around her shoulder, and pulls her close to his body.

'We won't be here long anyway,' I remind them. 'Paul said he'll be ready for people by eleven.'

Earlier in the week Paul ran into David, the same David the two of us met that Saturday scorcher in the Park months ago. David reads his own poetry at an open mic every month at a coffee bar in Stuyvesant Town, so he invited Paul to come and check it out. Paul, in turn, dragged us out to some artsy-fartsy place filled with bona fide fakes who sip five-dollar mocha frappaccinos and try to convince you that they are tortured souls.

'Eleven? That must be pretty soon, huh?' Julian asks.

'Probably,' I reply, unsure.

Allison pulls back a sleeve, revealing a watch. 'It's not even ten yet,' she corrects us. Julian moves in as if to examine the time closer, then grabs Allison's hand and shoves it into his mouth. Allison exaggerates an *Ow!* and Julian starts laughing. I have to roll my eyes. Julian nudges her, and after counting her fingers to make sure they are all intact, Allison returns a smile. She has this strikingly wide, Julia Roberts smile. It starts off like a normal smile but then it stretches out on the corners into the shape of a Venetian gondola.

Allison looks good tonight. Her hair is up, drawing out more of her face. A black turtleneck sweater nicely flatters her perky bosom. A silver chain hangs quietly on her neck. Classic, yet chic. She's done up a little, probably some makeup on her face but not enough to notice. She has that pretty girl next door look going on. UPN now, or FOX in the earlier days—you know, a Katie Holmes kind of shtick.

Paul returns to the table and warns us that someone is waging biological war in the bathroom. I slide out of the booth to let him in. He sits, and I point to a pint of condolence.

Something in the game has the weekend warriors celebrating. One guy with curly hair throws up his jointless arms and does his best Olive Oyl impersonation. He tips, the stool goes with him, and both end up on the floor. His pals completely lose it, and the entire bar turns it head to find out what all the commotion is about.

I take a long sip and gawk at the two, painted Barbie dolls on the other side of the bar. I hate these chicks. These are the girls who spend three hours getting ready to go out, head to the bar, confirm that every guy in the bar wants to sleep with them, and then spend the rest of the evening talking to each other about how much they love each other's new hairdos and bags. These girls can score tonight or any night that they want because for every horny moll in this town, there are six gangsters waiting to draw pistols.

Paul grabs his beer and gets up to monitor the jukebox. Julian slides out to attend to some business in the bathroom, leaving me stranded with Allison. I gulp, and she sips, both silent to each other's techniques. A group of men pass in front of us on their way to the exit. One turns his head our way. No, donkey nuts. *She-is-not-with-me-you*, I telegraph to him, tapping my glass on the table.

Allison slides over so that our legs touch under the table. I feel the fabric dig into me. She smiles. She wants me to talk to her, but I never initiate conversation with a tied-down woman. I think it constitutes flirting, and that's just sleazy. So I am minding my pint right now.

Allison puts her paw on my forearm. All attractive women have to be the center of attention. 'So how long have you known them?' she asks me.

'Who?'

'The boys,' she clarifies, twisting her butt into the booth.

Annie uses the word *boys* the very same way to describe Paul and Julian. I think Allison could pass for a younger version of Annie. Odd, because Julian has no reason to be stuck in his Oedipal Stage. A man without a father is a man without paternal competition, and, thus, a man without maternal replacement needs. At least that's what Freud would say, he and his sick, Psychodynamic Theory incest talk.

'I've know them all my life,' I tell Allison.

'Do you know their mom?' she asks.

I let Allison know that I met Annie when I was still in diapers, and she seems to like that answer. Two girls walk past us and set up camp by the bar. They lose their gloves, shimmy out of their coats, unwind their scarves, and press their Benetton winter collections down on a stool. The astute bartender comes running and takes their orders. He takes off, and the girls take seats on stools and light up smokes. They lean in close to each other, look long and deep into each other's eyes, investigate every crevice, and then fall back to take sensual drags. Draw and release, draw and release. Oral Stage fixaters. I think to breathe with them. Everything is connected, even the gut. Mouth and nose, windpipe and lungs. Alveoli convene, argue on fundamental identification, crack the gavel. Abdomen sweeps over all. Conversion, absorption, displacement. Toxic product restitution, then repulsion. Up pipe and mouth and nose. Lips purse 'I want you now' assertive and 'Take me now' submissive. Some real S&M shit going down here.

One looks at me for a second, or three. Classic stranger eyefuck or penis envy—I can't be sure which one of the two.

'I think it's so cute that you've known each other so long,' Allison bubbles, teddy bear amused.

'I know just about everything about them,' I add. She needs to know that blood is thicker than water.

'That's nice,' Allison muses, that boat smile of hers moving up over a wave as her head turns back to the bar. She checks out the Dukie fans, as do I. Rocking forwards and backwards like balancing licorice, they throw themselves through the screen and on to the bench to celebrate the great shots and recoil away as a turnover becomes too unbearable to handle. Loathsome corporate pricks, but I'd rather be hanging with them than engaging in girl talk.

'You know, my sister and I are real close too,' Allison informs me, like I care to know. One of the lesbians is gawking at me again. She's really hot. Allison rubs her forehead where the skin meets the hair. 'We used to do everything together until she moved to Maryland,' she continues. 'We still talk on the phone a lot. We're like, *best friends*. I even took her to my prom when my dickhead ex decided to go to Cancun for spring break.'

I wonder whether Allison's sister is good-looking. Betting on the genes, the odds are good. Maybe she has hot friends too. Tough to tell. Lookers often travel with other lookers, but lookers will sometimes hang with lookaways for the sole purpose of creating the illusion that they are more attractive than they really are. It's a crapshoot. The hotter the woman, the greater the standard deviation in the friend department.

'He left me without a date to the prom, and for what?' Allison asks, clearly agitated. 'To hang out with his asshole friends from SUNY?'

I should intervene soon. Julian is one of my best friends, and I don't know this babbling chick, and I certainly don't want to find out what her personal fuck count is.

'Then out of the blue, like a month ago, my sister tells me that she is engaged to her cheating prick of a boyfriend.' Allison shakes her head. 'I couldn't believe it.' She flicks her hand up into the air, 'Like, I didn't know that she was *in love* with him.'

'Yeah, that's interesting,' I answer, tracing the rim of my glass with a finger. I'm more interested in the jerk standing between me and the two muff-diving princesses. The guy is in the worst spot imaginable.

'I could see that from a friend, but from my own sister?' Allison asks.

I sort of grunt an acknowledgement, and Allison rolls her eyes in 'tell me about it' fashion. Back to the guy who isn't moving an inch. I need something to throw at him: a coaster, a pint glass, anything. I lean left. I will get my view.

'I just couldn't believe it when she told me,' Allison continues. 'She just dropped it on me. You think that you know someone, and then they go and tell you something that completely blows your mind. It makes you wonder what you really know about a person.'

I sport a deeply profound look on my face. 'No one can ever truly know another person,' I tell her.

Allison shakes her head. 'It makes you wonder whether it's worth the effort getting to know anyone,' she says.

Her words actually strike a chord. I actually think about them for a moment.

'What is Paul's deal?' Allison asks, interrupting rumination. She looks over to Paul, who has his face plastered to the jukebox glass. When he was kid, Paul would spend entire afternoons taking apart radios and clocks, examining each and every part before reassembling them. He can work on crossword puzzle books for hours at a time. The boy has a tremendous attention span. He reminds me of my dad. He is the only person I know who can sit in on a town meeting from start to finish.

'What do you mean?' I ask.

'Is he seeing someone?' Allison asks.

'Who, Paul?'

I can't remember the last time I thought about Paul's love life, and there's a good reason for that. Unlike Julian and I, Paul tends to leave out the good, morning-after stuff. He is annoyingly shy on the topic. If Paul were sitting here right now, he'd be blushing out of that vanilla milkshake complexion of his.

'I don't think he's dating anyone,' I answer truthfully. 'He's really picky.'

'He'll find someone.'

My boy Paul does just fine for himself, thank you very much. 'He gets along,' I inform her. Screw Paul. Does she have a friend for *me*?

'Maybe he hasn't met the right guy.'

'What?'

'The right guy,' Allison repeats.

We meet eyes. 'What do you mean?'

'He's gay, right?'

'Paul?'

She searches my face. 'Isn't he?'

'No.'

'Really?' She raises her beer to her lips. 'That's surprising.'

'Why is that?'

'I dunno, he just gives out that vibe.'

'Vibe?'

'Definitely.' She says it like I'm the king of all ignoramuses. She sips, and I look at Paul. He looks pretty straight to me. No floating hands, no flamboyant bounce in his step, no butt wagger in his swagger, not that I'm spending a significant part of my day staring at Paul's ass. No lisp. No infatuation with Madonna or floral arrangements. No 'Boy, he must work out' comments. No dreams of opening a clothing boutique in San Francisco or P-town. No, there's nothing gay, homosexual, queer, or flaming about Paul. He doesn't fit the profile.

I look over, and Allison is biting her lip. I think she should be more concerned with her boy-toy, Julian. That hot pink Modo shirt he pulls out of the closet on special occasions screams Christopher Street.

'You think he looks gay?' I ask Allison.

'I think he does.' She turns to me, and her eyes grow hawkish. 'Don't you?'

'Not at all,' I answer.

'Whatever.' She drops into silent bitch mode.

'Paul isn't gay,' I tell her.

'If you say so.'

'He's isn't.'

Allison shrugs and returns to the less opinionated company of her glass. Julian returns, relieved. The closet case makes his way back to us. I need another drink.

* * *

Separate the sounds of the street, and the inanimate becomes animate. Pavement cracks organize and form a Risk game board. Battery begins its bombardment, the infantry holds while the cavalry rides hard to the flank. When the booze is flowing, the creative juices are flowing, and I'm a little kid again. And there you go—the reason why it was OK to totter in the middle of the road.

I snapped out of it just in time to spot an old man in a wheelchair bearing down on me. Behind him was a boy, maybe in high school. I sidestepped right into a fire hydrant. I tried to avoid it, but the quick adjustment baffled and buckled my legs, pitching me headfirst into a stack of cardboard. I ended with a full, Pete Rose layout. A burning sensation pierced my palms as I heard a 'Sorry!' bark out of the deep purr of the night. I looked up and saw my assailants wheeling away in perfect synchronicity—inline skates digging deep into the pavement, shirt flapping in the air, tightened fist leading the charge. Meanwhile, Paul and Julian laughed at me like a couple of gassed hyenas. Allison stood there perplexed, blank, otiose.

That brought me to where I am now, shit-faced, unable to focus on a thing except the pain sizzling from my hands. Best I can judge, we've been here in Paul's apartment for a couple of hours. I'm not sure it's been that long, but it certainly feels like it. I'm bored out of mind. I think I've memorized every crack, tack, spot of spackle, and knick knack in this place.

I think the apartment was once part of a factory. The place has what it takes to be industrial: exposed piping, unfinished floors, banana-peeled walls, and a peculiar odor of burnt rubber and brick. The ceiling are high, and bedrooms play a chess knight's move through narrow hallways. When I walked in the apartment, I immediately pictured its owners as starving artists who wipe their asses on leases and adopt hostel-friendly tenant codes. You can tell that a fair number of vagrants have dropped by here to moan their hunger pains before picking up and transporting them elsewhere. It has that self-righteous, emaciated look.

The apartment is a walkup, which fits in perfectly with the disconnected character of the place. My apartment is a walkup as well, so hiking up five flights wasn't a problem, though I did expect to find a monument at the summit. As I walked them, I noticed that every metal door had been eroded of its Indian rust red skin, revealing the underlying azure muscle.

Paul disappeared sometime ago. Julian and Allison are talking to this unbelievably tall guy wearing a white trench coat and a colorful Rastafarian. The guy could easily pull off a Halloween get-up as one of those click-click, multi-ink pens that eight year olds love. A couple of dressed-to-impress chickies are smacking their lips and adjusting spaghetti straps. They are the beautiful people of the room, and they know it, but they will never say it. All they do is whisper. Their intentions, however, are no secret. They came here to test the fine line between sectarian celibacy and communal whoredom. They tease with hungry eye shadow, clinky earrings, and tops that sculpt their chests into temples of lewd. Uncomfortable funky shoes and tight lowrider jeans keep their legs slippery, their hips shifty and inviting. They have the sick behavior perfected. But wait. We have competition here. Two other girls spot the Studio 54 bitches and cringe. I know this type too. A couple of years ago they donned white puffy jackets and furry boots, but now they think that they're all grown up and mature. They took every Women's Lib class offered at their respective colleges, and they know it only takes one woman to set back the revolution a hundred years. They'll be damned if it will be one of them.

As far as I'm concerned, they all have nitroglycerine packs wrapped around their pelvises. Explosive on contact, corrosive with retention. Sexual irony is all around me. I'm sure my life is full of sexual irony, but I can't prove it now because all irony needs a context before it will pop up and reveal itself. I expect to have a great sexual realization when I'm around fifty or sixty years old, and I'm willing to bet it will have something to do with loyalty and wiener dysfunction.

A five-footer with a fro has a herd of people engaged with his run-in story about Chazz Palminteri, a famous actor from The Bronx. He met him on a street in—you guessed it—The Bronx, filming the movie—guessed it again—*A Bronx's Tale*. Good story so far. He tells it well, but I don't believe a word of it.

The music is thumping in my brain, in threes, BOOM BOOM BOOM. I bend over and feel the bass swell through a speaker sitting on the floor. The attractive brunette next to me tells her fugly male companion that he looks hot in Lycra. Ugh, I need a barf bag.

* * *

I've wandered out of a bedroom to escape the vapid talk of vapid folk. I push past people to the big common room. Everyone is drinking and smoking and engaging in clicky conversation. Bright primary color flashers cast a kaleidoscopic, acid-tripped life on a wall and the white leather couch pushed against it. Soft light emanates from hallways and bedrooms and mixes with passing plumes of cigarette smoke. Together, they slow the action in the main room to a crawl—not in the way a strobe light freezes speed-frenzied dancers and Time itself, but in the way a late night fog settles on a streetlight post, saturating the actors and water-logging their garments, effectively prolonging the scene for the audience by stretching out Time.

I walk down a short corridor to the kitchen, dodging obnoxious elbows and careless footsteps. BOOM BOOM BOOM. On the wall is a black and white print of a fat guy riding a unicycle. I sense a presence, and turn. Chazz. We exchange disinterested nods. Wisely, he takes a walk. I was here first.

A standard refrigerator—freezer compartment on top, refrigeration unit on the bottom, all painted a spicy brown mustard color. The front is sprayed with word magnets, the ones sold in supermarkets and purchased by exceptionally bored housewives. Densely concentrated in the middle, the magnets thin out as I move out on the door. My eyes see a pinwheel Milky Way. I take a step forward, and the inner core deepens. Distances shorten but extend at times, orbiting one and the other and the other's other at times, confusing the synodical revolutions. I struggle to read the words as they loop around in difficult circles. My head fills with upside down air. I feel a jerk on my body. Careful now. You booze, you snooze, and then you awake in a morgue with an even worse headache. A skull chisel awaits. The coroner and pathologist are arguing about whether a toxicologist should be present for the autopsy.

Back to the refrigerator now. My eyes work their way to the nucleus of whatever atom I am penetrating, and there before me, one phrase stands alone in the middle. The image I have is clear, offering no room for reading error:

LOVE LIFE

I stand there for a moment, read it again, then a third time more slowly, gnawing on the words like beef jerky. **LOVE LIFE.** I read the words backwards because the cop will ask me to do the Alphabet later and I ought to practice now. **LIFE LOVE.** 10x, 40x, my eyes focus in on a smaller area. BOOM BOOM BOOM. My eyes blur, refocus, blur. Letters blend. Others disappear and then reappear off to the side. Left eye, right eye. *How's my stigmatism, Doctor? Not good, son. Not* *good at all. You may need surgery. Unpleasant business, this is.* BOOM BOOM BOOM. **LIFE LOVE.**

'Excuse me.' I turn and look behind me, then down. A girl with long, black hair stands in front of me, her arms folded across her chest. She barely makes it up to my chin.

'Oh sorry,' I apologize, stepping to the side.

'Sorry to wake you,' she says. 'Do you see that too?'

'What?' I answer. The light in the kitchen sucks, and darkness has a cruel way of flattering faces, but I'm pretty confident that she's a pretty girl.

'Over there,' she specifies, pointing.

I look left to right and back. The performance is a punishing one. I can feel the booze pumping through me, flooding my vital organs.

'In front of you,' she says, pointing.

'The magnets?' I scrape at **LOVE** with my fingernail but am unable to get underneath it. I try nudging it, pushing it to the side.

'Magnets are things you use to stick notes to your refrigerator door.'

'Words?' I answer.

She smirks a giant smirk. 'Try again.'

BOOM BOOM BOOM. 'What do you mean?' I ask.

'Give me your hand.' She unravels her hand like a party trick blowout. I put out my hand, and she takes it. The initial contact is a painful reminder of earlier handshakes with Mr. Pavement. But her weave of alabaster is soft and warm, lubricating, erotic but without the dirty. She slides her hand down to my wrist, grabs on tight, and pushes up my arm. My hand drops open and rotates, and my palm moves to the ceiling and lines up parallel to the refrigerator door.

'I see something,' I say, as a cute girl has my hand, showing me what to do, 'I see—'

'Just look,' she cuts me short, not willing to hop in the sack without a little warm-up from the vibrator first. My hand begins to move with hers over the refrigerator's surface, first in tight, semi-circular motions and then opening up into wider, swirling patterns. We work around and over the words, stirring up the bottom of an ocean, scouring for hidden treasure. I try to focus, but I can't see through the murk. I consider a new objective: my lady. Her face looks like a raindrop.

She turns to me. 'You are cheating,' she says softly, using her free hand to give my cheek a gentle push back to the refrigerator door. She digs me. She wants me.

'Mind telling me what I'm looking at?' I ask, trying to be charming.

'You tell me what you're looking at. And don't tell me what you think I want you to say.' Her words are lightly splashed with penal authority, and I like it.

'I see black and white,' I tell her.

'You sure?'

She's teasing me, testing my resolve, working me over the way Regis works over contestants by asking whether their answers are 'final'. 'Black and white,' I repeat, basically drooling out the words.

'And?'

'A line and a circle.'

'What else?'

'Chaos.' I'm just making up stuff now.

'Now close your eyes.'

'Huh?'

'Go ahead. Close them.'

Alright, Helen Keller. I'll play.

Her milky opals fade away as I close my eyes. The world goes black. White spots begin to float up and away like bacteria that appear when you get up out of bed too quickly or knock your funny bone. I want to reach out and grab them. BOOM BOOM BOOM. My body sways. I need that crutch again. I need an old lady to help me out of this apartment and into a cab.

'What do you see?'

'I don't see anything,' I answer.

'Look some more.'

'Everything's black,' I explain. 'What am I supposed to see?'

'Not with your eyes. See with the rest of you, not just with your eyes. See with what you *feel*.'

'I see—'

* * *

Consider a dream, a very bad one. The bowl is wobbling, the water rippling. Feel the frappe, the leftover casserole. Feel the stomach spasm in the throat. Feel the pressure building. Feel it push as you push back. Watch a glacier of red oatmeal slide down the white slope and into the lake, spread out, and begin to circle the globe. Watch it. Look to the sky, to a sun that blinds, calls me 'Saul' and speaks of persecution. The world eclipses. Feel legs slide up along yours. I feel it. Jeans of blue left and right are my sidecars, jet engines. Strap 'em, Bruce. Fingers dig deep into my back, finding muscle leather and then spinal rock. I feel them rubbing and smoothing, sanding my bones into polished stones. I feel my hands on the frozen floor, the grooves between its white tiles. The road intersects a road, then another, and then another.

* * *

Down the stairs I go. Down and down the endless stairs. There is no bottom because the bottom is the stair in front of me, and it is never the last one.

I feel the chill of the night. I feel my own breathe. I can hear. No more BOOM BOOM BOOM. Call me a Night Kid. Soho, I am here to stay, or maybe I'll head due east to the land where the cloaked man hunts the Women of The Night. Mind the Gap, and hit the Eurorail. Rice, mystery, slanted serenity here and now.

Lights are different now. It's dark. The waves of heat, the rays of people, burning and judging, have all left me. Buildings fly. The world won't die.

* * *

We're not moving anymore. Now we are. Down stairs, up stairs, through a door that swings like a door, feels like a door, must be a door. Lobby, elevator, lots of buttons. I want to hit them all. Out and through another door. Dark, then light. A bed. I could stay here forever. Lights dim, dimming, with and without my eyelids closing. Shirt up over my head, tug on my leg and then the other. Covers. Lights. I can feel a thigh and it's not mine. An arm wraps around me. A hand takes my hand. Soft breasts push against my back. I can feel them, cool and warm, perfect. Shhh. Sleep.

Chapter Fourteen

WAKING UP IS arguably the most frightening moment of the day. In a flash you leap from exquisite ignorance to bewildered terror. The closing time lights come on. Out on the dance floor, you finally get a good look at your dance partner's face.

Fortunately, familiar comforts of home moderate the shock of the new morning. Your mold of a body fills with the distinctive funk of your pillow, the hum of the computer left on all night, the crispness of your sheets, and the light that pushes through the curtain to hit your left eye. It all mixes with the trepidation running through your veins and dilutes it. Home makes everything OK.

But when you wake in a bed with which you have no shared memory, you can't help but expect the worst. The paranoia is caused by your half-knowledge of the past and completely unlearned present. You are trapped in the most horrible dream imaginable, yet you are fully awake and fully in control of nothing. You pinch yourself, wince, and start asking yourself questions like 'Where am I?' and 'What time is it?'. When the reference section draws nothing but blanks, you settle on an 'Oh crap' and follow it up with an unanswerable, 'What have I done?'.

I imagine myself sitting on a chair during the taping of an after-school special, surrounded by a swarm of makeup artists and costume designers. Within ten minutes, I'm sporting rosy cheeks, a blonde wig, and a borrowed vagina. I also have a new character, a new persona, a new role. My father is an abusive drunk, and my best friend recently committed suicide. I now prefer a sordid life of drug use and whorish moonlighting, all in the name of glorified disenchantment and delusion, or so the director advises. This is my life, and horrible clarity visits as the camera fades in from black and zooms in on me as I lay flat on my back, eyes lustless and lusterless, staring into the endless black of a ceiling without a ceiling. I hear nothing but the sounds of a snoring one-night-stand and a careless dolly grip. I wonder why and how, and I think about changing. *Cut.*

I look under the covers. I'm wearing my glow-in-the-dark, smiley-face boxers, the pair I swore no one would ever see. I'm tamed to a TV-13 rating under the covers, but I'm sure that a few minutes ago the parents were skirting the term *NC-17* as they pushed their children out of the viewing room. Fortunately, this isn't television, and best I can tell there isn't a camera pointed on me. Or so I hope.

The bedroom looks like a female's college dorm room, only bigger, brighter, and better considered. At the foot of the bed stands a dresser pockmarked with big, black tree knots. On top of it sits a rectangular mirror. In front are books, plush toys, fist-wide candles, an open jewelry box, and a hairdryer big enough to groom Bigfoot. Above the dresser are large, colorful prints that fan out cartoon surprise lines from an unclear protagonist. By default, I would guess them to be the works of Monet, but chances are they are from the hand of Pissarro or Renoir or Cezanne because I once learned that these artists prefer people to flowers and water. A paper scroll of a mountain landscape covers a vertical stretch of wall to my left. To my right, an open closet. Clothes and shoes push out of its top shelf like crowded condiments in a pita. Below it, a row of clothes hits all the colors of the rainbow, and below that, small boxes mingle with mismatched shoes on the wood floor. Two nightstands stand guard by the head of the bed. A Venetian lamp and a digital clock on one, a telephone charger and a velobound book on the other. I roll over and grab the book's spine. *Finnegans Wake.* Not the easiest read in the world.

The apartment smells like a diner during brunch: bacon and eggs turning over in unison, carnation arrangements cooking in the late-morning sun. Light is pouring in from two windows, and I can see tree arms bending and snapping in the wind. I feel a draft move in and out like destruction-minded waves crashing into rocky cliffs, sliding down off the rocks and back into the ocean to organize new efforts.

'How are you feeling?'

My hostess appears in the doorway wearing a pink I LOVE NY T-shirt and a pair of blue scrubs that, rolled over once at the top, offer a milky-white teaser. I lay Joyce on the nightstand and flap up the sunflower-print comforter to give my feet some breathing room.

'I'm OK,' I answer, lying to throw her off my scent.

She sniffs it out. 'You look terrible.' She uses the spatula in her hand like a teacher would a yardstick, pointing out the relevant illustration on the blackboard. 'You look like you've been hit by a truck.'

'Of course I look terrible,' I reply, self-deprecating to ingratiate her. Her lips part slowly, dramatically introducing a mouth full of soap-white teeth. She has a great smile. She hands me a glass of water. I sit up and take a sip. The icy water shocks and cools as it slides down my throat. I look up and see her watching me, looking satisfied. 'I hope you like dogs,' she says.

'Huh?' I ask, carefully resting the glass on the nightstand to my right. 'Smells like bacon to me.'

'By dogs I mean—' A dog bursts past her leg, leaps up on the bed, and jumps on me as if I were a shot-down pheasant. The beast swabs my face with a sloppy hello. 'Clancy seems to like you,' she says. I stick my head out of the carwash, 'I'm glad to hear that.' She laughs and walks out of the room.

I give Clancy a rub on his bony head and encourage him to get off the bed, which he does with little cajoling. Down on the floor, he looks up at me, his dark marble eyes studying my every movement as his tongue flaps like a scarf whipped by the wind. I stare him down for a bit, and he responds with a stare of his own. He starts the tail slapping against the bed frame. I reach for the glass, take another swig of it, and use the comforter to dry off the condensation that rubs off on my hand. Clancy continues to watch me, probably waiting to finish what he had started. I shoo him off to the side, swing my feet over and touch them down to the floor. I snap left and right, successfully cracking my vertebrae both times. Clancy slaps my leg with his tail. I'm up, you mutt.

And I am, standing now. Up and at it, beginning the shameful deed of searching for the rest of my clothes.

* * *

I pop a couple of Tylenol and wash them down with a handful of water. I feel awful.

This bathroom is too bright with morning happiness to be mine. The walls are pink, the floor is gleaming white. A wicker basket sits on top of the toilet tank. It's filled with cedar chips, cinnamon sticks, miniature pine cones and artichoke-looking purple flowers. My eyes drop down to the toilet bowl lid, which is covered with a red lawn. This bathroom has old woman written all over it.

Something tells me the nameless woman in the kitchen will not easily be forgotten. She joins my short list of unforgettables. For years I hated this one kid because one day in the fourth grade he stretched my tightie-whities beyond repair. So high and viciously he tugged, I bled out of my delicate brown star for days. I'll never forget Anthony, the man who owns Anthony's Variety Store, my neighborhood Pop store where I bought penny candy and baseball cards. I still conjure his face whenever I watch the Red Sox lose a nail-biter. I still remember that look of anguish on his face as the ball dribbled, REWIND, dribbled, REWIND, dribbled through Buckner's legs and into the history books. I'll never forget Ronald Stubbs, and Tina. I'll never forget the young woman who cried on my shoulder as we stood and watched from First Avenue as the poles bents, the Twin Towers fell, and Antarctica dropped into the Arctic.

If someone holds my head up over the toilet bowl while I am puking, that person gets a separate page in my *Memory Book of Shame*. I can only pray that that person is someone like . . .

Lena Wang, 49 Street and 7 Avenue, the pill bottle reads. *Brooklyn.* Naturally, I had to end up in another fucking borough. You pass out, and 212 becomes 718.

* * *

Lena picks up a slice of bacon with a fork. The grease dips and explodes on the frying pan. I clear my throat, and Lena lifts her head up from the eruption. 'Find yourself something to drink,' she says authoritatively. 'There's OJ and milk in the fridge. If you can't stomach that, have some water.' She offers a grim smile to acknowledge my return from the dead and then falls back to the pan. I open the refrigerator.

I remember so very little of last night. A white light—I remember that. A bright and white light, not unlike the one just above this Minute Maid carton.

December

Chapter Fifteen

HOLIDAYS USED TO be momentous occasions filled with festivity, noise, and commotion. Not anymore. Now, holidays are quiet days shared with my father, the TV, and microwaveable pizza.

But I haven't forgotten the excitement holidays once brought me. I still remember what it was like to be a kid and absolutely love the holidays.

I see it now. It is Christmas morning, just after seven o'clock. I am huddled in my sheets, bleary-eyed but wide-awake. Minutes pass before I get up enough coverage to brave the cold. Finally, I get out of bed, and goose bumps the size of golf balls instantly bubble on my flesh. I slip into a pair of gray sweatpants and a t-shirt, fly out of my bedroom and down the hall, and jump on my father, who is fast asleep in his bed. I dodge a sleepy left hook and drag him over to the Christmas tree in the living room.

After unwrapping presents, I find a sweatshirt and a heavy coat, put on a pair of boots or sneakers—depending on the color of the ground—and grab a pair of gloves. 'Put this on or you'll catch pneumonia,' my father warns, handing me a hat. I complain, but eventually give in. Down the street I go.

I arrive to find Paul and Julian drowning marshmallows in mugs of cocoa and Annie scrambling around to find an extra roll of film for her camera. Paul, Julian, and I rock-paper-scissor to see who gets to pick the first present. I end up third, again. Julian goes, then Paul, then me. Every 'From: Santa' is selected carefully. I know full well that 'Santa' means Annie; my mom told me at a very early age that

St. Nick was a phony. Annie sits on the floor, watching us, smiling, pointing and shooting. Once the entire world has been unwrapped, we test-run the toys, subjecting them to everything that might break their warranties. When we grow tired of that, we wrap up in coats and scarves, hats and gloves, and head outside. We have snow, but it's a dry powder—not very good for packing snowballs—so we gang up on each other for white washings. We tire ourselves out just in time for Annie to hand us shovels and point to the buried driveway. We split the driveway into three sections and get to work. I throw some sky white on a fresh patch of dog yellow and start to hum that 'Jeremy' song on the radio. I hit a crack in the pavement, the handle slips from my hand and falls down the front of my chest, all the way to my nut sac. I double over like a circus freak gutted by a cannonball. It will be a miracle if I father children.

I leave and head back home. Uncle Jack and Aunt Lily arrive predictably late, running on something other than East Coast time. Little do they know that in just a few years, they will be living in Portland, Oregon. Aunt Lily has a new hair color, again. My cousin Eli follows closely behind them carrying an enormous tower of cakes and pies. Grandma and Grandpa won't be here today. They recently moved to Ft. Lauderdale, and Dad says that they are getting too old to travel a lot. I think the last time I saw them was at my mom's funeral. Kisses are exchanged. I don't have to count them on my fingers; I can *feel* another one missing. My grandmother—my dad's mom—died of pancreatic cancer earlier this year, and everyone feels the unspoken. I think about my Mom. She's been gone almost two years now. It's just the five of us today.

We go right to the food. There's enough for an army. All the holiday staples are represented: turkey, butternut squash, stuffing, green beans, sweet corn, and mashed potatoes. I finish the first round, then keep it going with a handful of Tums and a slice of apple pie topped with whipped cream. Uncle Jack begins to tell his stories, many of which end with my teenage father locked out of the house, his naked body covered only by a towel. Uncle Jack is my crazy uncle for sure. He's always on, always over-the-top. At one wedding, my father had to pull my Uncle Jack off the DJ after the man defied his order by playing the 'The Electric Slide'.

The sun drops in the window, Annie and the guys arrive, coffee replaces the punch, and Monopoly begins. I start off with a bad run of Community Chests. I shake it off. I always have a bad run of Community Chests. My father, who sits to my right, gets fired up quickly. Every time he is tossed in jail, my father flips out because the only person willing to sell him a Get Out Of Jail Free card is Annie, and she is determined to price gouge him. People aren't playing fair, but this is Monopoly. My father holds up the game to consult the instruction manual. My Uncle Jack gives him plenty of hell for this.

Two hours later, I develop a devastating cash flow problem. After landing on Paul's hotel strip for the fiftieth time, I have no choice but to sell my assets—purple plots, shitty utilities, everything, save the shoes on my feet and the one clopping around the game board. I eventually go bankrupt, push away from the table, grab a cup of eggnog, and watch the action from a distance. I catch Uncle Jack and Julian passing orange bills to each other under the table as Annie makes change with the bank, Eli. Paul is licking his chops at Park Avenue, which somehow has not yet been taken. My Aunt Lily, droopy-eyed and yawning, counts her bills and sips on what must be her tenth coffee. Suddenly, my Dad accuses Eli and Paul of illegal cartel activity. Words are exchanged, and everyone but my Dad loses interest in continuing the game.

We move from the kitchen to the living room and settle in to watch the same cheesy holiday movie we watch every year, the one that would always make Grandma cry. Snores are quickly heard, so the hugs begin, the plates and bowl are covered, and the coats are retrieved. The house clears, and my father and I go through a roll of tin foil and half my mother's Tupperware collection to put away the leftovers. My father washes the dishes. I dry them. The record player spins Duke Ellington for a couple of hours.

'Want another slice of pizza?' my father asks.

I can't eat another thing. 'Nah, I'm good,' I tell him. 'How about a beer?'

'We're only drinking whiskey tonight,' he reminds me, smiling.

'I tried.'

He squeezes my shoulder on his way to the kitchen.

It's 9 PM, and the only thing keeping me awake is the TV. TNT has *It's A Wonderful Life* running on a loop. I think this is the third time it's been on today. Earlier this afternoon, my father and I bet on the sequence of events leading up to the final credits. Two hours later, we had our winner. Harry arrives, George finds the copy of *The Adventures of Tom Sawyer*, the bell rings, and then Zuzu chimes in with her teacher's take on earning your wings. I don't know how I screwed that bet up. I must have seen that movie fifty times. It cost me a snow-filled driveway and today's choice of liquor.

I'm not much of a whiskey guy, so my father took it upon himself to educate me on the nuances of the drink. I was surprised to learn that Jack Daniel's is not a Kentucky bourbon, but rather a Tennessee mash. I mix up the Southern states all the time, so I guess it makes perfect sense to me that I would mix up their official state beverages.

We talked about Tennessee for awhile—the whiskey, Elvis, the intricate network of dams. I don't know too much about Tennessee, but I did meet a Tennessee local the first week at NYU. I distinctly remember how he introduced himself to the orientation group: 'Hi, y'all. My name's Troy. I'm from Knoxville, Tennessee, and I collect coins.' I started laughing. The accent I could handle, but the coin collecting was too much. Coin collecting isn't something you do when you're young. It's a utilitarian hobby of the old, a pill used to slow the degenerative disease called aging. Anyway, I felt bad about laughing, so later in the day I humored the soon-to-be Classics major and took a look at his coin collection.

'This is a 1938 D Indian Buffalo nickel,' Troy explained, leaning over to the side so that I could see the coin in the light. Troy was partial to Indian coins, and he had enough to fund the construction of a casino. 'Fifteen years ago, it was valued around three hundred dollars,' he told me. 'It's still in mint condition, but it's only worth about fifty dollars now. Oh, and this one. This is a 1923 coin. See its incuse design? The print is recessed into the metal, so it won't wear out very quickly.'

Troy carefully put down the nickel and then picked up a small copper coin.

'Don't you think you should put these coins in a deposit box?' I asked him.

'Why would I do that?' Troy answered, looking confused.

'To keep them safe,' I replied.

He looked at me funny. 'How would I be able to show them off if I did that?' Troy took a moment to admire the coin. 'That's where all the value is . . . ' he said, looking back at me, 'being able to show them to other people.'

The week of midterms, my junior year, a roommate found Troy on his bed, not breathing, not beating. The administration, the students, the media—they all said that Troy had a bad heart. I remember hearing that for the first time and getting angry. I only hope that they had the good sense to cover young Troy's eyes with a pair of coins.

January

Chapter Sixteen

THAT'S A TRAIN. Hurry up. MetroCard, GO, turnstile, Manhattan Bound, stairs. Get there. Shit. Missed it.

The 2 train, creeping away. Double shit. A couple twists around a subway pole like a barber shop welcome. Their eyes join the blur as the train rumbles noisily down the track. Another train screeches as it pulls into the station on the other set of tracks. Doors open, no one gets off, the doors close, and the train starts up again, heading the opposite direction, deeper into the belly of the Brooklyn animal.

I grab bench. Across the tracks is a lifeless platform, squeezed to the rails by a tiled wall the color of discolored teeth. I look left. Farther down the platform, two men are sitting on a bench. A bald man, wearing a shiny orange vest lined with black trim, balances a bump cap on his lap. The man's white-haired companion, dressed in similar clothing, is talking, but I can't hear what he is saying. The radio in his hands is drowning out his words.

I bring my attention back to the Uptown platform. The rusted supports between the tracks stand side by side, tall and dark with unmovable authority like guards of Your Royal Majesty. A shy poster on the back wall peeks from behind one of the metal beams. I hear coughing. The bald man is patting his head with a white handkerchief.

I stand up and slowly inch my way over to the men. I stop at a subway map and pretend to examine it. I find Clark Street station threatening to fall into the mouth of the East River just as the snippets of their conversation begin to make sense.

'This opera was written in 1860,' the white haired man explains to his companion. 'Many critics say that Isabel's voice is perfectly suited for the role. Not just technically, but emotionally. Others don't think so highly of her, but that de Vries wouldn't know good musicianship if it bite him on the ass.'

I tap the display case, look away, and peek out of the corner of my eye. Nothing. Another tap. Still nothing. I might need to drop trou to get these two to acknowledge me.

'Listen to the way she carries herself,' the white haired man says, tugging on his buddy's arm. 'It's amazing. You can't learn that. You have to be born to sing Federica.'

I feel like the unwelcome guest at a house party. I turn to flee but am too late. 'You taking the train?' the bald man asks me. His eyes are heavy. His face is dotted with a day-old beard. 'I hate to break it to you, but my boss just called in,' he says. 'They're about to start working on this track, so there are no more trains heading into Manhattan out of this station. You have to take the train heading the other way.' He grabs the white cap on his knee and uses it to motion over to the other end of the station. 'Take one stop to Borough Hall. From there you can take the train back into Manhattan.'

I thank the bald man and walk up the stairs. On the top, I see a man sitting on the ground, picking through the coins in a Styrofoam cup. He's busy counting the day's take and wants nothing to do with me. I walk up another set of stairs and out of the station.

The wind whistles through the intersection, right through a red light. Across Henry Street, several shops are dark, their retractable metal grill gates up and locked. To my right stands a kiosk that casts an eerie, greenish light on the street. Hanging bird decorations are trying to escape their string moorings. I walk over to look at the flower bouquets standing upright in white buckets. Roses, daisies, and funny-looking blue flowers. I ask the man on duty what they are. 'Blue delphinium,' he tells me.

It's after six o'clock in the morning, and I don't see a cab in sight, so maybe I'll walk until I find one. I'm feeling limber. I'm not drunk. I've passed that point. I've settled into a post-drunk buzz where I'm too tired to be tired. I get this way sometimes after my first cigarette of the day.

I continue walking on Clark Street, slicing through the intersections of Pineapple, Orange, and Cranberry. I must be in the fruit section of Brooklyn now. The liquor flowing through my veins makes every little thing intriguing. Sounds demand pause and investigation. Swaying shadows back me off, and oil and gum pressed deep into the pavement have me swerving. The trees that line the streets are ghosts, and the buildings behind them are their mansions.

An obscure entrance leads me up a set of stone stairs to the beginning of the Brooklyn Bridge footpath. All at once, the calm night is replaced by clip-clopping cars. Two stone sentinels with the same head stand tall on the bridge and hold on to the wire ropes with jungle gym pleasure. Recess. Whistle. Stubbs.

I ignore the yellow painted symbols that break up the path for walkers and those traveling by other means. I see a shadow up ahead. I can't believe there are other people of this bridge right now. It's too cold. It's too early.

The shadow becomes a man draped in a full-length coat. He gives me the willies, the kind that stop you dead in your tracks after a horror movie screening. He is harmless, but the terror maintains its snare until he looks down to his feet. We pass each other, and I keep my eye on him to ward off any attack he may have planned. He keeps straight, his eye on native Brooklyn flesh this morning.

I walk on, and the Municipal Building comes into view. A strip of yellow light rips up through the building's midsection, reaches for open sky, grabs it, and pulls up into the heavens. The Manhattan Bridge shines bright to the right. Down below, a patrol boat sends a stuttering red signal refracting off the East River, up to building tops, graphing the irregular pulse of my heart. Through the spaces in the bridge's wood planks, I see cars whiz by, and I think to whiz on them. I could explode everywhere right now, but I'm not an animal. I can wait. I'll walk faster and outrun the urethra. I just need a distraction, something to look at, something to think about.

I stop at the first bridge support and look up to see the Red, White, and Blue engaged in battle with the wind. For no particular reason I look back behind me. Time and Temperature take turns on the Watchtower Clock.

'Hello there.'

I look right, then behind me.

'I'm over here,' the ghost says.

To my left, on a beam extending from the walking platform and over the bridge's roadway, is a man dressed in a bright orange coat. A baseball cap hides his eyes. 'Don't worry about me,' the man says, puffing away on a cigarette. 'I do this all the time.' The man takes another puff and sends up a cloud that is immediately ripped apart by the wind.

'What are you doing?' I ask him. 'How did you get out there?'

'Slow down,' he answers. He tips up the front of his cap with his hand. 'There will be plenty of time to field questions later.'

Laugh it up, buddy. Any moment now you're going to fall off that beam right into oncoming traffic.

The man flicks away his cigarette. 'Beautiful view, huh?' he says, taking off his hat. I see his face for the first time—dark, mysterious. He looks older, late thirties or just into his forties. He might be bigger than me, but on account of his gargoyle pose on the beam, I can't be so sure.

'It is a nice view from here too,' I inform him.

'Nah,' he replies, shaking his head. 'I've tried both, and this is much better. Let me show you something.' The man swings one leg up over the beam, joins the other, and swings to the other side, finishing a perfect 180 degree turn that faces him out toward the south side of Brooklyn and Manhattan. He looks over his shoulder and finds me. 'See that?' he asks, pointing over with his hat. 'The bridge over there? The Verrazano?'

I take a look. Rows of light run lengthwise along what appears to be warehouses. I switch to the right. High-rises shoot up and down on the pale sky and black water. I look back at the man, and then to the water. I wonder what it would be like to do a banana split off this bridge.

'It's over there past Governor's Island,' the man clarifies. 'It's been cloudy all day, so it's difficult to find it if you don't know what you're looking for.'

I see the lights now, right pyramid of the two, arranged in an obtuse, lower case N.

'They say that if you drop anything off that bridge,' the man explains, 'there's a fifty-percent chance it will ride a current back into the harbor and float in circles for weeks, months, maybe even longer, and a fifty-percent chance it will be swept out to sea and never be seen by anyone on land again.'

'I'm sure you get a good view from there too,' I say, thinking I might convince him off the beam.

'Oh yeah,' he replies. 'I think the engineers realized that too, yet they still didn't put a footpath on it. What a gyp, huh?'

I nod. I'm sure they did that to discourage base jumpers, but I'm not going to tell him that.

'When it opened in the 1960s,' the man continues, 'it was the world's largest single suspension bridge. The whole world travels in and out of the City underneath that bridge. Cruise ships, cargo boats, trash barges, the military—'

'It's quite a bridge,' I say.

'I always wanted to check out the view from that bridge,' the man says, rubbing his chin with his hand, 'which is why I did the New York City marathon three years ago.'

I really need to drain the lizard. 'You ran the marathon just to see the view from the Verrazano?' I ask him. A homeless man running a marathon? Now I've heard everything.

'Hell no, I didn't run the marathon,' he replies sharply. 'But I wanted to get on that bridge, and the only day it's open to pedestrian traffic is the day of the marathon. So I signed up, won the lottery, paid the fee, and found the back of thirty thousand people.'

'You didn't run it?'

'Nah,' he replies, shaking his head. 'I got my viewing time in, then walked back to the Old Town station and caught a train back to Manhattan.' He looks down to the road. The cars are gathering in numbers, drowning out everything but our voices. 'I'm done running. I'm retired. So tell me,' he puts his hands in the pockets of his coat, 'what brings you on a morning stroll over the Brooklyn Bridge?'

'They closed the inbound track at Clark Street,' I explain, 'so I started walking this way and continued on to the bridge.'

'Kinda cold to be doing that, don't you think?'

'Yeah, it was a probably stupid decision,' I concede. The wind's dance has slowed to a retired waltz, but it's still damn cold out. Fucking Canada. It all originates up north. One day I'd like to reverse the jet stream and send this shitty weather back to those hosers.

'It's usually the regulars who pick this time of the day to take in the view,' the man says.

Here I am, walking across the Brooklyn Bridge at six-something in the morning, freezing my ass off and crumpling a twenty in my pocket, and it takes a crazy homeless man tempting Death on a bridge to serve up my first helping of common sense.

'What about a cab?' the man asks. 'Are you short on cash?' He starts to pull something from the pocket of his coat.

'That's OK,' I answer quickly. 'I thought I'd just catch a train at City Hall,' I explain. 'There's no sense turning around now. It's not too much farther.'

'You live in the Village?' he asks.

'How did you know that?'

Shrugging, 'Just a guess.'

'I feel like I've seen you before. Have I?'

'You might have,' the man answers. 'People call me a "willing vagabond". I prefer a "moving construction site".' He grabs the collar of his orange coat to explain the joke.

'You're homeless?' I ask him.

'The City is my home.'

'I mean—'

'I don't have a permanent address, so if that makes me homeless, then you're correct.' The man smiles mischievously, sensing the pity brewing inside me. 'Don't worry,' he chimes. 'I've learned to look at it as an opportunity to avoid junk mail and telemarketers.'

I'm starting to fell OK about this guy. I think it has something to do with his manner, his eloquence. He seems so confident, so self-assured, so *proud*. I've never seen that from a homeless person. During high school, I volunteered at a soup kitchen in Springfield. As I scooped out dinner plates, I watched homeless people stuff their pockets with bread rolls, then walk up to me and ask for their third helping of supermarket brand ice cream. Those people were never afraid, never too proud to ask for more. When you are homeless and hungry and broken, pride goes flying out the window. It has to, otherwise you don't survive. This guy doesn't sound broken, or homeless, or even hungry.

'What happened to you, if you don't mind me asking—'

'In a little bit,' he says, waving off my question like a pesky fly. 'Look.' He points. 'The sun is coming up.' He twists around to take in the view to our left. I follow suit.

The world is taking back its color. The water is a swirl of faint silvers and deep blues, the land a patchwork of broad greens and scribbled blacks. Gaps in the gray clouds hang over the land in a stubborn haze of fog and pollution. Farther to the north, smoke crawls up the sky, belched up deep in the bowels of Long Island. Its lead end winds up seductively like a viper out of a piper's basket. A thin layer of pink separates the earth from the sky at the horizon. The air there is folded and rippled, gassy, a steam that rises from a desert road, and the land is a piece of melting glass from a building caught in a sunset.

The minutes are passing like hours. I've never had to go to the bathroom so bad in my life. My bladder must be the size of a zeppelin by now. 'What do you do after watching the sun come up?' I ask, utilizing the blast of a truck horn to break our silence.

'That's easy,' the man says, looking over his shoulder and finding me. 'We go to breakfast.'

'And where's that?' I ask.

'We go where the day is.' He points to my left, toward the land of the rising sun, the same land which was once cast in a great shadow of commuter blackness.

Brooklyn.

* * *

I was under the impression that bakers stopped making pumpernickel bread years ago. Up until the moment Ryan ordered it, I had no idea that they still made the shit.

Ryan and I talked the whole way to this diner from the bridge. I almost passed out from holding my bladder together, but I made it to a toilet on time. I think I heard Ryan's entire life story along the way.

Eight weeks into his first semester at Northwestern Law, Ryan showed up at his parents' door in Canton, Ohio to tell them that the Socratic Method wasn't working out. He told them that he wanted to pursue his passion, painting. Ryan's father, a Northwestern law man himself, was outraged and showed him the door. The two never spoke again. But for several years Ryan and his mother kept in touch. In his letters Ryan would let her know what he was doing, where he was living, how things were going. Over time, Ryan received fewer and fewer return letters from her mother. Eventually, the letters stopped coming.

His first year in New York, Ryan struggled to make ends meet. He jumped from one lousy part-time job to the next, and he never seemed to have enough time to paint. After a year, Ryan decided he needed to start working full-time. A friend at his alma mater, Ohio State University, suggested that he apply for a position as a runner on the New York Stock Exchange. The money was awful, but the future prospects were terrific. After some deliberation, Ryan put himself on the waiting list. He caught a break, and six weeks later, Ryan made his Wall Street debut as a floor runner. His job was simple: run slips of paper from one person to another. And that's what he did, from opening to closing bell, for an hourly wage considered competitive by the fast food industry.

A couple of months later, a trader assistant blew up into a 'Fuck that, Fuck you, Fuck everyone' tantrum, and suddenly Ryan had a new job. Ryan started a training program, and his investment firm sponsored him to take the Series 7 and 63 tests. After earning certification, Ryan quickly developed a specialty in commodities trading, particularly in utility goods like oil, gas, and electricity. A couple of years passed, and Ryan got into futures trading, where he would saw gain and loss like nowhere else. He watched fortunes made by double-downing on the Blue Chips, and he also watched fortunes disappear in a flash when the bubble burst and, effectively, raked in the entire pot. He witnessed big-shot investors panic and instruct slash-and-burn traders to cash out of their positions just as Wall Street did on an overcast Thursday in 1929. He watched as the uncertainty wildfire spread, consuming white and blue collar alike, swallowing up 401Ks and releasing the ravenous animal of unemployment.

Tougher times compelled Ryan to move his business outside the boundaries of the investment world that had failed him. He sought and discovered a satellite game, one that thrived on unlawful or ethically 'questionable' means of wealth building, one whose key strategy was to turn over small projects quickly without asking questions and without falling in love with the method. A trusted colleague, not quite a friend but more than a common acquaintance, helped put Ryan's foot in the door by spilling the beans on the existence of the off-Vegas biz, which, so they say, is headed by a man people call 'Mr. Green'.

Many people in the trading community know the name 'Mr. Green' and have rubbed business elbows in one form or another with the shadow behind the name, but few will admit that they have coffee with the man. Everything about the man is totally sketch. He is one of those freelance consultants of information who puts people in touch with other people for a price. Payment for his services is never in the form of traditional green and white currency. Rather, Mr. Green uses his indebted customers as intermediary vessels for other transactions. His price is favors, and lives.

Building a business relationship with Mr. Green is not unlike the process of procuring a dime bag from a local drug dealer for the first time. The exchange is weaved together by a delicately arranged system of not-so intransitive associations by which A knows B and B knows C but A never *considers* the existence of C, and vice versa. Adding a limb to Mr. Green's tree is no easy task, for it involves a series of decisions and actions that cannot be trusted.

According to Ryan, no one seems to know how Mr. Green dreams up his business synergies, finds and organizes his contacts, acquires his information, and makes money in real terms. But no one seems to care. Those thrust into the Green machine wanted a quick way out of a financial predicament and could have cared less how it happened. They wanted salvation, and with Mr. Green, they got just that. The weak, the cowardly, the unsure—all leave the herd early. But the rule remains the same, irrespective of the player involved: once you're in, you're in. Step out from underneath Mr. Green's umbrella of control and influence, and you won't just get wet—you'll drown.

Ryan's acquaintance began to funnel the whirl of the conversation by throwing extra weight on the cons, perhaps hoping to turn Ryan on to a 'Thanks very much, but I'll pass' position, but Ryan picked up on this sloppy jump to sophistry. He started to see real opportunity. I can do this, he thought. I was made to do this. I've been trained to do this.

Ryan entered the game as a nobody, a sub-letter in the underground circuit, a patsy for ballsy B-manipulators. He started with a pump-and-dump of a company with small 'float', which is defined as the number of shares publicly owned and made available for trading. The gig worked like this: a small group of conspiring financiers would instruct traders to buy stock shortly before making a positive recommendation to investors. News of the company's recent acquisition would create a quick spike in the stock price, followed by a quick drop. The traders would sell when the stock price peaked, and they, along with Ryan, would collect terrific profits.

The operation was a success, and Ryan was hooked. He began hearing tips in the halls and acted on those tips. The gains were always fairly modest, so the regulatory world paid little attention. Ryan marched on, moving into the world of Internet predation, investing in a pyramid Ponzi scheme that involved a 'Prime Bank,' which usually refers to one of the fifty top banks in the world that trade high quality, low-risk instruments like Federal Reserve notes and International Monetary Fund bonds. The perpetrators used an off-shore management vehicle and an 'unfortunate' computer glitch to escape the wrath of those promised trickle-down greatness.

The frauds ran smoothly for months. Ryan's exploits became more risky, both in terms of their size and complexity as well as in their lengthening window of time in which Ryan would be caught between a rock and a hard place, anxiously awaiting confirmation that his legal deniability was still intact.

Then the boss found out, and everything got *really* bad for Ryan Townsend.

'I've met all types of people on the streets,' Ryan continues, 'and not one of their stories is exactly the same. But they do share similar characteristics.'

'What kind of characteristics?' I ask, watching him leave large pats of butter on a slice.

'Drug abuse, violence, tragedy,' Ryan answers. 'Mental illness, paranoia and depression.'

'How long have you been on the streets?' I ask him.

'Well, that's hard to say,' Ryan muses, resting the butter knife on the side of his plate. 'Over the past two years, I haven't stayed in the same place for more than a couple of weeks.' He shakes off crumbs from his slice. A few specks miss his plate and land on our cheap, white paper tablecloth.

'You've been homeless for two years?' I ask.

'Not exactly,' he answers, taking a big bite.

I let him chew and swallow, then ask, 'What do you mean?'

'It isn't necessarily an either or situation. People move on and off the streets all the time.' He launches his lecture prepense with his toast into the air. 'I see a lot of people go in and out of shelters. You have the recently released psychiatric patients, the convicted felons, the people out of detox. And you have the less dramatic examples—the people who lost their jobs, those who got evicted. For all of them, life is very transitory. Living in a shelter doesn't really change the homeless status of that person.' Ryan takes another bite. 'The person can't stay there forever,' he continues in between chews, 'and he isn't paying rent.' He puts down the toast and rests his hand on the table. It's white and shiny, and completely hairless.

'A shelter may not be great option, but at least it's a place to stay,' I tell him.

'Yes, but does that give him a home?'

'I'm not getting you.'

'Homelessness is a tricky topic. It depends on what you're talking about and who you're asking. The law seems to define "home" as a place of permanent residence, but that definition is problematic. A person might have a car and use it the way you or I might use a house or an apartment. He might sleep in it and use it for storage. If he can afford to buy gas, he can heat the car. And if he has a key, he can lock the car, and the car becomes a secure dwelling. You could say that that car is a form of shelter, but can you really call it a home? A person may stay at a shelter where he has a roof over his head, a lock on the door, and three squares a day, but would he call that a home? How about the streets? Can you call skid row home? A clergy man let me sleep on his couch for a few nights—was that my home? When I was a trader, I crashed at my friend's place while the superintendent repaired water damage to my three-thousand-dollar-a-month apartment. I still had stuff in my apartment, but I wasn't living there because it was uninhabitable. Does that mean my home was temporarily displaced? Or did my home change?

In this country, you are homeless if you don't have an address. The IRS, junk mail senders—they all need to know where to harass you. To them, address equals home. To them, a car does not qualify as a home. To most of us it doesn't, but I don't necessarily agree. I believe there's more to it than that.'

'If we are talking semantics, how would you define *homelessness*?' I ask.

Ryan reacts to my question with a grin. I feel like the arrogant student challenging his Nobel Prize winning professor. 'When I first came to New York, I moved into an apartment in Williamsburg,' Ryan explains, 'but it never felt like home to me. I moved a half-dozen times in a less than ten years, but I never really considered any one of those apartments to be my home. For the longest time my parents were the only constants in my life. Everyone else would come and go in my life. For that reason I felt like my home was with my parents, wherever they were, no matter where I was. I guess I started feeling this thing you call "homelessness" when I stopped having contact with my parents.'

'Do you still consider yourself homeless?'

'No, I don't.'

'Then where is your life now?'

'Here, in the City.'

'Do you live with other homeless people?' I ask him.

'You don't need to be on the streets to be homeless. Homeless people are everywhere.'

'Let me get this straight. You worked on Wall Street, and you did very well for yourself—'

'Financially,' Ryan qualifies, sipping his black coffee.

'OK, *financially* you did very well for yourself. You made a ton of money from an illegal deal, lost your job when you came forward, and now to avoid an associate of Mr. Green you live on the streets?'

'An associate of Mr. Green *is* Mr. Green,' Ryan replies, 'but yeah, that's a good summary of it in a hundred words or less.' He sticks his nose back into his mug.

'Why come forward?' I ask.

'It was the right thing to do.'

'But why then?'

'A lot of *whys* you are throwing at me,' Ryan says, his grin much wider now.

'Seriously.'

'I realized what I had done. I realized that I had taken advantage of people I should have been helping.'

'But the decision to tear down those buildings wasn't yours to make.'

'It doesn't matter. When all was said and done, I was rooting for it to happen. I was cheering on the bad guys. *I was on their side.*'

'Why not just move and find another job?'

'I guess I could have moved west, bought a gas station out in the desert or something. But the thing is, my work here is too important to be running away from my past.' Ryan takes a moment to look around, unintentionally suggesting that his job is to serve breakfast in this very diner. 'It's—'

'What's worth staying here in New York?' I interrupt. 'Why take the risk?'

'Some things—no, some *people*—are worth the risk. And no one really pays attention to people on the streets anyway.' He stops to examine the bisque-colored curtains drawn left and right on the silver rod above our window. The curtains match the color of the napkins on the table. Ryan looks back at me. 'The role is a disguise in itself,' he explains. 'Believe it or not, staying on the street is a protection in itself—for me, and for everyone I know.'

'It wouldn't be a problem if you moved out of the country.'

Shaking his head, 'I couldn't see myself anywhere else. This is where my work is.'

'What work?'

'Helping people find homes.'

'But how can you do that if you don't have a place to live yourself, or money?'

'That's just it,' Ryan rings, excited that I have finally invited him to go there. 'Who said you need a permanent place to live?'

'What about money?'

'What about it? Who said I didn't have money? I traded on Wall Street for years. I'm not exactly broke.' Ryan chuckles and then antes up more serious. 'But money isn't the whole story here.'

I know where this is going. 'There are people who give money and others who give their time,' I say.

'That's the rule,' he says with a nod. 'I-bankers open up their wallets so that they don't have to sacrifice two hours a week to tutor a child. Others pinch their pennies and volunteer their time.'

'But at least they do something,' I remind him. I feel like the world is under attack, and I am in charge of the counterattack. 'And time is money,' I continue, 'which means money is time, so it's all the same thing.'

'That's true,' Ryan concedes, 'but there is a danger in making tradeoffs based on convenience. Time and time again, we are the priest and the Levite who pass the robbed man on our way to Jericho. We walk by because we assume someone else will be along shortly. Our logic clouds our compassion. The idea of what our roles should be prevents us from taking action. And sometimes, in the end, no one stops to help the robbed man. That's the tragedy. Humanity is about the giving of yourself, whatever that is, whenever that is. The real cost of living isn't based in dollars. It's not even based on acts and decisions. A good Samaritan doesn't stop because he has the time or the money. He stops because he has the compassion. That's what most people are missing—compassion.'

'How do you get it?' I ask.

'You have to get out of your own comfort zone,' Ryan replies. 'You can't begin to understand another person unless you try to live his life, even if only for a day.'

'Can you really do that?'

'The question isn't whether you can do it. It's whether you *will* you do it.' Ryan points to me. 'Are you willing to switch lives with me? Are you willing to switch lives with a blind man, or a paraplegic, or a paranoid schizophrenic? Are you willing to switch lives with a poor person, a black person, a woman, a Palestinian living in Manhattan? Hell, an Afghani after 9-11? A Moslem in America *now*? Compassion is hard.'

'So how do you get there?' I ask.

Ryan's eyes begin to glow. 'Listen,' he says. 'And to do that, you need to give up everything material you cherish.'

'Everything?'

'*Everything.*'

February

Chapter Seventeen

No page limit. Write about a unique high school experience. You should not be the subject of this midterm assignment. We all know how wonderful you are. Tell us how wonderful someone else is. Do not hold back.

* * *

I REMEMBER THE game as if it were played yesterday. It was a preseason basketball scrimmage. I missed most of the first half because I was in the lab.

Science had never been my forte, and very early into my senior year of high school, I discovered that Chemistry was a tough pill to swallow. After bombing a couple of quizzes, I cut a deal with Mr. Lyman. In exchange for a 100 quiz score, I agreed to help out Mr. Lyman with his after-school program for students bused up the hill from the nearby elementary school. For a month I spent Tuesday afternoons in Mr. Lyman's chemical dungeon, rinsing test tubes in sink wells and scrubbing microscope slides—basically, mindless monkey work that served no purpose other than to remind me of my academic shortcomings. The kids were the worst part of the job. They liked to squirt me with pipette droppers and click their Bunsen burner lighters in my face. There were days that I thought about ducking into the backroom, digging up the largest bottle of acid I could find, and writing out on scrap paper the epitaphs for a dozen twelve year olds.

The scrimmage started at 4:30 PM. The class also ended around that time, but I had to stay longer to calibrate the electronic scales. Twenty minutes later, I walked into a quiet gym through a side door. On the other end of the court, a kid stood at the foul line with a basketball in his hands, studying the basket for a decade. Metal halide lamps dripped from the ceiling, leaving splotches of light on the backboard. The basketball rim looked distorted, like an overexposed 3-D film print.

Not unlike most small high schools, Billington had a small basketball gym. The retractable bleachers hugged the court lines and sat back only eight or teen deep. The court was old and dusty-looking. The rims needed to be replaced. The whole thing gave off a *Hoosiers* vibe. And like Hickory, Billington loved its high school basketball. During season games, spectators fought each other for a piece of lumber. For playoff games, people were standing.

On this day Billington had a scrimmage, so the gym was fairly empty. People sat together in small clusters on the bleachers. Preppies mixed with off-season Athletes, Dorks kept their distance, and a Goth couple pleasured themselves in the back. I also saw a few "Boots"—the students who, irrespective of the season and weather, arrive everyday at school dressed in a black Metallica t-shirt, ripped jeans, and a pair of work boots. Frank and Joe, two booger-flicking guys I knew from band class, sat underneath the 1983 State Baseball Champions banner on the wall. The snot rocket launchers were like pasta and potatoes—likeable dishes when kept separate but a starchy overload of gnocchi annoyance when brought together in the same meal. A few students down from them sat Mr. Barry, a white-haired willow who taught history. Mr. Barry rarely addressed his students properly; he merged their names with those he come across while watching the History Channel. "Major General Andy Burnside!" he'd address Andy Burns, my bordering left flank and perhaps the dumbest soldier in the Billington High School regiment. "You will meet defeat in The South if you pass on this homework assignment!" I always thought it cruel to have his intelligence thrust into the limelight like that, and by the same teacher who taught us that the name "Burnside" was synonymous with rollover defeat on both ends of the Mason-Dixon textbook. But the material was genius. My friends and I often spoofed on Mr. Barry's name-play outside the walls of the classroom, giving each other names like "Butt Jugglin' Jules Hung Daddy," "Tim Lucky Nuts" and "Billy Boy Chips Ahoy."

Mr. Barry made me laugh, but he also made me uneasy. He loved war and gangsters, and he often replaced his lectures with rather violent videos. After popping a tape in the VCR, Mr. Barry would spray the room with a Bugsy uh-uh-uh-uh-uh-uh-uh of homework instruction and then follow it up with his best Jimmy Hoffa disappearing act. Rumor had it that somewhere in the building Mr. Barry had a secret office where he moonlighted as a CIA operative. I believed it then, and I believe it now.

I finally spotted Paul sprawled over two rows of stands, a Notre Dame cap hiding his face. I took advantage of a break in the action to hurry over to him.

"Good of you to show," he quipped, half sitting up to acknowledge me.

"Lab," I replied. "How's Julian doing?"

"Awful," he answered without hesitation. "I don't think it's the ankle either."

"Does he have it taped?"

"Yeah."

"Sometimes it's worse taped."

I played soccer on the high school team and had a pair of glass ankles, so I knew all about Ace bandages. You couldn't move in them. They made you feel like you were running a three-legged race.

"Maybe," Paul responded, sounding very unconvinced, "but Julian stopped icing it days ago, and he said it was feeling better today. He's running up and down the court fine. He's just playing timid."

"It is preseason you know," I countered.

"Smeeshun preseason," Paul growled. "His jumper is off, and the rest of the team can't be shooting anymore than twenty percent from the field. They've been missing easy buckets, taking wild shots, throwing up air balls—they look really bad out there. And their defense hasn't fared much better. See Number 30 down there? The red-headed kid?"

I followed Paul's finger down to the court. Two opposing players were working hard in the paint, coming off screens and looking for the ball. Our tall guys tried to keep up with the maroon shirts, but they were always a step behind. They looked like the bad guys chasing Scooby Doo and his buddies through a corridor of doors. On the far side of the court, a short kid with a floppy mess of strawberry red hair stood off to the side and behind the three point line, waving his hands in the air. Number 30 looked like a leprechaun yelling at the thief that had just made off with his pot of gold.

"What about him?" I asked Julian, who looked with me at the bankrupted Irish midget.

"That kid is lighting it up from the three point line," Paul answered. "He must have fifteen points already."

"Have we been playing zone?" I asked.

"Nope. Man-to-man."

"Maybe we should. Maybe a box-in-one or something."

"That would be embarrassing."

"Why?"

"Are you even paying attention to this game?"

I shrugged my shoulders.

"Julian is guarding him," Paul explained. "Sure, let one or two of them go, I can see that. Take away the drive and see if he's up to the challenge. See if he can actually—" taking a pretend shot, "—shoot the rock. But that kid has been connecting all over the court, and Julian is letting him set up in the corner all by himself. He's being lazy."

Rusty, maybe. No one bothered to play defense during summer pickup games, so players always looked shaky when they got back in uniform and tried to coexist with whistle-blowing officials. Still, Julian was a defensive maniac. He hated to be beat on the ball or off the ball.

Julian was a two-season athlete. His best sport was football. He started throwing bombs to Paul and me during recess. He knew I couldn't catch a football on the fly to save my life, but that didn't seem matter to him. The balls kept coming. I guess he figured that sooner or later Murphy's Law would kick in and somehow I'd pull one in for a score.

Julian was a fierce competitor. He challenged his teammates. He challenged his coaches. The football game against rival Jefferson High is a prime example of that. People still talk about that game. It's legendary. I have heard the tale so many times that its details are surgically burned into my brain tissue.

It was the last week of the football season, and Billington High was in contention for a post-season bowl game. The team cruised into its final regular season week on a roll, having won its last six games. Jefferson High, the reigning conference champions, lost its starting quarterback to an early season injury but still headed to Billington with an identical record of seven wins and two losses.

The game featured two high-powered offenses: Jefferson High had its running game, and Billington had Julian's arm. The game stayed tight for three quarters. With less than three minutes left in the fourth, a Jefferson miscue handed the ball over to Billington deep in Jefferson territory. On the next play Julian and Wally Fallon, an orca-fat tight end with hands too sure to be stuck in the facemask of a defensive linemen, hooked up for a pretty score running from play action. With that, Billington moved to within a point of Jefferson. Our field goal kicker, Toby Higgins, who we called "The Mule" for his trusty foot and massive overbite, finished warming up on the sideline and came onto the field.

Two months earlier, Billington had squeaked by Jefferson, 21 to 20. Because overtimes were not observed in conference play, Jefferson needed to win its second meeting with Billington to force a rubber game to determine who would play in the bowl game. A point-after by Higgins and the tie would seed Billington above Jefferson in the final regular season standings by virtue of that early season, one-point victory, and everyone knew it: journalists, players, coaches, spectators, even the lazy-eyed geezer running the concession stand.

But Julian thought differently of the situation. Realizing that his teammates were tired and that Jefferson still had two timeouts to work the clock, Julian proposed in the team huddle that they fake the extra point and go for a two-point conversion. I have no idea what Julian said to win over Coach Barker, who also taught shop class and once threatened to remove my hand with the table saw after examining the notch cuts on my crooked nightstand. Locals still hotly debate what was said. The call was the right one, Billington won the game and the following bowl game. Collectively, it all makes for a colorful addition to the town's mishmash of self-fabricated mystique.

Back to the scrimmage. Both teams were playing sloppy ball. During one sequence, the point guard on the other team tried to dribble the basketball between his legs but bounced it off his foot, right into Julian's hands. Minutes later Billy Bane, one of Billington's starting forwards, received a pass while unwittingly standing out of bounds and attempted to call a timeout. The coaches continued to jump off the bench, mixing in experimental trap defenses that sometimes confused their own players.

The game started to become interesting when Billington made a run late in the second half, cutting Pickering's sixteen-point halftime lead to five with as many minutes clicking off the clock. Julian continued to play "timid," as Paul had put it, allowing Ronald McDonald the space to launch bombs from behind the three point line. The Billington-heavy crowd became inspired by the comeback and started yelling words of encouragement to our players. They also taunted the opposing players and jeered the officials. Each affront sent the crowd writhing as if their collective head had been hacked off with an ax. Paul and I remained in the minority, laughing inside but never allowing our amusement to surface.

"They're going to lose this game if Julian doesn't get his shit together," Paul warned me.

Billington called a timeout, and Paul put away his book. He was too busy scrutinizing his brother's play to have organic chemistry split his attention.

Paul loved sports. He followed records, conference standings, press announcements, and playoff races because he loved the process of collecting information. But Paul wasn't much of an athlete. He made the football team his freshman year, but a nasty tackle during his debut scrimmage sent him to the hospital for a leg splint and a painkiller cocktail. Almost three months later, with Paul's fibula nearly healed and the season all but over, Annie, a mother only nervously tolerant of her baby's participation in such barbaric games, decided that it was best to pull him from the roster altogether. Naturally, Paul did not object, knowing that leaving behind his football career would provide him more time to crack open other pursuits.

With his brother dominating sports, Paul took it upon himself to excel in everything intellectual. He became a classic academic overachiever, the kind of student who completes the same homework assignment four times to get it right. Literary awards, certificates of excellence, college scholarships, gilded plaques and maple-cured, cob-smoked Vermont hams galore—you name it, Paul held a monopoly on it. In eleventh grade he took on the planarian. For eight weeks Paul spent his afternoons and weekends holed up in his cellar, hacking away at defenseless black slugs with a straight edge and taking notes in a three-ring binder.

His work paid off in the form of a cheap trophy and a fellowship offer from the regional Chapter of the Amateur Scientist Association. The honor was thought to be one of great distinction by the Billington academic community, but Paul decided to pass on the fellowship because had already decided to spend his summer studying Eighteenth Century Parisian architecture. His science teacher, Ms. Simmons, thought the snub insane and called Annie. She politely listened to Ms. Timmons' plea, but she made it clear that Paul would be the one to make the decision. Not one to change his mind, Paul maintained his resolve, extending his middle finger in good baise toi fashion. By hop-scotching from one pursuit to the next, Paul closed the window of opportunity on anyone who wished to shower him with shallow praise or vulgar awards. He wasn't capricious, for he would see through to the end everything he set forth to do. But once he had crossed the finish line, Paul was nowhere to be found. He was a phantom in his own extraordinary world of achievement, and he seemed to enjoy it that way, perhaps fueled by the power that comes only with modesty and anonymity.

"CATCH THE BALL, DICKHEAD!"

I looked up. Julian took a long rebound out of the air and charged down the court to begin the counterattack. The making of a spectacular play seemed to be in the works. Ty Simmons, our super-tall center, extricated his limbs from a defensive player and streaked down the court. Julian broke loose from the pack, made his way to the middle of the court, and spotted Simmons. The ball left Julian's hands, and the air seemed to grow thin as the crowd sucked in a collective breath of anticipation, waiting for the ten o'clock highlight. But Julian's alley-oop pass was low, and Ty couldn't meet flush with the hoop. The rim clanged noisily as the ball jumped out of the cylinder and out of bounds.

The crowd exploded. Back on the court, Ty flashed a hungry look to the bench for approval, but his teammates were already on their feet cheering. I saw Paul cover his eyes. He was too horrified to watch the circus show.

All of a sudden, Ty's face greened. His coach—a new coach that year, I think his name was "Smith"—had him locked in a stare. A few seconds passed. The coach looked down, then up, and then shook it out. Blood returned to Ty's face. Sporting a fresh pair of shorts, Ty managed a cautious smirk as he found his way back on defense.

Play resumed, and we all took a valium apiece and settled back into our seats. Coach Smith called for a quick timeout when Number 30 hit another long jumper, this one right over Julian's outstretched arm. The team returned to the bench, and Coach Smith pulled Ty aside for a quick chastising, wrapping it up with a tap on the rear.

Coach Smith and his coaching counterpart had handled the entire scrimmage lightheartedly—a few yells here and there, but nothing to get overly excited about, other than when they decided to examine their players' butt cheeks. They expected their players to screw up. They needed questions to ask themselves post-game—the What Went Wrong, the How It Fell Apart, the Who The Hell Does This Kid Think He Is. Coaches are hired and paid to pain the critique.

I waited for Ty to sit on the bench with the other players currently in the game, but he never did. Coach Smith had yanked him.

"NOT YOUR FAULT TY!" Paul yelled.

He caught me by surprise with that comment. No one could argue against the coach's move. Ty had killed Billington's momentum by handing the ball back to Pickering, indirectly manufacturing three quick points against his own team and forcing our coach to use one of the team's two remaining timeouts. He could have controlled Julian's pass and laid up the ball for a sure two, but instead Ty had showboated, looking for style points before he had scored acceptable marks on the technical component.

The officials leaned over the scorer's table. Someone yelled "Scoreboard!" I looked at the clock. Both teams had 99 points. Something was amiss.

"IT'S JULIAN'S FAULT!"

The words rang in my ears. I turned to Paul, half-expecting him to no longer be there, having been replaced by an imposter. Who could be so bold as to speak out against Julian, the best player on the team, and in our house? Surely not his own brother?

Heads began to turn our way. It didn't matter that I hadn't said a word; I was guilty by proximity. So I looked for an escape. To my left an elderly couple sat quietly and continued to watch the players, evidently unaffected by the ensuing drama. No luck there. To my immediate right sat students spaced apart by piles of coats and knapsacks. No luck there either. No, there would be no hiding from this. We would have to stand together and proclaim our folly, and if necessary, beg on our hands and knees for forgiveness.

Paul removed his cap. His face paled death in the blazing gym lights. Julian looked our way to identify his nemesis, and soon enough, he looked right at us. He cocked his head to the side, an inquisitive hook and dot drawn up on his pink-splotched face, and then slowly walked to the bleachers in front of us. Sweat glistening on his forehead, Julian took a moment to wipe his chin with his jersey. He then put one foot on the pine and a hand on a knee. He leaned in toward us as if ready to deliver a halftime speech.

"What are you doing?" he asked.

"What are *you* doing?" Paul responded, not missing a beat.

My palms began to sweat. This was not the petty domestic squabble that I had seen so many times before. This was an event, a town happening. We were in the middle of the Billington High School gymnasium, the town on hand, invisible microphones sucking in whispers and gasps like a giant vacuum.

"You're pissin' away the game," Paul snorted. "When are you going to start playing defense?"

The gym sat silent like a deserted barn. It seemed to reach an unprecedented quietude as I heard the drawn-out hiss of compressed air leaving a soda can. Light appeared to fragment into its base elements, its photons crackling and burning out ribbons of memory like the smoke left behind by firework explosions. Time seemed to slow down, its seconds framed in snapshots, the individual images pieced together like a flipbook, appearing and disappearing at the crawl of a baseball soaring through the air during the climax of a sports movie.

Julian followed a pesky invisible mosquito moving about him. I kept my head moving from him to Paul, feeling just like the kid who chases after a ball tossed back and forth by his older siblings. I watched and pleaded, my eyes the arms that reached up and begged for participation. I thought to break the silence, but Julian beat me to the punch.

"What are you trying to do?" he asked Paul. "Make me look like an idiot?"

"Someone needed to call you out on this," Paul answered firmly, his words floating off his tongue with self-importance. "That last pass to Ty—" he started to say, and then motioned over to the court with his hand, "—how could you expect him to put that dunk down when you threw it behind him? That was terrible."

Out of the corner of my eye, I caught the old couple staring at us, their jowls dropped to their shoulders as if weights were tied to the skin on their faces. Apparently, the old folks had checked their hearing aid batteries and rejoined the rest of us.

A whistle blew.

"Hear that, folks?" Julian said. "My little bro has a few tips for me. Go ahead. Tell them."

Julian had a really bad habit of calling Paul "little bro." Technically, the label was accurate. The chance scout of the two fraternal twins, Julian was the first to step beyond the great EXIT ONLY sign. But Paul hated hearing the words *little bro*, and Julian knew it. Paul came to his feet, arms intertwined in a display of defiance. Julian's face tightened into a grimace. Both stood tall, a recalcitrant to the other.

"I can't let you do it," Paul declared, full of conviction. "I can't let you continue out there." He pointed to the court, and then met up with his brother's eyes again. "You're embarrassing yourself out there, and you're embarrassing *me*."

I looked at Julian. His eyes were stretched to an unnatural length as if metal forceps had pried them open. His nostrils flared, allowing invisible steam to escape the boiling pot. I turned back to Paul—stiff as a board—and then back to Julian, who shook his head a moment and then looked over his shoulder as if he had left something behind him. A strange gurgling noise bubbled out of him. I split back to Paul, who with arms still folded tightly, remained unmoved by his brother's sudden amusement. I started to laugh.

"You dumb jackass," Julian said. He turned away to rejoin his teammates.

"Coward," Paul muttered, the corner of his mouth curling up a little as he took his seat.

The game ended with Billington winning by four. I walked out of the gym aghast, squeezing through the double doors in a herded daze. I thought about what I had just witnessed: a brotherly spat, a clash of fraternal wills, a nonsensical display of sibling chicanery and subversity. I tried to make sense of it.

Julian and Paul never fell into the category of failure. They always seemed to find a way to succeed. Ask them to keep three Ping-Pong balls in the air for ten minutes and they would find a way to do it. Julian would learn how to juggle, practicing for hours until he could break the ten-minute mark without breaking a sweat. Paul would sit in a chair, think about vectors and physics, run over to the bathroom, fetch Annie's hairdryer, and put on a dazzling aerial show.

They were both winners. Annie was the first to see it. She never compared her children, and seeing their parity in her eyes must have cheapened the fun considerably for Paul and Julian. Denying a competitive spirit the satisfaction of being better than your only brother must have been a serious party foul. Paul and Julian exchanged noogies and wedgies, looked to Annie, she shook her head, and they grimaced.

Looking back on that Pickering scrimmage, I can see that something much deeper than adolescent frivolity was at work. I see jealousy and admiration coexisting peacefully. I don't understand how that could be, but I witnessed it with my very own two eyes, and I still see it now, and I hope that means I *could* one day have that too.

I stopped at the soda machine across from a stretch of lockers. Paul trudged off to round up the rest of his books. Across the hall, a young boy with fuzzy, copper-colored hair eyed him suspiciously as he sucked on a lollipop.

"Do know that guy in the stands?" he garbled.

"What guy?" I replied.

The boy pulled the red sucker out of his mouth and looked at it. Cherry or strawberry flavored, I guess. Maybe watermelon. Very likely a Charms.

"The one you were sitting with," he replied. "The one with the Notre Dame hat."

The perceptive imp looked to be about ten years old. Maybe he was a younger brother of one of the players.

"Yeah, I know him," I told him.

The boy's forehead crinkled. "What was his fucking problem?"

I couldn't help but laugh at his potty mouth. The boy flashed me a menacing scowl. "What does he have against numbah twenty-two?" he asked.

"Nothing," I answered, taking a quick look at his Sesame Street t-shirt.

"Are they enemies?" he asked cautiously.

"Not exactly."

"Then what?"

"They're brothers."

"What?"

"Brothers," I repeated.

The boy looked at me as though I had something wrong with my head. "They're really brothers?" he asked.

"That shirt . . ." I pointed, changing the subject. "Where did you get it?"

March

Chapter Eighteen

YOU HAVE TO love the bus. It is always slow going from green to red and red to green, always dirty, always crowded. It takes you on trips through the seediest parts of town, where people drive stolen boom boxes on three hubcaps in a never-ending, right-hand turn. And you have to love the guy who is always behind the wheel—middle-aged and disgruntled, hormones like a teenage boy. The man will race anything that moves. And when the action dies down, he'll start playing homicidal-lane-change chicken with big rigs.

This driver is no exception. Two minutes ago, I witnessed a pedestrian dart out of the way to avoid being shoveled under an inch of asphalt. The driver responded to the middle finger with a peace sign. He knows he's protected by Federal Law. Read the sign on the window: **Assault on drivers is punishable by prison terms up to five years and fines up to ten thousand dollars.**

Today, I'm working on my sixth trip to The Delton Shelter in Jersey City. A week after our meeting on the Brooklyn Bridge, Ryan and I rendezvoused in the Village, and over surprisingly decent sixty-five cent coffees, we talked Paskell and poverty politics. A tremendous feeling of guilt hit me hard that day. I had lived in the City for almost five years, yet I had no memory of walking by any one of its one hundred shelters—strike that—any one of its one hundred *family* shelters. Ryan quickly sold me on the idea of volunteering my Saturdays to help out at the shelter, which provides emergency housing for the local homeless. That was early January, and now here it is, mid-March, and I'm still doing it. My level of commitment is amazing. I deserve a damn medal.

Omar Everett. When Omar was nine years old, Social Services stepped in and placed him in a home with a Long Island City couple. But things didn't improve for Omar. Omar's foster father was an alcoholic who often came home from work drunk and beat his wife.

The Delton Shelter puts out a monthly newsletter that it distributes to workers, local churches, and private contributors. Henrietta Garwood, the shelter's long-time director, a middle-aged woman with a thick English accent, somehow found out that I was a Literature and Writing major, and last week she pulled me aside. She asked me to sit in on support group meetings, interview recent arrivals, collect their testimonials, and write up their biographies. I agreed to it, and after her one hundredth 'Brilliant!', Henrietta handed me a copy of last month's newsletter and suggested that I read it over to get a feel for its content. Just as I was about to leave my apartment this morning, I realized that I had forgotten all about the homework assignment, so I grabbed the newsletter on my way out the door, thinking I'd do my research on the bus.

The woman standing next to me is wearing a lemon-colored warm-up suit and a silver tiara. Good call. If you don't know me and you're not hot, then you might as well go heavy on the Weirdo. Entertain me, and you will get noticed. A middle-aged man, dressed in a suit, carrying a briefcase—he will behave himself, and I will forget his face the minute he steps off the bus. But a dirty, disheveled man yelling, 'It's a fucking conspiracy, I says! A fucking conspiracy!', will have me at hello. The involuntary reflex to chaos stimuli binds us all. Some of us do a double-take. Others stare. A few even silently applaud and cheer for more. I'm one of them. I'll spend a dollar-fifty any day of the week for a few good laughs. I like to watch people, but I *love* to watch Weirdoes.

The trouble begins when you stop watching Weirdoes and start interacting with them. A week ago, these two Wierdoes boarded the bus and dove straight into a discombobulated critique of the Star Wars movie *The Phantom Menace*, which had come out in the movie theaters about two years earlier. The two managed to screw up everything, taking characters from *The Empire Strikes Back*, sticking them on planets discussed in *The Return of the Jedi* and fitting them into periods of time clearly befitting *A New Hope*. Princess Leia suddenly became Anakin Skywalker's mother and Jar Jar Binks started 'acting like a pussy' when he refused to work for Jabba the Hut on the planet of Endor. I closed my eyes, fell into a Jedi trance and worked on collapsing the floor underneath the morons' seats, but they finally gave it a rest. A few minutes later, the one in Starter gear turned to 'Slips' and said, 'Yo, Slips. Been thinkin'. Don't you think Chewbacca could be based on Bigfoot?' Slips, probably the younger of the two, fingered his pencil moustache and replied, 'Shit yeah! Chewbacca's frightful woman too, shure nuff.' I kept quiet, but Slips' pal spotted my marquee grin. 'What the hell you lookin' at?' he asked with a snarl. After giving it some considerable thought, I answered, 'Dementia of the Sacred Femininity.' 'Huh?' was his turd-brained response.

The bus comes to a stop. God, I hate buses. They are so damn slow. Every time I ride one, I'm reminded how luxurious subway travel is. Subway lines feed commuters transportation with the consumptive ease of a sausage link breakfast. They work together to deliver passengers train-to-train quickly and frequently. Buses, on the other hand, are sloppy logistically. They run independent from each other. One delivers the blueberry jam, one the bread, one the toaster—and they arrive in that order. If you don't plan wisely, you may wait 20 or 30 minutes, maybe even longer, for a bus to show. Add a connection or two, and you are looking at one, long-ass journey. So, when you take the bus, you have to plan ahead. And it's for this reason that each bus line develops its own ridership community, broken into families according to time periods and geographics.

After boarding the Number 37 bus every Saturday morning at 10:13 for six straight weeks, I now have the faces of fellow bus riders tacked to my brain. I now have an ongoing relationship with these people. I'm starting to get to know them.

I get to know them by watching, not talking. I'm a quiet bus rider. I squeeze, suck it up and in, and stare at people and Attorney-At-Law advertisements and bulletins written in—let's see here, I'm thinking *Destinos*—yes, *Español*. I don't strike up conversations with people; I just watch. A 'Normal' doesn't talk unless a happy-go-lucky guy boards a half-empty bus, takes a neighboring seat, wraps an arm around you, and decides that it is important for you to hear his take on rising bus fares. Normals won't even talk to other Normals. I think this is because we Normals spend so much time and energy shedding off the intrusive behavior of Weirdoes that we are exhausted by the time we actually cross paths. When we do, we invoke an implicit agreement: *Yeah, I know you're cool, but let's just read our newspapers and books and let this idiot who smells like garbage gab away, OK?*

Most of the regular Weirdoes on this bus are harmless entertainment fodder for Normals. There is this one woman that I like to call 'Dancing Queen'. Dancing Queen probably wouldn't hurt a fly, but she stands out like a sore thumb because she is *freakishly* tall. She also has a very masculine face, which she tries to hide with pounds of cheap makeup. She likes to wear skin-tight outfits that reveal things that should never be revealed. She makes people stare, especially when she starts singing along to the music spitting out of her headphones and tap-dancing in her red knee-highs. Her heteromorphic height, fleshy peepshows, and tremendously bad dancing exhibitions demand attention. No one is too worried about The Bus Man either. He is an older gentleman—late sixties, if I had to guess—who always wears a taxicab hat and a tweed suit coat. As the bus rolls from one stop to another, The Bus Man nibbles on a pipe he claims a Native American carved and points out different buildings and landmarks. He doesn't talk to anyone in particular; he just talks: 'Walter owned that print shop before he sold it to the Cortez brothers . . . . I did construction on this road once . . . ' I've also crossed paths with Ms. Complainer two or three times. Ms. Complainer bitches about *everything*—the bus stopping, the bus moving, people boarding the bus, people leaving the bus, people hitting the yellow tape to signal the bus driver to stop, dirty bus windows, the temperature inside the bus, her lateness and the causes of it. She's annoying, but I find her easy to tune out.

Not all bus regulars are harmless. A few downright scare the shit out of me. One day, as I made my way down the steps of the bus, a man left the curb, climbed up the stairs, and pushed me aside. Before the door swung closed between us, he turned around and yelled,

'Fucking Asshole!' The next time I saw him, I almost went out a window. Fortunately, the bus was packed, Fucking Asshole Man was on one end and I was on the other, and eight or so passengers stood between us, eight or so passengers that he would have had to 'Fucking Asshole!' to reach me. Then there is Sad Woman. She is *psychologically* scary, as opposed to Fucking Asshole Man's I'm-gonna-lop-your-head-off-with-a-machete scary. At our introduction, I thought Sad Woman was a Normal. I even considered taking a seat next to her. It's a good thing that I didn't. For a short time Sad Woman just sat by a window and said nothing, but suddenly, as if her world had been dropped into a pot of boiling water, she began to wail, big Humpback Whale wails that could probably be heard across the Atlantic. Then, without clear reason, Sad Woman stopped. A couple of minutes later she started up again.

Omar ran away from his foster family to live with his mother. Like his foster father, Omar's mother was an alcoholic. She often left her kids unattended for hours, even days at a time. When the summer arrived, the neighbors caught on, the police came, and Omar found himself back living with his foster parents.

Woman with the Killer Right Elbow is at it again with her bag. I want to kill her. She's not a young woman—mid to late thirties, I think. She is certainly old enough to mind her Ps and Qs. The woman sitting across the aisle is younger. Late twenties, early thirties—I don't know, everyone looks younger these days. She's a big girl, built for consumption. All that Twinkie eating has made her tired. She has her head on her shoulder, eyes closed, headphones curled around her ears. She's wearing a purple, short-sleeve shirt with *SUBWAY* written on its right breast. The polo flops over her round stomach and bunches up just below the waist, hiding the top of her black work pants. Polyester Dickies. A harsh acid could eat through them, but balsamic vinaigrette wouldn't stand a chance.

The bus stops, and I count the new passengers as they walk the aisle. Five of 'em. The last is a good-looking woman with caramelized Latino skin and a head weaved together with bleached curls. She stares a moment at the space between Subway Lady and a vertical steel pole before squeezing herself into it. She shoots Subway Lady a quick glance and then looks forward, slightly to my left, over toward the Woman with the Killer Right Elbow. A truck pull even to the right of the bus. An American flag flies from the radio antenna. The man inside the pickup punches out a long honk, picks up speed, and passes.

'I guess she has a problem with me sitting down,' Hair-Dyed Woman cracks sarcastically as she smoothes out the lapels on her camel-colored, suede faux fur coat. She makes eye contact with Woman with the Killer Right Elbow, then adds, 'I'll take whatever I can get.'

'I hear that,' my neighbor replies, smiling with some pained effort.

The bus breaks hard. I look out the window. Texaco station. A man pumps gas into a maroon gangbuster ripped straight from the pages of *Car and Driver*. He's wearing a black t-shirt and a pair of white pants. I think he was an extra in *Miami Vice*. Someone needs to tell him that he's not in Florida.

Hair-Dyed Woman looks out the corner of her eye to check on Subway Lady. 'You run around all day at work,' she tells Woman with the Killer Right Elbow, 'and then you can't even sit down on your way home.'

Subway Lady opens her eyes slowly. She turns slightly to the side. *Sandwich Artist* reads in gold across her shoulder.

'I wouldn't mind the space myself,' the Hair-Dyed Woman continues, not aware that Subway Lady is now watching her, 'but that's how it is.' She starts fussing with the cheetah cloth handles on her black bag. Subway Lady slides off her headphones. The bus driver uses his horn to yell at someone on the road. He drops his lead foot, the bus buckles, and the short man standing to the right of Hair-Dyed Woman stops a nosedive by slamming one foot forward.

'You know how it is,' Hair-Dyed Woman says, giving the bag a rest to unknot a lock of hair.

'Uh huh,' Woman with the Killer Right Elbow agrees, nodding her head. 'You work two jobs for five years, and sooner or later you start thinking you should rob a bank or something and then go buy yourself a car.'

The two of them laugh.

'Gotta work,' Subway Lady says, breaking her silence. 'Gotta make da money to feed d'em mouths.'

'Where do you work?' Hair-Dyed Woman asks, brushing away a blond curl.

'Ridgefield.'

'Bergen Boulevard?'

'Yeah.'

'My cousin lives in Fort Lee. How long you been there?'

'Lord, been a year now or so, goin on a lifetime.'

'How old are your kids?' Hair-Dyed Woman asks Subway Lady.

'Seven and fifteen.'

'Gettin older, huh?

'Mm hmm, and dem gettin big. Real big. Just to feed and cloth'em is a check. Shoes alone. Basketball shoes, skuhl schools, church shoes . . . ' I examine her sneakers. A rushed checkmark. Nikes. 'Shoes this, shoes da. My older one's up to a twelve now.'

'Twelve!' Hair-Dyed Woman exclaims.

'My whole family has big feet,' Woman with the Killer Right Elbow pokes in and says. 'My mum, my sister. Me. I've had a size ten since the day I was born.' She laughs. 'Swear to God. And you can't just go to the mall and get size tens. Nut uh. Not when your feet are this big.' She lifts up one of her heels and wiggles it.

'My cousin Leslie,' Subway Lady says, 'she's big, not like me, but ya know, big in da bone—she either too tall, or too long, or too much woman here or d'ere.'

'I know, I know,' Hair-Dyed Woman bellyaches. 'I walk into stores, and there are these little girls in there, and they start talkin the minute they see you. They start talkin, uh huh.'

Woman with the Killer Right Elbow laughs, shakes her finger, and says, 'You don't worry what they say.' She gets into a groove. 'You keep shakin your thang. You lookin fine.'

They laugh. The bus idles at the corner of JFK Boulevard and Communipaw Avenue. Down on the left side of Communipaw, a woman dressed in a traditional Indian sari waits patiently on the sidewalk. Yards of red material whip back, suffocating her legs like a snake would its dinner. A shopping bag weighs down one arm, a stubborn kid the other. The boy is putting up a fight, stretching himself out like a taut elastic band. Traffic doesn't want them to cross. God bless mothers.

For several years Omar dropped in out of treatment programs, but whenever he sobered up, he realized that he was miserable at staying sober. He moved to Newark, where he continued to battle his addictions tooth and nail. Barely able to scrap together enough money to keep a roof over his head, Omar decided to make a little extra money breaking into houses and businesses.

One night, Omar broke into an electronics store. The storeowner unexpectedly showed up, pulled a gun, and shot Omar in the leg. Omar managed to get away in his car, but minutes later he pulled over to the side of the road because the pain was too much to bear. He got high, then passed out. He awoke in a hospital a few hours later.

After leaving the hospital, Omar tried to overdose on aspirin but failed. Days passed, and the landlord posted an eviction notice. After an altercation with him, Omar left and found a shelter in Jersey City. There, it took two days, a woman named Flo, and a black book to shatter his pride. Two weeks later, Flo told him that he should pack his things and head to Manhattan because she had made other arrangements for him.

When he walked through the doors of St. Steven's Christ Shelter, Omar met Ryan Goodspeed, one of our regular volunteers.

The bus starts up again, only to come to an immediate stop. A young man with a crooked weasel face makes his way to the front to exit. Following him are two women. The first one is quite pretty. The second one has an enormous ass.

Woman with the Killer Right Elbow points to Subway Lady and says, 'You know, my first job was at a Subway.'

'Yeah?'

'Montgomery, Alabama. Years ago. First job I had, first job I was fired from.'

I have to stop myself from saying, *Fired from Subway?*

'What happened?' Woman with the Killer Right Elbow asks.

'I got caught doing something bad, really bad. Back then I had some problems, you know. I moved to Jersey, but it took ten years to leave that life behind, if you know what I mean. But now I worry more about the size of my feet.'

My body shakes as Woman with the Killer Right Elbow laughs. The bus driver crashes to a stop, drops off more passengers, and accelerates back into traffic. The bus is clearing out. A clown a few over from me is going to town on a bag of candy. I should intervene. Jellybeans are to be eaten and not snorted. *Eaten,* not snorted.

I check my cell phone: 10:28 AM. I close my eyes and imagine this bus crashing. I can hear the news report. *We have breaking news for you. A young man is fighting for his life today after a horrendous accident in Jersey City. En route to a day of community service, a twenty-four-year-old man was badly injured when a New Jersey Transit bus ran a red light and broadsided a trailer truck. Sitting at the point of impact, the victim was crushed between two bus poles. A witness called the scene a 'war zone'. Another witness described an explosion of metal and glass that 'sounded like a bomb went off'. The young man was rescued by Jersey City fire and police with the help of a Jaws of Life. He was rushed to the hospital, where he is said to be in life-threatening condition. The bus driver survived with minor injuries and is now being questioned by authorities. At the time of the accident, the bus was not carrying any other passengers—*

The bus engine revs. I open my eyes and look out the window. Woman with the Killer Right Elbow and Hair-Dyed Woman are walking shoulder-to-shoulder, working on something that I never imagined could begin on a bus: a friendship.

Subway Lady puts her headphones back on and closes her eyes.

April

Chapter Nineteen

COLLARD GREENS AND iceberg lettuce heads, celery stalks and broccoli florets. I have no patience for perishables, so scoop up the bargains. Bags of miniature carrots for $2.49 apiece, portobella mushroom baskets for $2.99 a pop, crates of mandarin oranges for seven dollars, and rubber-banded cords of asparagus at $3.49 a pound.

A mist shoots out of the sprayers, and I unleash an April morning yawn for public consumption. I'm tired today. And hungry. Shopping on an empty stomach should be speeding up this process.

Usually, I'm a real man in the supermarket. I don't shop, I purchase. As soon as the automatic doors slide open and Michael Bolton or some other easy-listening crap invades my auricles, I push in the clutch, grab a shopping basket, find what I need and what I know and what I can afford, forget the receipt and get the hell out of there.

'Sorry,' a woman apologizes, brushing up against me as she scoots down the aisle, a box of cereal in one hand and a carton of milk in the other. Total Type A.

Live in the City, and you may as well be Forrest Gump with a speeding Buick on your tail. Move fast, think fast, act fast, talk fast, live fast, or life will gore a hole the size of Pamplona in your ass. The City teaches you to run-walk, and run-walk I now do, even when my legs are not moving. NYU Life prepared me for Corporate Life and all else that is City Life, which is based on seconds rather than minutes or hours. Consulting isn't consulting without deadlines. 9 AM means 9 AM and 3:45 PM means 3:45 PM, which means my home and office clocks are running five minutes faster than me. I am late or running late for everything, even if I am not really late at all. For this reason I now think, act, talk, and live as I walk—in fast forward.

Outside of the office I'd like to ease up on the rocket burn and drift to a slower speed, but I have found that it is less taxing to move at a consistent five miles a second. If you don't think too hard and don't try to switch mindsets, then the conformist routine of City Life takes charge, stripping your memory of the ability to change, and life becomes an effortless, downstream ride on a fast moving river. You don't even have to steer.

I ride that raft, baby. I keep my cell phone calls short during peak hours without cutting down on the money content. Fast food is fast—fast food, and restaurant food is fast food. If I hit a light, then I take a left and head uptown because I'm heading that way anyway. Hit another light, and I skip back east. It's all about anticipation. And jaywalking.

It is the spoiler who slows me to a thinking crawl. Lena stands not too far from me, comparing the colors, shapes, and textures of two tomatoes. She is *my* supermarket spoiler today. Her composed shopping manner has a catastrophic effect on my blitzkrieg assault on City commercialism. She pays special attention to unit prices. She'll pick the 2-for-the-price-of-1 $2.50 carton of eggs over the $1.50 carton of eggs if I agree to eat nothing but omelettes for a week. She buys in bulk, repackages and freezes. She leafs through supermarket flyers, folds over pages to compare items side-by-side, and tears out coupons. She likes to hunt. She'll circle like a vulture, waiting for the perfect moment to swoop down and collect her prize. She can walk into an Ann Taylor, pick up the same shirt she picked up two days earlier, feel its material, try it on in a dressing room, and leave the store without buying it.

I think Lena's restraint has something to do with her family background. In 1930, a year before Japan declared war on China, Lena's grandparents left China for the United States. They made it to San Francisco, only to be immediately shuffled off for processing at Angel Island. For a month, they lived in crowded communal living spaces, haggled with attendants who drilled their testimonies and dissected their paper credentials. With no end in sight, Lena's parents resorted to bribing officials with the last of their possessions. They were released, but they ended up floating in and out of California for the next several years in a perpetual prison of nomadic poverty. They eventually settled on a potato farm in Oregon. There, they delivered Lena's mother into the world and found God with the help of a house servant who had jumped the Rio Grande border as a teenager and headed north to the land of infinite eyes.

Lena's grandfather lost his life when a tractor turtled and crushed him, leaving Lena's grandmother with a six-year-old daughter to raise. Lena's mother and grandmother eventually moved to Lassen County in California, where Lena's grandmother married an American-born car salesman who died ten years later, at which point mother and daughter relocated to Sacramento. Lena's mother lived a quiet life until she married a charming Chinese-American, whose felonious past caught up with him just weeks before Lena was born. Lena's mother quickly filed for divorce, and she has since balked at remarrying.

Her family's history of sacrifice and survival appear to have had a profound effect on Lena. I think her meticulous shopping is just an extension of her mother's stance on waste and superficiality. Lena cooks her own meals most of the time; thus, she shops. The new clothes in her closet are twice as expensive as the clothes she bought in California; thus, she shops. Lena is paying her way through Brooklyn College; thus, she shops.

'What are you doing?'

Lena drops a bunch of clear, plastic bags into the basket I'm holding. Tomatoes, bean sprouts, and scallions. She puts scallions in everything.

'Huntin' wabbits,' I lisp, holding up a bag of carrots. She blows away a bang escaped from the rubber band holding her hair in a ponytail. She's wearing a t-shirt—plain white, baggy, wrinkled, mine. Her jeans balance on her favorite pair of sandals. She has on her weekend look: casual, messy, and beautiful. She pokes me in the shoulder. I pretend to ignore her. More pokey. 'Yes?' I ask, real cutesy.

'You're dripping water all over yourself.'

And so I am.

'We should find a cart,' she says, looking in the basket. 'This isn't gonna cut it.'

The basket *is* getting heavy. I'm such a weakling in the morning.

A cell phone rings. 'That yours?' Lena asks.

'I left mine in the apartment, remember?' I answer. 'I took yours.'

'Go ahead and answer it, will ya? I need to grab some tampons.'

It started off with the toothbrush, followed by a change of clothes. Now it's time to usher in the tampons. Wow. This is starting to look like a relationship.

Lena clogs down the aisle. I find the cell in one of my seven pockets. I love these cargo pants. Flip up, TALK. 'Feldman.'

'Um, hello?'

You're not at work, stupid. 'I'm sorry, can I help you?'

'I'm trying to reach Lena Wang,' the woman on the line says.

'She's busy right now. This is her boyfriend. Can I take a message?'

'This is Beatrice Turcotte from Fuller Hospital in Sacramento. Will you please put her on the phone? It's very important.'

May

Chapter Twenty

THE NEIGHBORS ARE at it again. I can hear them.

'¡NECESITO ALIMENTO!'

'HACES TU . . . ALIMENTO.'

' . . . '

'MI AMIGO ERA EL DISPARO EN EL PARQUEST . . . THAT BITCH!'

'¡LA CALMA! ¡PUEDO NO ME . . . PENSADOR.'

' . . . '

' . . . QUE VENDÍO EL ENDROGA . . . ¡Y LA POLICÍA! . . . CABEZAS COMENZÓ, BANGING AND ASKING ALL THESE FUCKING QUESTIONS.'

' . . . YO . . . MAURICE . . . MI HERMANA. PIENSAS QUE EL PUEDE VENIRE . . . '

'NO!'

'YES! YES! . . . A MÍ CASA Y ÉL DISCURSO A MÍ COMO ESO? ¡DIOS MIO! . . . SHIT!'

' . . . LO ADVIERTO, WOMAN . . . NO! . . . NO ME . . . FUCK NO! . . . FUCK NO!'

'WHAT?! ¡PIENSO NO TAN! YO LO GOLP—'

' . . . '

' . . . '

' . . . '

' . . . LA CABESA CON ESE CALENTADORA DE ESPACIO . . . PIECE OF SHIT! . . . A FUCKING PIECE OF SHIT!'

Chapter Twenty One

JULIAN POINTS TO my TV as a crowd helps a little girl finish the Star-Spangled Banner. 'Cheer up!' he says. 'The Red Sox are on, and they're not even playing the Yankees. Do you know how rare that is?'

'That's because they're playing the Mets,' I point out.

'Don't ruin this for me, OK?'

'Whatever. Leiter is pitching. He's hot, and the Sox are not.'

'I know,' he concedes. 'Just in time for inter-league play too.'

'Didn't you pick him up for your Fantasy League team?'

'Yeah, I'm torn on his start today,' Julian says in an ultra-sincere way. 'I could go for a one-nothing win by the Sox and a complete game and twenty strikeouts for Leiter.'

'Twenty bucks says they tag him for runs early and he's out by the fourth inning.'

'We both know I'll be waiting a year for that money.'

'I'll keep that bet on the table.'

I crack open a bottle of cheap domestic and take a small sip. Ugh. I can't drink this warm. I walk back to the kitchen with the bottle and the rest of my Italian sub, open the freezer door, sidestep the back-drafting steam, and look in. There has to be a good, four or five inches of frost inside. It looks like someone is constructing an upside-down igloo in here. A few weeks from now, I may sublet it to a bunch of Eskimo bats.

I twist the cap back on my beer bottle and carefully slide the brown guzzler in between two ice cube trays. 'Do you want me to throw a couple beers in the freezer for you?' I holler.

'YOU DO THAT!' I hear.

I fit three more bottles in the freezer by stacking a bag of curly fries, a package of chicken nuggets, and a couple of microwavable dinners. I can't believe I eat this trash. I should learn how to cook, but there really isn't a point to learning right now. I usually don't come home from work until seven or eight o'clock, and at that hour I usually don't have the energy to cook. Fortunately, I have feeding troughs like Louie's Stop. Located two blocks from my apartment building, open 24 hours a day, rain or shine—oh, I'm in love. The father and son duo make the most amazing subs there. They will make you anything, I mean, *anything*, if you ask them for it. On a dare I once asked Louie's son for tuna fish, pickles, mustard and hot peppers, all squished into a hero, and he didn't disappoint me.

I close the freezer door, grab a 99-cent bag of pretzels off the kitchen counter and pop it open on the way back to my bed. Julian is sitting on my red fuzzy chair, watching the tube. A hick lights up the screen. He laughs, and I laugh. 'Trailer trash', we call them, but we should know better than that. The truth is, we are *all* trailer trash. Some of us just happen to be hidden from the public, too ashamed to wear our colors proudly. This guy is smart. He's embracing his color. America loves him. Reality shows are all the rage now.

Julian is rubbing the back of the chair with his hand as if it were his wife of fifty years. I always offer my guests the fuzzy red chair. I wouldn't call myself a great host, but I do what I can to make the very few visitors I have comfortable. Julian hardly qualifies as a guest, but I still find myself sitting on my bed, which makes watching my fifteen-inch something along the lines of bird-watching without binoculars.

My vision is so bad that these corrective lifesavers curled around my ears are thick enough to bulletproof the teller booth of a commercial bank. Without glasses or contacts, I can't accurately distinguish objects placed more than a few feet away from my face.

Best I can tell, I survived three, maybe four years, half-blind. My Stevie Wonder went undetected because quality of vision is in the beholder of the eye. My parents failed to detect it, as did the school system. After the fourth grade, the school lost all interest in sponsoring the nurse's annual eye examinations. The days of sitting on a stool and playing peek-a-boo with a beach ball or the letter E facing left, right, up or down, disappeared. No more lice inspections and throat cultures too. I guess the dirty kids started showering and parents got a clue and kept their sick kids home. Absorbent lost a spot in the janitor's daily rotation. The phase-out continued. A couple more years passed, and my class moved to another wing of the school building, where the teachers were more interested in catching students smoking in the bathroom than making sure students washed behind their ears. The literature changed, and students were advised against going on shooting rampages, starting families, and spreading diseases. No longer in the health inspection business, the school faculty became a loose association of law enforcement agents, unlicensed psychiatrists, and auditors for the local center of disease control and prevention.

It wasn't until junior high school that I realized I had to squint to read the blackboard. My only viable solution was to sit next to the good note-takers. Unfortunately, the good note-takers tended to be the nerds, who loved to sit up in the front, so I ended up drifting away from the cool kids in the back and toward the uncool kids up front. The move should have helped me visually and academically, but my vision only worsened and my grades remained stagnant. But it beat the humiliation of reading the words *It's best to test it with a fork or knife for consistency* off the blackboard in front of fifteen Home Economics students waiting for a reason to send their candy apples airborne.

Freshman year, I cracked. Enter my first pair of glasses, two monstrous telescopic lenses held together by a heavy cast of twisted metal. Surely, it was the most sophisticated piece of optic instrumentation in the world, one capable of measuring the cosmic shifts of the Universe. Whenever I wore them, I looked like that kid with the hot air balloon head from the movie *Jerry Maguire*, but without the million-dollar smile and the hot mom.

I blame the salesman. From the moment I walked into that eyeglass store, the guy was ON. 'You look good in them,' he told me as I tried on pairs. 'They make you look older.' For nearly an hour my father and I deliberated over the frames. Mr. Four Eyes behind the counter finally stepped in between us, threw out some more marketing garbage, and sealed the deal. He bent his sales pitch to win my father over to the more expensive set of frames, and the artifice worked to perfection.

Two hundred and ten dollars was the price that I paid to return to the back of the classroom. Fortunately, dropping prices in soft contact lenses rescued me later in high school, and I now wear the little guys all the time. Maybe when I hit the Mega Lotto I'll check out that laser surgery business, but for now glasses and sex will have to share limited time and space—late at night and behind closed doors, where no one can see me at my very worst.

I'm listening to the television more than I'm watching it, sitting on my bed, flipping through the pages of a *Rolling Stones* magazine with Britney Spears on the cover. Apparently, she just graduated from Catholic school. Good for her. Julian starts clapping. I look up and see Pedro Martinez warming up. A good sign for baked beans lovers. Mister Cy Young two years in a row, 35 plus victories and well over 400Ks. You can't count last year because he was hurt with that torn rotator cuff. He is back, and I like our chances this year.

The game commentator moves the audience to a commercial. Julian leaves the chair, walks up to the TV, adjusts the volume, and returns to his seat. He turns his head around and looks at me. 'How's work?' he asks.

'Crazy. They fired another guy this week.'
'What happened?'
'Another tool found the end of a work boot.'
'What?'
Bad joke. 'Poor performance, I guess.'
'Someone you know?'
'Not really.'

I remember the day that Feldman walked into my life. The interview with Phil. Two days later, I received an envelope, Fed Ex Next Day. It was on a Thursday. Blah blah blah, Feldman loves me, they want me to start the following Monday. They offered me a crappy salary, long hours, and medical a month into employment. They must have been desperate. Feldman was my ninth interview, so I accepted the offer immediately. I was desperate too.

A few weeks passed, and one morning I awoke with tonsils the size of oranges. I looked like a kid who had returned home from a camp run by Jonathan Swift. Off I went to the ER. Poke poke probe. Dr. Rye pre-diagnosed me with Strept Throat. I'm allergic to penicillin, so the doc gave me something else. Steroids, I think. Something in tablet form—I dunno, I wasn't really paying attention. For a week I couldn't eat solid foods, so I drank apple juice and ate Gerber peaches out of a jar. I had always been an apple juice fan, but I was nervous about the Stage Three baby food. The regurgitated nourishment had an appalling consistency, but I was surprised by how tasty it was. Three weeks later, an envelope arrived in the mail. Contained therein, elegant hospital letterhead. 'HMO ball jugglers,' my Dad explained to me on the phone.

'So how is it working Downtown?' Julian asks. 'I bet it's pretty cool,' he continues, 'being down by Wall Street and The Seaport.'

'I guess.'

The novelty of working Downtown has worn off for me. Downtown, they talk nothing but BIG business, BIG moves, and BIG paychecks. A company beats another company like a baby seal into signing on the dotted line, and industry experts call that 'genius'.

Downtown, they discuss networking, the expansion of consumer markets, and business card stylings. They recite department goals as if they were back in the sixth grade grinding out state capitals. They practice explaining the nuances of 'The Consultant's Creed', e.g. the popular, 'If you take a month to take a step forward, then you should give yourself ten to take one back.' 12 point Times New Roman font runs through their veins, and I hate Times New Roman. It is not uncommon to take an original and photocopy it into middle office oblivion. They sell paper for paper, hit PRINT, and then throw the page in the house safe, or, screw it, entrust an Intranet database to work *pro bono* as its *au pair*. Downtown, you cannot separate yourself from the page because you and the page are conjoined twins. Both are alive for each other. They are cultured like whipped cottage cheese, pressed into notarized squares, sorted and paper-clipped. Look at the paper. Three cheers for us because we print on 100% recycled dreams.

Downtown, they like to talk about the over-ambitious guy who launched a startup in Silicon Valley and had the college graduates running. 'Oh oh, me! I'll take worthless stock!' Downtown, they trade souls for equity, but I am hardly familiar with the value of human derivative swaps. I find nothing mutual about mutual funds; thus, I've decided to wait it out another quarter before enrolling in Feldman's 401K plan.

Downtown, they jump on the bandwagon, betray King Chemical, smoke the evils of Big Tobacco publicly and tap it into a tray of self-righteous media ash. Then they turn around and inflate the stock prices of those very same Fortune 500 companies, the ones developing the cancerous products which will one day drag our grandchildren on regular visitation walks to Radiology. When things get bad, they tell the papers, 'No comment,' and point to the bathroom, where their lawyers are busy powdering their noses on the counter sink.

Speaking of lawyers—I'm on the business side, which means I have to hate lawyers. And why shouldn't I? Downtown, lawyers string together class action lawsuits, send the media into feeding frenzies, collude with the enemy, distribute fifteen-dollar certificates to the real victims, and then cash out at five hundred dollars apiece, per hour. Corporate lawyers live a swinging life in a picnic basket, assuming by definition that 'life' constitutes the legal, valid, and binding obligations of its bearer—'Life Bearer'—to himself or herself and to, collectively but also singularly, each 'Party', or also in the singularly plural form, to compare individually each 'Party' to the 'Parties', all of which are terms that have not been previously defined, such is *my life*—referred hereinafter as the 'Agreement'—to be duly executed and delivered and bearing all of its legal, valid, and binding obligations, enforceable in accordance with the respective terms hereunder and thereunder, except that the enforceability thereof may be limited by insolvency of the body or similar laws of applicability affecting the general enforcement of the Agreement rights of the Life Bearer or made impermissible by certain laws of nature, including, but not limited to, laws of biology and physics or by a higher authority's discretion in relation to equitable remedies.

Sure, no problem. Make a point to remind me not to be unduly burdensome and unreasonable. Remind me to transmit to the world by telecopier a duplicate of my authorized signature to the Agreement, complete with applicable power of attorney, official signature specimen, and notarized cover letter, assuming such duplicate copy shall be deemed to constitute due and sufficient delivery of my binding legal commitment to the Agreement, provided that the Party or Parties so receiving such binding legal commitment shall promptly after such delivery deliver to my attention an original copy of their own authorized signature or signatures to this Agreement, complete with supporting documentation as necessary to deem such authorized signature or signatures to be of equally binding legal commitment to the Party or Parties of same. Blah blah blah.

But I am a Life Bearer. My burden is what it is. Bear I do, though I part not or with the fault, crown, and give rise to a life other than mine. Six billion ready to receive redemption through umbilical cord charity, but I rise up from the fetal and stand alone, beleaguered by the Life Bearer's task, beset by what is mine and mine alone, all around and upon me.

Do I like Downtown?

'It's overrun with stuffy old men,' I tell Julian.

'Have you heard?' he asks, changing the subject.

'Heard what?'

'About Paul and David.'

'What about them?' I ask innocently, not that I am in the dark. I know exactly what he's going to say, but I'm not going to say it.

'They're officially dating now. I talked to Paul last night.'

'What did you tell him?'

'What is there to say?' Julian brings himself around on the chair. His knees stick up over the back and reach up to his chin. 'I think it was a long time coming. Why? Are you surprised?'

I shrug my shoulders. I am, but I'm not. I, too, saw this coming, but I never prepared for it. I couldn't have. I know a few gay people, but I'm not close to any of them. They're not family, not close friends. My cousin Freddy is a little off. Last time I saw him—which was years ago—he was playing 'house', cooking and cleaning and all that eyelash-raising girl stuff.

But for all I know, domestic fancy might be very normal for an eight year old. I haven't seen Freddy in years, and maybe he has since given up dolls, but how can I be so sure? What if he sent Barbie and her hot pink convertible on their merry way and then picked up Ken?

I wonder what Annie thinks about all this, assuming she's heard. I bet she'll handle it well. I think my Dad would laugh and hang up the phone if I told him I were gay. If my Mom were alive, she'd be devastated. The religion thing, the fact that I wouldn't be giving her any grandchildren, etcetera etcetera. Let's just say that it would have been extremely hard for her to watch her X and my Dad's Y match up with two other Ys. Throw an X up on the Family Feud board and ask 'Why?' for a lifetime. No, my mom would have wanted grandchildren. I'm her only child. Carrying on the bloodline is my job.

'He's gay, huh?' I say.

Julian grabs his knees and squeezes them together with his hands. 'I asked him about that,' he says, 'and he said that he doesn't really see himself as gay. "I still like women," he told me. "I just like David."'

'Hey, I liked Brad Pitt in "Fight Club", but that doesn't mean that I want to roll in the hay with him. I just don't get why he is telling us now.'

'Would you if you weren't sure?' he replies. 'Would Paul?'

'But this is pretty big,' I remind him. The word *reticent* comes to mind.

'F-ing right it is,' he answers.

'Time for a beer.'

I leave the bed and head to the kitchen.

'He told me that he had been thinking about it awhile,' I hear over the whirr of the refrigerator, 'so I asked him if he felt this way about men before, and he told me "No".'

'I think it's crazy,' I yell out to him. 'Paul has done some pretty off-the-cuff things before, but nothing like this. This is too much.' I grab my open bottle of beer as well as an unopened one in the freezer. The bottles aren't cold, but I want a beer, and I want it now.

'Is he serious about this?' I ask, handing Julian a beer.

'I guess so,' he replies, twisting off the cap and then reaching over to spin it on the coffee table. He takes a sip and cringes. 'Awful,' he reviews.

'But you'll keep drinking it,' I reply.

'That I will.'

'Quite the quandary.'

'You know this thing with Paul had me thinking . . .' Julian pauses for a moment. 'Do you remember Marina?'

'Marina?'

'Marina. Your Marina from NYU.'

My Marina, he says. Hardly. I met Marina in an African Studies class the first semester of our freshman year. She grew up in Savannah, and when she left Georgia, Marina left behind a boyfriend that she had known her entire life, one who had remained in the good graces of her parents for years and would have likely had their blessing. Marina's best friend got engaged shortly after their high school graduation, and Marina flew back to Georgia at the end of our freshman year to be her maid of honor and witness the lives of two nineteen year olds be bound together by holy matrimony. The event must have rattled Marina because she decided to cut her boy loose that weekend. The moment I met her, I could tell that she wasn't the settling down type. Not my Marina. Not anyone's Marina.

During his last year at Billington High, Julian came into the City to take a look at the NYU campus. I'm not so sure that NYU has a real campus, but anyway, I introduced Julian to Marina, and they hit it off. Let's just say that they exchanged more than their phone numbers that weekend. Shortly thereafter, Marina told me that she had started seeing a girl. I pushed for the meat and potatoes, but Marina handed over salad and bread. No explanation, no details, nothing. The next time I spoke with Julian, I messed with his head a little, telling him that his insensitivity had played a role in triggering Marina's abrupt conversion. I had Julian one phone call away from making a complete ass out of himself.

So I'm not a virgin to the conversion. Well I am, but I'm not. I've never known experimentation to be limited to the NYU chem labs, but I've also never heard of a guy deviating from The Scientific Method. I've met gay guys before, but I guess I've always assumed gay men to be born always and forever gay. Gay women, on the other hand, are open-minded, free-spirited nymphos. Straight, but bored with being straight. Paul ruins this perfect dichotomy. Now, sexuality is a sliding scale for men as well.

'Yeah, I remember Marina,' I tell Julian. 'Why?'

Julian doesn't respond. He just raises his eyebrows to the limits of the ceiling and smirks. The boos build. The Sox must have scored a run.

'I should have picked up on this a long time ago,' I say.

Julian shrugs. 'Maybe he deliberately kept it from us.'

'I don't see why he would. You wouldn't.'

'You'd be surprised.'

'What?'

'It's a need-to-know basis with you,' Julian explains, tone out of the flippant and into the serious. 'Trust me, it's not hard to keep things from you.'

'What things?'

'Things.'

'Like what?'

'Like why I decided to go to NYU.'

'You told me that BC didn't offer you an athletic scholarship.'

'That is what I said.' Julian takes small sips from his beer, keeping his eyes fixed to the television.

'What?'

He turns to me. 'BC offered me a scholarship,' he says, blushing. 'A full one. To play football.'

'Are you serious?'

'As a VD.'

'You never told me that BC showed you some love.'

'I didn't tell anyone.'

'Why not?'

'I didn't want people to know.'

'Why?'

'I didn't want to play football anymore. I was tired of it.'

'How could you be tired of football? You've loved football since you were five years old.'

'I wanted to enjoy college.'

'But you played basketball—'

'Yeah, D-3 basketball—*at NYU*. You know how different it would have been if I had played football at BC? That's Atlantic-10 ball. D-1 players are like professional athletes. If I had gone to school there, I wouldn't have had time to do anything else, and I would have spent all four years on the bench too.'

'I doubt it.'

'Those players would have ripped me up. Football in high school is one thing, college ball is a whole other thing.'

'You could have been a taller Flutie with blonde hair.'

Julian shakes his head. 'I'd be lucky if I got a Rudy moment, never mind a Miami moment.'

'Great movie.'

'Do you remember that concussion I got against Theston Academy?'

I nod. Sure do, senior year, toward the end of the football season. Julian took a big hit and left the game in the third quarter. He returned in the fourth and finished up the game. Little did we know that he was playing with a mild concussion.

'I remember getting food poisoning from a bad hot dog,' I tell him.

'That day I realized that I would never play football at a division one school.'

'Why?'

'I blew it. I totally misread their defense. I should have called an audible and thrown a quick one to Wally. That's what I should have done. And when I got hit over by the sidelines, everything just went black. When I woke up, everything was so clear to me.'

'But that was one play!' I appeal. 'You made a mistake. Big deal.'

'That's all it took,' Julian responds, not at all swayed by my argument. 'At that moment, I started thinking differently about my ability. I started to realize what I was and what I wasn't. You know what I mean?'

'You know what I think? I think you've taken one too many hits to your head.'

'When BC came to me with that one and only option, it wasn't a tough decision to make,' Julian explains. 'If I went there, they would have made the decision for me. It would have been like I was stuck in high school with the same expectations, the same challenges, the same bullshit. Nothing would have changed. I'm glad I made the decision I did. I don't regret it.'

I give him a hard look.

'I don't.'

'You Andersons are something else.'

He lets out a dismissive grunt and turns back to the television. Piazza homers, tying up the game at one-all. I kill my bottle and find a colder one waiting for me in the freezer. Back to my bed.

'You know what happened to the other quarterback BC recruited that year?' Julian asks.

'No idea,' I reply.

'He died from alcohol poisoning.'

'No shit.'

'What are the odds?'

Chapter Twenty Two

SOMETIMES I THINK my dad wants me to suffer.

'You just get up?' he asks me.

'Nah, I've been up awhile,' I reply. I'm lying, but that's what happens when you feel guilty. My dad is the King of The Morning, and I'm not the best heir to assume the throne when he passes.

'How are things?' I ask him.

'Not bad,' he answers. 'I got a few things done early today, so I'm happy about that.'

My dad insists that success is tied to the time of day you wake. It all begins with that stupid saying about the worm, and believing it to the very core. On a day like today, a Saturday, my dad jumps in his SUV, plows down the street to Billington Donuts, and scoops up a half-dozen favorites before the metal racks empty. It's like a contest to my father, a contest between him and all of the other Boston Crème fanatics out there. And while I'm snoozing away, my dad is finishing his coffee and third donut, taking his morning walk around the neighborhood, reconfiguring his sophisticated system of hoses and sprinklers, fixing the toilet handle, and polishing off the last two chapters of a book.

'So, what are you doing now?' I ask.

'Not much. Just standing around, watching that jackass neighbor of ours flood the bushes with a hose.'

'Don't you mean sitting around?'

'No, the hemorrhoids are flared up bad today, so I'm trying to stay off my butt.'

'Hemorrhoids? Since when?'

'A couple of weeks now. The proctologist said he's never seen hemorrhoids this big in his thirty years of practice—'

'Dad?'

'I looked in the mirror this morning, and one of them is getting real big.' My dad is totally fascinated with this topic. 'I've been monitoring it lately,' he continues, 'because it's been changing color and shape. It started out pink, then turned red, started small but then got bigger and then small again. It's starting to round out now. I've thought about naming it . . . '

My dad speaks with a sloppy fastness when he's excited. He's an employee-of-the month telemarketer and a horse derby announcer, fighting over a crystal meth pipe. You can't get a word in edgewise.

' . . . I looked through that baby name book your mother bought before you were born. I'm thinking "Henry" or "Harry" or right now.'

'Can you hold on a second?' I interrupt.

'Why?'

'I'm going be sick.'

'It's just inflammation. It's perfectly normal.'

'I don't think so.'

'Sure it is. You know Peter from my office? The man with the extra toe on his right foot?'

'What about him?'

'He told me that his brother had them about six months ago, and—'

'Dad?'

'He seemed to think—'

'Dad!'

'What?'

'Can we talk about something else? How's work? How are all the other accountants treating you down at the office?'

'Fine. Go ahead and change the topic.'

'But—'

'Why can't you talk to me about these things?'

'Because it's disgusting.'

'Because you're talking to your father about it?'

'No, I just don't want to hear about the things on your rear end.'

'If you can't talk to me about these things now, when will you? What happens when I lose my hearing, huh?'

'I guess I'll just have to speak into a megaphone when that happens,' I answer. I like to fit in my jabs. I think it keeps things more interesting that way.

It doesn't take long for my dad to digress and get all Ann Landers with the *Trust Me On This One*, *Let Me Tell You Something*, and *When I Was Your Age*. But I'm slowly learning to turn it against him. The other day, I told my dad that I recently hired a scribe to record our conversations, that way I can go back thirty years from now and revisit his lessons on paper. My dad laughed. I think he knows how crazy he is.

'Before you know it,' my father marches on, 'I'll have to subscribe to one of those services where an operator types everything you say into a computer and the words pop up on a screen for me. I'll have to read your words off a screen, and then what? Will you start talking to me then? Will ya?'

I tend to drift in and out a lot when I'm on the phone, and this is never a good thing when you're talking to someone like my dad. He'll be in the middle of a monologue, and all of sudden my father will ask a question like, 'Did you know that diamonds are a girl's best friend?' —you know, as a test to see whether I'm paying attention—at which point I'll realize that I haven't, and then I'll try to come up with a generic response to cover my butt. Unfortunately, 'You've told me that a million times, Dad' only makes occasional sense in the middle of a conversation. If my timing is off, I get to listen to him lecture for twenty minutes about how I don't have any respect for my elders.

'They have that on the Internet now,' I tell him. 'They call it "IM".'

'You know what's strange?' my father asks, ignoring my swings.

'Dare I ask?'

'Peanut butter and jelly in a jar.'

'Huh?'

'Are kids buying that now?'
'Dad, they've had that for years.'
'I could see it if you had no kitchen utensils. But everyone has kitchen utensils. You know, your mother used to . . . '

. . .

'Dad?'
'Yeah?'
'Nevermind.'
'Thinking about your mother?'
'Yeah.'
'Me too.'
'How are things with you and Lena?'
'Terrible. She's going back to California.'
'What? Why?'
'Her mom was having these headaches,' I explain, 'and one day she fainted at work. They ran a bunch of tests and discovered that she has cancer. The doctors want to start chemo right away, and Lena wants to be there when it starts.'
'How is Lena doing?'
'OK, I guess.'
'When is she moving back?'
'In a few days.'
'And what do you think about that?'
'It sucks. She's leaving me.'
'She's not leaving you. She's leaving to be with her mother.'
'I wish I could see it that way.'
'What's going to happen between the two of you?'
The million dollar question. 'I don't know,' I reply. 'What can I do?'
'What do you want?'
'What?'
'Make it work if you need to. You show up everyday at the office and work hard, don't you?'
'Yeah.'
"How is a relationship any different? And jobs are replaceable, people are not. Remember that. Jobs are replaceable, people are not. But you have to want it to work. That's the first thing.'

'But Dad, she's moving three thousand miles away.'

'So? When you love someone, no distance in the world should keep you away. You find that right person, and suddenly your life stops being all that complicated. You no longer have to puzzle over the little decisions. And once you get the little decisions out of the way, trust me, the big ones become much easier to make.'

'I think it's more complicated than that.'

'Is it? That's the thing. When it's right, it's simple.'

'I don't see how it could be.'

'You will.'

'Dad, I'm sorry to cut you off, but I have to go.'

'Heading out?'

'Lena is taking me out for breakfast.'

'You better go then. Best not to keep a lady waiting.'

'Right.'

'Happy birthday, Son.'

'Thanks Dad.'

'Have fun.'

'I'll try.'

Chapter Twenty Three

IT IS NINE o'clock, and people are pouring into David's apartment as if it were a bomb shelter and the Armageddon ball were scheduled to drop at 9:01 PM. Anyone and everyone that I don't want to see is here, including those who witnessed my hurling exhibition at David's last party a few months ago. I wish they would all disappear in a massive nuclear blast. NO VACANCY, except for scientists and hot girls.

I picked up a **CALLER ID UNKNOWN** call on my cell phone this afternoon, and by the time I realized what was happening, David had already recruited me to help throw together a last-minute surprise birthday party for Paul and Julian. I couldn't gather up the nerve to say 'No', so I showed up at his apartment, put on a happy face, and asked him what he wanted me to do. I think I cut enough lemons and limes to prevent world scurvy for a year. When my cuticles started singing, I left the fruit rolling figure eights on the cutting board and started looking around.

The apartment looks a lot different with the lights on. I can actually see the color and detail of the walls, the kitchen cabinets, the furniture. Last time I was here, everything looked dark and blurred, flat and completely plebeian. It was as if I had passed that night on a speeding train. But now, I can see the deep greens swirled in with the blues on that canvas on the wall. The ceiling has the color and texture of rotten cottage cheese. There's also a dartboard on the wall next to the door leading outside to the stairs. I missed all of this the first time around.

The door opens, people walk in, and the door closes. I can't put any of them together with a job, a major, a funny story, or anything else. They are Paul and Julian's friends from school, people that I merely exchange empty hellos with at a bar or at a gathering like this one. When I was in college, I hung out with the more interesting of the bunch, but even then I neither invested the time nor the energy to get to know any of them well. I'm paying for it now. I'm the loser of the apartment, the Queen of Spades. As an implicit rule, everyone passes me off to another guy at the very beginning with the hope that the other guy has a poor hand or plays a suicidal 'Hi, my name is Antonio. What's your name?'

David invited his regular posse, a peculiar mix of burnt-out artists with names impossible to pronounce and trust fund babies blessed with doormat friendly names like 'Jason', 'Michael', and 'Timmy'. These are people that I can't imagine befriending because they are either too bizarre or too perfect. You need to be an enthusiastic extravert, a man with charms and stories to survive them, and I have been the worst kind of socialite and storyteller lately. I just don't care to care, care to fake it. I don't want to be here, and I don't want to pretend that I want to be here.

A knock on the door. I have no idea how I landed door duty.

A smiling Dan Grimes stands in the doorway, holding a plastic grocery bag. 'Grimsy' is a good guy, a year or two older than me. Up until a few weeks ago, he worked in Feldman's accounting department, which is located on a different floor than mine. A couple of times a day Grimsy would stop by my cube to chat, usually about basketball and how great Allen Iverson is. On his suggestion I joined the company's intramural team. Once a week, seven or eight of us would head to a high school in the Village or on the Upper East Side to have the absolute snot blown out of us. Not all that good, I spent most of the games on the sidelines, watching our out-of-shape white collars be torn apart by teams pieced together with neighborhood hip-hop players who breathed basketball. I enjoyed watching Grimsy play though. The kid played D-1 scholarship ball at Hofstra. His first step was lightning-quick, and his stop-on-a-dime jump shot was amazing. He made everyone else on the Feldman Tigers look like a bunch of arm amputees rolling around in a fleet of broken wheelchairs.

Grimsy left the firm about a month ago. The story is, he got into a shouting match with his boss and was shown the proverbial door. He liked to listen to music through headphones—a no-no ripped straight from Page 13 of the *Feldman Associates Employee Handbook*—and I'm sure that contributed to his demise as well.

I haven't seen Grimsy since he left Feldman, so maybe we'll have something to talk about, say the recently sedated March Madness, or take shots at Feldman. I say hello, and he sort of slaps and shakes my hand in one motion. I take the bag from his other hand and replace it with a cold Corona I just opened. 'Thanks buddy,' he says, turns, and walks away. So much for that.

I guess he's still bitter. That's understandable. I've heard stories about the dreaded, 4:45 PM Friday call. The man upstairs sends in an HR rep who sugarcoats the slap in the face with a sliver of the company petty cash box. Here's your ten-day consolation prize. Please sign here. In small italic font, *Good luck suing us.* Years of service are fed through a paper shredder. Time to head to the back of the unemployment line.

When it comes to firings, the little guy suffers and the bigwigs thrive. No one thinks twice before filling the backyard pools of objective-failed executives with cash and stock. 'What a guy! He served the company well!', they say, but they are really thinking, *Hey Johnny! Hand that man a multi-million dollar parting prize! He sucks as much as that poor fuck in the Documentation Library!* Pop the cork, I've found my calling. Executive gypsy life is for me. I'll pack my things. Will you be so kind as to hold the elevator?

But first you have to climb this so-called corporate ladder, and do it quietly. Make a ruckus, and you might set off an alarm. *May I have your attention please! May I have your attention please! This is your fire safety director. This is not a drill. Everyone please make your way in an orderly fashion to the lobby of your floor, where you will receive further instruction as to proceeding down the stairs to the ground floor. 58, 57, 56...*

People like Grimsy are heroes. They are the few that have a systems breakthrough. They rediscover their conscience. They remember that a soul is behind the brain that crunches consolidated statements. They rise up, and are put on permanent administrative leave within the week. That's justice. Some even say holiness.

I still say that I am next to go. I'm not lazy. I just have I nothing to do most of the time.

I check the bag Grimsy handed me: Natty Light, Official Beer of The Unemployed. Oh well. Beer is beer.

I began drinking the minute I arrived at the apartment. A stupid idea when you just ate a really bad buffalo burger. My decision to flood the village came with the idiotic thinking that if I drank enough, I might just be able to flush the fucker out of my body. I started off with Coronas, but up around the third of fourth beer I moved to a light domestic brand after accidentally spraying a girl while sinking a lime. I've turned up the charm tonight. I should be drinking from a sippy cup.

David, looking ostentatiously dapper in a pair of black slacks and a fitted long sleeve shirt, rallies together a group of partygoers for tequila shots. I have no intention to let the show-off drink me under the table, so I take the libation like a champ, killing the bite with another lime wedge before bounding away to find something else to drink. It has become sickeningly obvious that I have reverted back to my old college lifestyle, drinking for the sake of getting drunk, not because it is a socially accepted thing to do at a party but because it is something to do.

I think it be best that I continue the downward spiral. I crack open a bottle of gin, coat a beer cup, add some tonic, and garnish the kerosene with a couple of green wedges. I draw a steak knife from the drawer and use it to mix the rocket fuel.

I move out from behind my Maginot Line, making my way to a group of ladies I recognize to be Julian's friends from NYU. I'm sure Lena won't mind me trying my hand at flirtation seeing as our relationship is in ruins, torn apart by the reality of one life moving forward to the future and the other life running circles in the present. Truth is, I might be ready to move on now. And I *am* moving, chugging on this gin like a train feeding on black coal. I'm rolling, consuming with reckless abandon. I stopped keeping track of how each companion appears in front of me, and that's all fine and dandy with me. I am willing to accept the magical element of it all without asking questions.

The girls exchange knowing glances; they've pinpointed that guy in the crowd who hides behind a cup because he doesn't belong. My kind stands out like a sore thumb. But I don't care. Having a drink in my hand at all times ensures that I remain occupied, both mentally and physically. You never feel alone when you have something in your hand, holding you as tight as you are holding it, depending on you as much as you are depending on it.

I drool a Hi to Justine, an attractive blond whose heart and chest are unfortunately much bigger than her brain. The tractor beam tugs, but she has little to say beyond awkward pleasantry, and her twin wingers offer nothing but gormless looks, so I fire up my thrusters and speed away to another star system.

The room falls to darkness. A loud SURPRISE! ruins my hearing, directed not to me but to Julian, who stands in the illuminated doorway. Shadowing him is Vinay, a painfully nice kid whose Psychology major sits him in on many of Julian's classes. Paul pops his head in, followed by Lena, who gives him a friendly push. I feverishly gulp the gin on hand and run away to the kitchen to scoop up another antacid. The refrigerator door closes ever so slowly. I spot a bottle opener sitting on the counter next to a four-slot toaster. I pick it up, crank off the bottle's silver cap, and take a swig.

Avoid Lena, hunt down Paul. Cat and mouse, mouse and cat. Hide from that who seeks, seek that who hides. But first, there is one matter of business that requires my attention.

DARK LIFE

* * *

Look at Paul, all pleased with himself, saying his hellos and howyadoins. He'll take a drink, but unlike me he'll drink in celebration, victorious in beating the joy out of me.

Lena bounces over and gives me a kiss. I feel the heat on her lips because I'm an emotional snow cone. Exothermic and endothermic reversed, two measly letters removed. Lena looks at me funny, seems to know that something is up. She sees me looking at Paul, who is making his rounds, embracing his beautiful people. She must know that I am drunk because I wear my lack of sobriety on my shirt. Drunk, I may be, but I've seen drunker. My brains are clothes thrashing together in the middle of a spin cycle. The battle has its initial instigator but no clear continuator. I have nothing to do with this. I'm way too drunk to fit the quarters into that little hole.

Paul returns to joke with Lena about the surprise. Lena laughs and hugs him off. What a farce. She doesn't know him. She didn't grow up with him. She wasn't the one to drag him home from the reservoir after he twisted his ankle falling off a bike. She didn't share a limousine with him on prom night. She can't understand why I feel betrayed. My world has been shattered, and here I am trying to piece together the shards with hands already bludgeoned.

I know my anger has nothing to do with Lena or Paul. Lena is going, and that's that. And I know that Paul is neither gay nor straight nor even bisexual. He lives as he wants to, the way it should be. He's out there in the open, not hiding anything, just living his life, following his heart and allowing it to take the lead, but I know I can't do that because I'm a coward. I'm too afraid to call a spade a spade, too afraid to order a nip of sake in a Japanese restaurant, too afraid to say what I feel and be who I am. I can't rock the boat. I'm not a rocker. I'm not a shaker. I'm not a mover. I could turn this whole thing upside down for me, but I can't get beyond the rules and the constructs that are embedded in my head. The law of unhappy mediocrity is my law. Paul's law is Paul's law. He is Paul, and he has always been Paul. And I'm not Paul. And I'm not his brother, a guy who can say no to BC, no to scholarships, no to instant popularity, no to a free boat, no to anything, no to everything. But this is about Paul. Yes, what I really want is for something to go wrong in Paul's life, for some piece of his life to not fit perfectly. No, this is about me. This is about my life and how imperfect it is.

Lena pulls me to the side and has the audacity to ask me whether I'm feeling OK. She knows that I'm not. I can see it in her eyes, and I'm sure she can see it as it reflects off my eyes.

'How the fuck are ya?' I ask, pointing to what appears to be the middle one of her faces.

'What did you say?' Lena asks, leaning back. She hates it when I drop the F bombs. I can get away with a lot, but not the F word for some reason.

'Can I ask you a question?' I ask in the nicest tone I can muster.

'What is it?' She rests her hand on my chest. I want none of that.

'Why are you here?' I ask her.

'What are you talking about? You told me to bring Julian and Paul here.'

'Yeah, the birthday boys are having a great time.'

She looks. 'I guess so,' she says, shrugging. 'I hope they are.'

'That so?' I parry.

'That's the point of throwing a party.'

'Fill my cup, frauds.'

'What?'

'Frauds.'

She takes her hand off me and looks over my shoulder. She returns puzzled. I help her. 'Them and Paul, that's who.'

'What?'

My feet are working like anchors, trying to keep the boat in one place. 'A fraud, and you love him for it. It's too bad he's gay and Julian is dating someone.'

'What are you talking about?' she asks. Her hands start moving. She becomes very animated when she's angry.

Keep it coming. 'Fucking frauds.'

She searches my eyes for humanity, or just for that guy she calls her boyfriend. But that guy is long gone. 'Fucking frauds.' I match perfidy with alliteration. *Y tu, Brutus.*

'What is wrong with you?' she asks. Her eyes cower away from me as if my eyes are headlights clicked on high.

'What what,' I drub. 'You sound like a broken record.'

'Why are you acting like this?'

'You tell me why I'm acting this way,' I fire back. 'Tell me how I'm acting. Tell me how much you love me. Go ahead. Tell me.'

She breaks into Mandarin.

'That's right, sweet cheeks.'

'You're such an asshole!' Lena screams.

I can't believe she pulled out the Mandarin. Want to curse me, fine, but do it in a language I can understand. She turns away, but I want to get in the last word. 'The greatest asshole in the world deserves a parade,' I tell her. I am so eloquent.

Lena turns back but says nothing. Her revulsion disallows speech. She's looking at me, into me, through me, locking in. E-5. Open the torpedo hatch.

David walks by us with a tray in his hand, and I reach out and grab something off it. I sink my teeth in, bite long and deep. A gooey wonder rolls with the buds of my tongue. My nostrils fill. I break the indulgence to show Lena my conquest. I'm a three-year-old on his birthday, posing for the camera, tickled pink. Shocked statues look in on me from left and right. Their glares are meant for kibosh, but they can kiss my ass. I'm having my fifteen minutes right now. I'm commanding the stage, inside and outside. Sir Olivier, Pacino, the sweaty girls swinging around thong-buffed poles—it's Andy Kaufman genius!

Something feels hot on my nose. I pull my hand away from my face. A flame on a wick. I look deep into the orange fire. It burns savagely, stares coldly. Everywhere there are eyes watching.

Chapter Twenty Four

I DON'T KNOW why the birds are chirping. This morning is nothing to get excited about. My head is pounding. I feel like crap.

I think I became unhappy when I stopped enjoying the small pleasures of life. I wish I could go back and remember what gasoline smells like. I know that might make me a little Columbine disturbed, but still.

It's a good thing to have 'a thing'. And it's a good thing to have beliefs. I believe in dreams, and in realities. Like a lot of people I dream about falling off of cliffs, having sex with hot new acquaintances, and fleeing blood-dripping beasts, but I only remember the dreams that I have with my eyes open. So I think dreams and real life may be the same thing. Sometimes I think TV and real life might be the same thing too, but then again, I am not an idiot. If you throw water on a Gremlin, its balls shrink, but that's the only thing that happens.

I believe in friends, and in enemies. I'd like to think that my best friends tell me when I'm acting like a total asshole, but I'm not so sure anymore. With belief comes a pre-requisite for honesty and truth, and people who have real tans are just as fake as the people who have fake tans; they simply tan differently. Lies are like adhesive bandages in that they cover and conceal but never reveal to the world whether they truly help the healing process. I've been doing a lot of lying lately. I hate my job, but when people ask me how work is, I say, 'OK'. I've been lying to people, and I've been lying to myself.

Lena reappears, freshly showered, her hair pulled back in a ponytail. She walks over to the far corner of the room, sits on a chair, and opens up a book.

The girl is my sleeping opposite. She goes to bed early, gets up several times during the night to ruffle a pillow or pee, and wakes early. At 8 AM, Lena is up and prancing about the apartment, doing what it is she does, and she does it with a gusto that normally doesn't hit me until the afternoon.

I could make an attempt at conversation, but I don't see the point. She's not interested in talking to me. I could write Lena a letter ripe of confession and repentance, but I have no reason to believe that it would be read and answered. Asking questions in a unilateral letter is romantic folly.

My bladder forces me to the bathroom to urinate. I don't bother to close the door. I go forever. A jiggle of the handle collapses the soup into a violent maelstrom. Mirror Mirror, on the wall, who's the ugliest fuck of them all? All fairy tale, no poetry in this place, just the stench of urine and shameful unashamed nudity. What you see is what you get, and damn I don't look so hot. My eyes are black. My cheeks are scrunched up. I rub out my slimy tongue. It feels like the bark of a wet tree.

A face a hundred times more beautiful appears in the glass of the medicine cabinet. 'How are you feeling?' it asks.

'Miserable,' I answer, wiping my hands on a towel.

'You drank a lot last night.'

I don't understand how she can be so calm. It drives me crazy sometimes, her calmness.

'Have you talked to Paul today?' I ask her.

'No.'

'I'm such an idiot.'

'You were drunk.'

'I said a lot of things I shouldn't have,' I say. 'Things I didn't mean.'

'People tend to tell the truth when they're drunk.'

I look at Lena through the reflection of the mirror. She's not going to believe the reflection anymore than the flesh, but I don't want to look directly into her eyes. 'I wasn't angry at you,' I explain. 'I was angry at myself.'

'No one owes you anything,' Lena says. 'You understand that, don't you?'

'I'm beginning to.' I locate my toothbrush. The taste in my mouth is overnight decay.

'I'm not going to feel sorry for you,' Lena says, folding her arms. She looks ready to shell out a scolding of a lifetime. 'We both know this has nothing to with me moving,' she continues. 'I wouldn't be leaving if I didn't have to.'

I gather some courage, turn, and reach for her waist. She brushes my arm away angrily. 'I feel like everything is falling apart for me,' I explain, resting my rejected hand on my bare chest.

'You're not dying,' Lena says.

'I feel dead inside.'

'Listen to yourself! You—'

'I don't know what my problem is,' I cut in, 'so I can't expect you to know either. All I know is, the one person I really care about is leaving.'

'I'm not leaving. I'm just moving. And you've got Paul and Julian here.'

'After last night, I'm not so sure about that.'

'They're your best friends. They're not going anyway.'

'Even so, I don't have anything else.'

'What are you talking about? You have *so* much. If you could just open up your eyes and see it.'

'What do I have, Lena? What?'

'It's what you have, and what've you done. Look at what you've done at the shelter. Look at the people you've helped.'

'What good is that?'

'Don't you dare!' she exclaims. 'What you do for those people is important.'

'I expect to matter. I expect to—'

'Take my hand,' she interrupts, putting out her hand.

'What?'

'Just shut up and do it.'

I take her hand.

'Look at me.' I look up, into the white, past the tributaries of pink, past the white pearls and into the darkest and deepest parts of her eyes. 'I'm moving back to Sacramento,' Lena says, each word painfully slow. 'I need to be there. This is where my life is bringing me now, and you have to decide where yours is going. If you want to stay around here and feel sorry for yourself, then that's your choice. I can't stop you. But I'm not going to make that decision for you. You have to make it yourself.'

Chapter Twenty Five

AN HOUR AGO Lena handed me an index card, touched my cheek, and left.

Rewind 6 months.

My head rested in the toilet, and she sat down next to me.

Rewind 27 years.

On his way back to work, my father dropped a book on the library floor and into my mother's life.

Fast forward 15 years.

My father and I waved as my mother backed the car out of the driveway.

Fast forward an hour.

Sergeant Lucent introduces himself.

Fast forward, all the way.

Strike me down with anhidrosis. Remove me from sight, touch and memory. My life is in the crapper. I am shit. Flush me.

They say that what comes around goes around, and around and around. Bad things happen when you are coming, and bad things happen when you are going, and it goes around and around, and I am left with a dreadful feeling that this loop will stop halfway around again.

June

Chapter Twenty Six

LARRY WALKS IN and gives me a squeeze on the shoulder. Larry's right hand shakes a lot, so he tries to avoid handshakes.

I met Larry when he came to the house after my mom died. After that, he would arrive on the doorstep unannounced to smoke a cigar, talk politics and financial planning, and behave the way all family attorneys from small towns like Billington behave—self-importantly. He usually conducted his visits on Sunday afternoons, arriving at the house shortly after the New England Patriots had lost yet another heartbreaker of football.

We move into the kitchen. Larry slides a chair out from underneath the table, takes a seat, and gets down to business, opening up his briefcase, clicking his pens, and organizing sheets of paper on the table. He's one rigid S.O.B., a man who walks in right angles and knows everything he is going to say two hours beforehand.

Larry left California in the Seventies and moved to the other side of the country because he thought the West Coast had turned into a Mecca for slacker potheads and surfboarding amateurs. He started his own law practice here in town and began investing in real estate. How he ended up in Billington remains a mystery to me.

Whenever he talks about property owner's rights and interest rates, Larry definitely comes across as a well versed, erudite individual. He has a statistic and allegory for everything. Like a brilliant politician, Larry can surround boiled ham in a pesto wrap and get the most astute constituents chomping away. If you're not careful, he'll suck you right into his vacuum of convoluted dumb ass. But at times he becomes so ridiculous that even I know he is full of shit. His tendency to adopt adage as truth leads him to make outrageous claims. He once argued that a massive earthquake will cause California to break off the Continental United States within the decade. He still believes that Joe Montana is the second coming of the Messiah.

He definitely got to my father. After Larry would leave the house, my father would track down his copy of Trump's *The Art of the Deal* and, after a spirited reading of the text, he would lean back in his chair, crunch black leather in one hand and hardcover in the other, and curse his 'Act First, Think Second' approach to residential financing. As The Donald got it all out of his system, I would watch MTV and try to figure out how much it would cost to buy my own TV Room.

My dad wasn't dumb enough to buy into all of Larry's nonsense, but I think he found Larry's penchant for disputation and polemics entertaining. They fed off each other. Whenever you got them together, it was like you were listening in on a discussion between the author of the Encyclopedia Britannica and the voice from the *This is How the World Works* cassette tape series. Sometimes they brought me into their conversations, particularly when the topic of academia came into play. Larry terminally sided with my father on every issue, but Larry always had a desire to make himself a wholly loved individual and, thus, would make amends for his treachery by slipping a ten in my pocket on his way out the door or inviting me on a ski trip to Vermont with his family even though he knew full well that I didn't know how to ski.

I grab a chair across the table from Larry, drop my butt in it, and scoop my right leg under my left. Larry writes something on a legal pad. He reminds me of executives: white, tall, observant of the strictest grooming habits. His hands are smooth, his fingernails are perfectly manicured—everything you look for in a model Allstate spokesperson. A thick layer of gel keeps his thinning salt-and-pepper off his forehead. He dresses impeccably. He's always wearing a designer suit. He must go to fittings. Twice a year, he must stand around for a half hour and let a short, Italian man dance around him with a handful of measuring tape.

Larry puts down his pen and looks up with nervous eyes. 'I'm terribly sorry to hear about your father,' he says, playing with the gigantic piece of Stanford metal on his finger. When I was younger, Larry would tap me on the head with it. Damn thing stung like a motherfucker. He'd fiddle around with the ring constantly, knowing that I was watching him do it. 'Nice, huh?' he'd proudly ask, holding out his hand as if that thing on his finger were an engagement ring. 'Maybe one day you'll get one.' He'd breathe on it and then polish it on his sleeve. He had no idea that I thought him a complete asshole.

'My wife sends her condolences,' Larry says. 'I brought her along on a business trip to Chicago last week, and she wanted to fly back with me yesterday, but she came down with a stomach flu. I thought it be best for her to wait and let it pass before she gets back on a plane.'

I nod. It's become clear that I have become nothing more than just another R listing in Larry's fat rolodex.

Two weeks ago, I was in a taxi, zigzagging my way to the Upper East Side, when I learned that my father had died. After hearing the message on my cell phone, I yelled to the driver to take me to Penn Station. I dialed the 800 number programmed into my phone and checked buses leaving the Port Authority for Springfield. The next Greyhound left in twenty minutes. I showed the driver a crumpled Jackson and asked him to step on it.

Annie met me at the bus terminal in Springfield. She gave me a hug that almost sucked the life out of me and told me that Julian and Paul would be on a train first thing in the morning. On our way to Billington, I couldn't get myself to play Snake on my Nokia. I just stared out the window.

The funeral took place three days later—on a Monday, the first of June. No one told my father that people don't die on Fridays. We held the funeral at Sims' Funeral Home because I used to drive by the death venue in my Cavalier during high school and could think of no other place to hold it.

Annie handled most of the arrangements. She released an obituary notice to the newspapers. I briefly looked over what she had written and saw that she had focused appropriately on my father's family life. She also instructed the undertakers to decorate the funeral home and casket with my mother's favorite flower, the white orchid. Even the time of the funeral was perfect: atrociously early, 9 AM. I wonder whether she consulted my father on the matter before he died.

The coffin remained closed throughout the entire service. 'Don't let the world see you with your eyes closed,' my father often told me, 'because the world will give up and close its eyes to you.' I thought about that as I stared at the portrait of him on the easel beside the coffin. I am still looking for meaning in those words.

Uncle Jack and Eli flew in from Portland a day before the funeral. Aunt Lily was a no-show, as were my mom's parents. Uncle Jack delivered a long eulogy that brought the twenty-two guests signed into the foyer book to tears. I sat in the last row because I didn't want to feel the eyes burning into the back of my head. After the service, we drove to the gravesite, a small plot located on the southern edge of the cemetery in the middle of town. A drizzle became a downpour, and all but a few faithful ran for shelter. I ignored the wet and watched the raindrops explode on the coffin. Paul and Julian held two umbrellas above Annie. The Reverend closed his eyes. Peter looked like he had lost his best friend. I wanted to laugh. My father would have loved a shower requiem.

Larry clears his throat. 'I took the liberty of contacting your uncle a few days ago,' he says.

'Yeah, he called and told me.'

'That's good,' he says, picking up a pile of documents on the table and holding it up for my examination. 'I had my secretary pull your father's files and fax them to the hotel where I was staying in Chicago so that I could start reviewing them. The rest I'll have mailed to you in the next few days.' He stops to write something on his legal pad. 'In the package I'll send you,' he continues, 'you'll find a few documents and informational packets. We won't need them today to wrap up the important stuff, say, the deed to the house and the life insurance forms. I have those papers here. If you want, we can go ahead and handle this today so that we don't have to worry about it later. Sound good?'

'Sure,' I answer.

Larry explains to me how the house mortgage will be paid off with a flat payment, the funds taken straight from my father's bank account, at which point the house will become mine. He speeds through various insurance policies, using gibberish that only someone in the industry could understand. He becomes a little more excited as he explains that the will should be uncontested and that everything will be handed over to me pending certain official approvals. I nod and shake my head at the appropriate times, secretly fuming that he is putting a dollar figure on my father's death. Part of me is amused though. His situation is a precarious one. I have the power to dump him as counsel. I can see the fear in his eyes.

Larry's cell phone rings. An extremely important call from his wife, he tells me. I nod off the indiscretion as he walks out of the kitchen. I catch a bit of his conversation—something about 'transferring funds'. I guess the markets are open on Sundays now.

Larry returns and apologizes for the interruption. 'So where were we?' he asks, sitting in his chair and getting back to thumbing through papers. 'Oh right. Like I said, I'll send you a few things in the mail once I've had a chance to look them over. It will take some time to finalize everything, but I promised your uncle that I'd do everything possible to make this go smoothly. I assume you'll be in town the next few days?'

No, I'm catching tonight's last flight to Tokyo. 'That's right,' I mumble.

'Good. I think we can have you Hancock these, then I'll leave you alone. I'll have a copy made of everyting, and we'll be in touch in a couple of weeks. That work for you?'

'I guess.'

I watch Larry piece together a new pile of documents from his other piles. He slides the set over to me, and I sign on the dotted lines that he points to with his finger. Satisfied, he grabs the papers in front of me, shuffles the deck together, and heaps it on top of the others piled high in his open briefcase. 'I think we're done here,' Larry says, snapping shut the clasps on his briefcase.

'I'll see you to the door,' I offer.

'That's OK. I know the way.' He squeezes my shoulder. 'Let me know if there is anything else I can do for you.' He pulls out a business card from the inside pocket of his suit coat and hands it to me. 'In case you don't have my number lying around,' he explains.

I feel the coldness of the card in my hand. Larry heads to the door. 'I almost forgot!' He turns around and starts again for his pocket. 'Your father wanted me to give this to you when he—well, you know.' He pulls out an envelope and hands it to me. My name is written in the middle and underlined. 'I've had it for about six months now,' he explains, staring at the envelope now in my hand, 'but I'm not sure what it is.'

'Thanks.'

'I know this means a lot of responsibility for you,' Larry says with a very serious look on his face, 'particularly with all the money from the will and the life insurance policy. And let's not forget the house.' He takes a moment to examine its stuff.

'I'll manage.'

Larry looks back at me. 'If you need anything, please call me. I'm your man.' He shoots up a finger, clicks his tongue, and winks at me all in one motion. What a dick. I take his extended hand, his good hand. 'This is going to change everything for you,' he adds, squeezing my hand tight, driving home the conviction of a man who thinks he has read my future in an autobiography.

'I know,' I tell him.

And I do. It means my father is dead, and now I'm an orphan.

Chapter Twenty Seven

I'M SITTING BY the window with a bowl of cereal, looking out. It's cloudy, raining. The weather has been fucking with me all week. One day it's sunny, 80 degrees. The next day, it's a few degrees above absolute zero. The price you pay for living in New England, where the unpredictable is predictable. A couple of nights ago, a downpour had me scrambling from room to room, slamming windows shut, cutting off the floodwaters surging in. It was the most excitement I've had in days.

Click. I haven't been watching television all that much, but when I do, I avoid the news altogether because I prefer not to know what makes today any different than yesterday. It's probably better that I can't remember the last day that I showered. Ignorance keeps my rotting corpse smelling like perfumed flowers.

Volume all the way down. For once, it's quiet in the house, so let's not ruin it.

My neighbors have been using my house like a hotel the past couple of weeks, popping in at outrageous hours, dropping off casseroles and warming my toilet seat before heading back out. Their never-ending visits have kept the days unpredictable and unpleasant. I've greeted, hugged, listened and tolerated. I've also worked through the diplomatically neutral flower and fruit baskets left on the porch steps by UPS and FedEx ambassadors. I've unwrapped, sniffed, and chewed. Cheeses, meats, crackers, jams, fruits, flowers, cards—business is booming, the office is shrinking, and every time I pass within a few feet of the tower of crap sitting on my kitchen table, it thinks to buckle and crash to the floor. I could make certain structural adjustments to stabilize it, but I'd prefer not to.

I'm tired of the morbid routine. I can't do it. If I see another car pull into the driveway, I'm hiding.

The note on the front door of the house might help. I taped it up last night:

PLEASE LEAVE ALL PACKAGES INSIDE THE DOOR. THANKS.

Most of my neighbors are retired Italians who only emerge from their homes to go to the supermarket or visit relatives, which is why I'm not afraid that my note will turn my house into a showroom for thieves. When you're old and feeble, you can't get your bones motivated to break the law. I could leave the door wide open if I wanted to. A raccoon or another forest creature might accidentally wander in, but I'm more than capable of fighting it off with a baseball bat.

I'm on my third bowl of cereal this morning. Raisin Bran. Tastes phenomenal today. Two scoops of fucking unbelievable.

I've been eating like a blue ribbon contender for this year's upcoming King Fat Ass Festival. I've cleaned the shelves, all but emptied the freezer of its microwave dinner stock, and sampled most of the humanitarian aid packages sent by sympathizers with the energy of a starved boy introduced for the first time to a Costco sample aisle. I've kept up the charade on the drinking end as well, polishing off every bottle in the house resembling anything that could have alcohol in it. To drink is to experience death without dying, or something to that effect. One thing is for sure, drunkenness has played a crucial role in warping my time continuum. I awake at different times of the day, unsure of where I am and what time of the day it is. A photo frame or familiar piece of furniture helps me to regain my reality, at which point I usually wander back into the kitchen and remember where I left the Tums.

I hear my father's voice, then a woman's voice. It's the answering machine. I turned off the ringer on the phone, so the answering machine has been busy, handling telemarketers selling magazine subscriptions and family friends selling peace of mind. Go ahead, lady. Blah blah blah, your dad, blah blah blah sorry about blah blah blah, call me if you need anything, blah blah blah. It makes me sick when people come out of the woodwork after you die.

Earlier this week, I spent a day flipping through books and photo albums, weeding through boxes and dresser drawers. I thought I might stumble upon something important about my father, the man he was but never appeared to be, the things he did but never mentioned. I pulled the string, the ladder fell, and I monkeyed up the stairs to the attic. After wading through a sea of boxes coated with a half-generation of undisturbed dust, I began separating the flotsam into piles on the floor. Baskets, baby clothes, plastic trucks and other toys, books, blankets, Halloween costumes, a busted air conditioner that my father never fixed—a lot of junk, a lot of memories. I found a lot of my father's personal stuff too—black-and-white wedding pictures, old Christmas and baseball cards, a crumbling King James version Bible, a small stamp and coin collection—and I put it off into a separate pile. I had no business touching any of it, but someone had to sort it, and that someone was me. But what am I to do with a high school class ring? Keep it? Give it to a friend or a relative? Pawn it and give the cash to charity? I decided to filibuster the topic until I no longer think about disposing family heirlooms. My father tormented over such matters when my mother died, and I saw what it did to him.

Normally at this hour I would still be in bed, but today I'm tired of sleep, tired of my bed, tired of the length of the day. I could stay inside and do nothing but drink, but I'm not ready to walk that plank yet. The break is good for me. I've been bombed every day it seems. I'm not talking about casual boozing, the kind for which you book winter waxings at days spas in Boca Raton, twirl the umbrella in the sand and the one in your daiquiri for three and a half business days, and hit up duty-free airport shops to buy snow globes for the rascals at home. I'm talking real, destructive drinking—Jim Morrison, but without the mystical genius. I'm talking about a drinking that kills. I'm talking about puking and swigging, puking and swigging. I did that for four years and survived. And I'm back at it. I must be a god, or testing one.

If it were Sunday, I could give the Whitmans a buzz and ask them to swing by and pick me up on their way to church. I've recently thought about seeing the inside of the Father's house again, but right now I can't bear to sit in with a room full of sinners, talk uh-oh fires, and metaphorically bathe in public pools of disinfectant blood. It's too much irony for me to handle right now. Go tell it on the mountain as Ray lays down a carnival nightmare of chords to your stride. Consider the hide-and-seek tale of a man who tears out his hair looking for one wool sock gone astray and never makes it into the Promised Land. Let's consider parting the Red Sea once again, but let's rewrite the tale on location in Arizona, long before Barringer came across that big ass hole in the ground and said, 'Gentlemen, the peyote might be playing tricks with my eyes, but I do believe that's a big ass hole in the ground!' An eye for an eye, a disobedient wife for a sack of salt, a bearded man for a lamb—I'm dying here. I'm losing a sole purpose for the soul. I want a break from creating heartache. *And on the Seventh Day God rested*, Moses wrote, and a gospel choir fifty strong and five-ton organ lung blasted in unison, 'AMEN!' The clouds thickened, a crazy old man ignored his laughing peers and built a Royal Caribbean out of cypress sticks, saved his life and a handful of others, and all of a sudden sea travel becomes *smart* travel.

Yes, contradiction invites irony. God *did* rest, as well he should have. Sunday is a holy day that anyone can observe. In a way I stick to Sabbath obsessively, compulsively, even *religiously* in the most secular definition of it. I might be the last pure Creationist on Earth. If I could stop the involuntary blinking at the start of a new calendar line, I'd do it. I've birthed the miracle of continued existence all week long, and I'm tired of pushing. I present my battered frame as evidence. I'm a patriot. Give me peace and quiet, or give me death. I'm a human's man. Give me one day, and I'll give the world one day free from me. Heck, I'll throw in five more. Give me my Sunday mornings. This is all I ask, speaking as one tired man to another.

I think I will pass on church today. But I will definitely drink. It *is* Sunday.

* * *

A morning shower has left the earth with a healthy green color and a starter pot scent. On the phone line big, black crows are cawing bloody murder and snapping at each other with territorial cockiness. A couple of squirrels watch attentively. I walk on, my shoes crunch the grass, and the squirrels wake up, drop to fours, and quickly hop over the stone wall, into the safety of the underlying brush behind the garage. I slip on a patch of grass and go down to a knee to break my fall. The tight rope walkers laugh at me in Crow.

Today is a new day. That I do know. I could drop tears right now, but my head, hot and running on an empty tank, would dry them up inside of me before they can fall. Hunger has dropped a pain in my stomach that feels different than that of mortal loss, and rather than handling it in the kitchen, I pieced together a knapsack of food items to take on a walk: a bag of jelly beans, a slice of cold pizza wrapped in tin foil, a water bottle filled with cheap vodka, and a Zip-lock bag packed with mixed nuts from a jar I found shoved behind a box of pancake mix in a cabinet above the kitchen sink.

My steps take me into the woods. Maples materialize whenever, wherever they want. Farther up on the top of a bunny hill, I spot a black birch. Small birds, mainly chicks and silvery warblings, entertain me briefly, followed by a couple of robins and then an arrow of field sparrows. I attribute my ability to identify trees and animals to my father. On many afternoons, my Dad would return home from his walks through the woods, pull a book off the bookshelf, and point out his latest sightings.

I slip underneath a copse of pines. Flinty rock belches out of the ground where plates hiccupped in the past. Julian, Paul, and I often made trips this way when we were kids. A couple of blueberry shrubs live up on the hill. We'd pop the tart treat into our mouths until the juice ran off our hands and lips like Vulcan blood. When our stomachs began to sour, we'd fold our t-shirts into kangaroo pouches and gather a supply to take home. When we had returned to Paul and Julian's house, we'd stuff the fruit in a blender, add copious amounts of sugar and a little ice, push BLEND, and watch the birth of yet another revolting purple beverage, incomparable in foulness until Lena introduced me to taro tea.

A squirrel runs across my path without stopping for introductions. Dusty spotlights pop up on undergrowth nestled above newly formed miniature ponds of rainwater lying in depressions of root and rock. A weed splits a giant boulder and reaches vertically to the sky, extending a thank-you to the sun.

I'm walking because I'm drunk and need the fresh air. I'm walking because walking is associated with deep thinking and grieving. I wonder why that is. Because one is moving and not standing still, having no destination in mind but just moving and changing? Does exercise jog the mind and sweat out the inconsequential, or does it have something to do with the great outdoors, the revitalizing powers of its revolving air and evolving ecology?

I throw a handful of nuts to a watchful bird. It pauses to mull over matters. It must be a girl bird. She finally bounces over to investigate, pokes at one of the bigger nuts and manages to cradle it in her tiny brown beak before dropping it. She suddenly rejects the windfall and flutters off.

I stop at a tree to unload a stream of piss. An acrid steam hits me in the face, and I'm reminded of the odor of a stewing City gas vent. I twist and avoid the Jonestown disaster below, then rest my head on the bark. One eye presses into its rough grooves and the other slides down to admire my golden triumph. I'm not sure who or what is holding up what or who. My companion is old, twisted and mangled, blackened and deepened. Overlooked by many but forgotten by no one, this tree is the ruler of this place. It speaks on behalf of the others, guards and protects them.

I've seen this before, somewhere. Without color or scent, the poetry of memory fills my head. I stand in a ballroom, surrounded by black-and-white mannequins, fine China, silver cutlery, ice sculptures, flowers twisted into art, and service trays that glitter with champagne crystal. The room goes black, and all I see is the whiteness.

Only in my mind do I pass through the center of town, pass the store that might be general, pass a steeple that I only admire from the outside. Up above and to my left, a sharp slope leads to a set of train tracks that are silent all but once or twice a month, and this is one of those times. I pass to an underpass, pass the underpass. Birds find refuge from the cold wind under bleeding tracks. Leaves dance under broken black. There's a humming in my head. My hands are numb. The tracks lead to nowhere. They move around, up and over and around again. Back here, sometime ago again. I stand in silence and gaze at the endless portraits etched on slabs of rock and become as limitless as the gloom that pervades their very souls. I hear their wobbling again, the birds. They are laughing, crying maybe. Their tiny feet are glued to the world. Lethargic with the day's work, the birds sit idly by and 'bye' and never 'hi' to the busies of the day. A plane passes overhead, a bus, and then the quiet. A calm now, or maybe just a sequestered agitation. Another leaf, fallen months before it should have, makes it presence known. It hisses, venomous from being told what to be and what not to be. A chill follows, paralyzes my body, subsides, and mounts a comeback. I warm my arms with the motion of a mummy escaping its cocoon. Body alive, but the birds don't care, those miserable shitters. They've followed me all the way here. Let me check my sole.

I miss my Dad.

The envelope opens easily, having practiced this before. An invisible hand begins to write on yellow paper:

The future is entirely up to you.

I hear something running toward me. I look up, turn. The bird is back.

So this is God.

July

Chapter Twenty Eight

'YOU'RE REALLY LEAVING?' Julian asks, lopping the head off a French fry.

'First thing in the morning,' I answer, grabbing the saltshaker in front of him.

'You're finished packing?'

'Yep.' I salt my fries and then push a water glass away from my plate.

'You're really doing it?' Julian asks, amazed by my resolve. I smile back at him. I can't believe it myself. If everything goes to plan, my life will be hauled down four flights of stairs and shipped to Billington tomorrow.

'You called the moving company?' Paul asks.

'This morning,' I answer.

I'm paying some shady Brooklyn company a fortune to help me move. I didn't want to bother my friends, and I can't handle the big stuff on my own, so I had to get movers. I feel a little guilty about it. It's the same guilt I experience whenever I spend seven dollars for a box of Cocoa Puffs. I hate myself every time I leave a supermarket. But I always get over it.

'Are you keeping everything?' Julian asks me.

'Pretty much,' I reply. 'I might throw my mattress out. It's pretty old.'

'Put it on the street. Somebody will take it.' Julian decapitates another fry, double-dips, and watches the torso ketchup-bleed itself to death. 'Did the landlord give you a hard time about leaving?'

'We talked on Wednesday,' I answer. 'He asked me why I was leaving, so I told him, and he said it was fine. He even returned half my security deposit.'

'That never happens,' Julian says.

'*Never*,' Paul adds, stealing a fry off Julian's plate.

'What about work?' Julian asks.

'Fuck work.'

My words explode him into a hard laugh. He calms down enough to ask me whether I gave my notice. To that I respond, 'Not yet,' and I receive an incredulous stare from across the table. 'I thought I'd give them a call Monday morning when I have the free minutes,' I explain.

Julian laughs some more.

'You were always a good trooper,' Paul says, nodding his head and sporting a false 'I'm so proud of you' expression on his face.

'I could go days before anyone noticed that I wasn't in the office,' I let fly. 'Maybe three or four if the entire office decided to give up caffeine for the week.'

'Uh-huh.'

'Seriously, people in that office walk around in a daze. I hate that place.'

When you are kid, you can't wait to have a job. I was eight years old when I decided what I wanted to do with the rest of my life. My father thought my announcement amusing. He reminded me that a fireman is supposed to put out fires, not start them, and then he chased me around the house with a garden hose in his hand. My mom stood there and yelled something about doing whatever I want as soon as I finished my hotdog.

One day you are saving people from burning buildings, the next day you are driving a fucking NASCAR. The sky is the limit. But then you grow up, you start paying bills, and people tell you that you need a career. The next day you are pushing paper across a desk.

Once upon a time, you were quick to decide what you want. Now, you are quick to decide what you *should* have wanted.

A lot of people blame Corporate America, especially the socialists who drink it up at Village speakeasies. They say that Corporate

America is all about making money to consume, and they're right. Corporate America tells us that we need MORE MORE MORE and, in doing so, transform us into work machines. The problem is, no one knows when enough is enough. I'm guilty of it. I buy lots of things I don't need. And as a member of the workforce, I manufacture a lot of things people don't need. It's a vicious cycle. You work to buy from other people who work to buy from you.

I can't claim hatred for Corporate America. That's reserved for my Fourth Street comrades, who grew up on Trotsky bedtime stories. Still, my dissatisfaction is very real to me. I don't know when life started to revolve around making money, but I'm starting to despise it.

I've written and rewritten this conversation in my head so many times that my emotional wrists hurt from carpal tunnel syndrome and I have no choice but to make an appointment with my primary physician to make a later appointment with a specialist. It matters because it affects me. I'm part of it. Corporate America is a choice for all of us.

'I think you're doing the City a great service by leaving,' Julian says with a grin, wrapping his arm over the top of the booth as if to prepare a movie theater move on Paul.

'I agree with him,' Paul adds, joining in on my derision. 'Let's face it. Things are not working out between us.' He flaps his eyelids peacockishly.

'I thought I'd see a few sights, burn some cash,' I explain. 'I want to do a road trip, and for once in my life I can actually do it. The car I bought last weekend is sitting in a lot in Jersey City, waiting for me to pick it up.'

'You're heading to California, aren't you?' Julian asks.

'I'm leaving New York,' I clarify.

He smirks.

'But I never thought it would be under these circumstances,' I add.

'You don't always get to pick your circumstances,' he says, giving the table a knock with his knuckle, trying to wake me out of my drowsy pass to melancholy. 'You have to roll with the punches, give the world the ol' rope-a-dope.'

Paul punches Julian in the arm. The waitress witnesses the assault and gives me a questioning head tilt. 'Children,' I explain. She purses her lips and then offers me a refill. I nod, and she scoots off with my empty glass.

'Are you going to be OK?' Julian asks, suddenly serious, holding up a fry and contemplating another murder.

'Absolutely,' I reply. 'I have nothing going on in this town. I think that's when you have to pick yourself up and go.'

'Maybe,' Paul ponders, rolling around my question with a sip of soda.

'You might think you have nothing,' Julian says, 'but you at least you know what you want. Most people head in circles because they have no compass. They have no idea what they're running to because they're too busy running from something else.'

'That's beautiful,' Paul chimes in.

'You might be right,' I say, 'but I really don't know what I'm heading to. I only know it's not here.'

'Get going then!' Julian instructs.

'Be gone with you!' Paul seconds Julian. 'Here's to dismissal.' He picks up his glass and raises it to toast my exile. Julian meets it in the air with his own glass. I raise the saltshaker in elegant acceptance. We clink and drink in the moment.

'So what about you guys?' I ask, returning my salty beverage to the table. 'Are you going to be OK without me?'

Paul smiles big. 'I decided to take that paralegal job in Midtown,' he announces.

'When do you start?'

'August. Apparently, they need about a month to prepare for me.'

'Nice.' I turn to Julian. 'What about you?'

'I have an interview next week,' Julian says. He brushes something off the table with his hand. 'We'll see what happens.' He does a little 'I dunno' hand gesture. 'Maybe I'll take your job.'

'It's still my job,' I remind him.

'Not for long.'

'You'll find something. Don't worry about it.'

'I'm not,' he answers with a vigorous shake. 'The summer is young, and a few guys from school have tossed around the idea of renting an RV and driving to Myrtle Beach.'

I turn to Paul. 'You'll be sure to deliver that package I gave you?' I ask.

'I have it in my apartment somewhere,' he confirms vaguely.

'Remember, I need it hand-delivered.'

'Alright.'

'OK?'

'I got it, I got it,' he jingles.

'You have the name and address, right?'

'Something shelter, on something and something street.'

'Hardy har har. Make it happen, pal. Screw this one up, and I'll come back just to kick your ass.'

'This is Paul you're talking to,' he says, tapping his chest hard with a finger. 'I said I got it, which means I got it.'

'Good. So you know, I sent both of you something in the mail. Keep your eyes open for it.'

Paul and Julian exchange puzzled looks.

'Something sexy,' I tell them. I take a smug sip of my refill.

Julian gives up on the mystery and nudges me. 'If you say so.'

'It'll be more fun for me if you have to wait,' I explain.

'That still leaves one thing to do.'

'What?' I ask.

Julian slaps his hand on the table, shaking the cubes floating in our glasses. I look over to Paul, who is nodding his head. Back to Julian, who claps his hands together and takes a deep breath.

'What?'

'We can't send you off without a present,' he says, grinning ear-to-ear.

Chapter Twenty Nine

I THOUGHT ABOUT washing my hands in the bathroom, but I decided against it. No one cares about cleanliness when it comes to pit stop sodomy, and this place looks like it does more business than the vendors running a perimeter around Madison Square Garden.

I shatter a Dorito with my teeth. The noise hardly stirs the zombies standing like headstones in front of me.

I'm craving everything orange today. I think about my fourth grade health teacher, Mrs. Sullivan. Eating through a chapter on nutrition, Mrs. Sullivan warned my class that bright-colored food made nations fat. That always stuck with me: 'bright-colored food made nations fat'.

Mrs. Sullivan was one of those happy-go-lucky, hippy teachers who talked more about recycling than reproduction. She hated lecturing, so she never followed the book. She wasn't a big fan of standardized curriculum either, so she let her students pick the class' subject material. Mention something about football, and Mrs. Sullivan would talk about the evils of steroids and cortisone shots. Let out a sneeze, and Mrs. Sullivan would start in on the chemical factories and car manufacturers.

Mrs. Sullivan had no problem discussing the birds and the bees, so the shits in my fourth grade class took advantage of the Q&A at the end of every class to push the envelope. These were the students who found Playboys under their older brothers' mattresses and brought them into school for informal show-and-tell. The kids who sat in their sisters' closets and waited to catch Daddy's little girl doing anything but saving herself for a white wedding. These are the same perverts who probably drew boobs and dicks on the bathroom stalls later on in high school.

My classmates and I wrote the questions on pieces of paper and then dropped them in the fishbowl that Mrs. Sullivan passed around the room. 'It's fine if we laugh with each other, just not *at* each other,' she'd always remind us.

One day I thought I'd ask a question that didn't include the word *penis* or *vagina*. I wrote down the question and dropped the piece of paper in the bowl. It could have been luck that she picked my question, but maybe the pull could be explained by fate. I'm starting to think that such a thing exists.

Mrs. Sullivan looked at my question for a long time. Her lips rolled in tight circles as she read it to herself. After a minute or so, she cleared her throat, took a breath, and read:

Why do doctors say you die when your brain stops working but not when your heart stops working?

I looked around and saw everyone looking at each other. The Friday bell suddenly rang through the walls. As we scrambled to the door, Mrs. Sullivan promised us that she would answer the question the following Monday in class. The next day, as Mrs. Sullivan and my mom chatted on their way to pick up my birthday cake, a man hit a hairpin turn, crossed over the center line, and killed the answer to my question.

The woman at the cash register punches in my Doritos and Mandarin Slice. She asks me whether I want anything else. 'Twenty dollars of gas and a pack of Marlboro Lights,' I tell her.

'What pump?' the woman asks.

I turn back to the door. The bell rings as a man dressed in a red jogging suit enters the store. He picks his nose, real good and deep. 'The pump with the green Cavalier in front of it,' I clarify, pointing.

The attendant lifts the glasses hanging from a string roped around her mole-riddled neck. She looks to be about sixty, and blind as a bat.

'You see it?'

'I do,' she answers, looking through the glasses without resting them on her nose. 'That's pump number two.'

'Twenty on two then. And one of those road maps behind you.'

'That it?' she asks, turning away to grab a Rand McNally.

'Yep.'

'32-86.'

I find two Jacksons in my wallet and exchange the cash for a book of matches. The attendant scraps the bottom of the register tray, realizes she is short, and then picks a Lincoln out of the community tray. 'Where are you heading?' she asks, handing me back my change from forty.

I dig out of my back pocket an index card and a neatly folded piece of yellow paper. I hand over the index card. The cashier looks at the pretty blue cursive. 'Sacramento, California,' the cashier reads.

'Actually, I'm heading to Savannah.'

She hands me back the index card. 'Good luck with that,' she says.

'You know the way?' I ask.

'Head south until you hit a bunch of peach trees.' She cracks a smile that reveals two rows of gold-stained teeth.

'Peach trees, huh. That sounds easy enough.'

'What's in Savannah?'

'Me,' I answer.

She squints out her unconvinced. She wants to know what I'm hiding, but she has a job to do and starts to bag my groceries.

'Should be a good trip,' I tell her.

'Keep your gas tank full, and you'll be fine.'

'What about you?'

'Don't worry about me.' Her night owl eyes widen, and the brackets that frame her mouth elongate obliquely as the rest of her face pushes down on her jaw. 'I'm sure someone is leaving a town in Georgia as we speak,' she explains, 'and whoever that is will balance the scale.' She nods and hands me the bag. 'Have a great night.'

'You too.' I scoop up my bag and start for the door.

'Don't forget the people who know you.'

I turn back around. The cashier is looking down, fidgeting with her glasses.

'What people?' I ask her.

'I think you know the answer to that,' she says. There's a strange sharpness in her crumpled eyes.

'I do?' I ask.

'You sure do,' she replies. 'The people who watched you grow into a man.' She smiles, loving my veil of confusion and loving that she is the only person who can lift it.

'What people?'

'Why, your friendly gas station family of course!' she explodes, smacking the top of the register with her hand. She shows me the gold nuggets filed away in her mouth. She waves, as do I.

* * *

I've decided to stay on I-95 for as long as it will take me. You choose to stay on, but you also choose not to get off. You choose both, whether you know it or not, whether you want to or not. Decisions do not ride alone. They ride together in pairs, both driver and passenger, bi-simultaneously.

But do they both look to the road ahead of you? Are your eyes fixed to the North as five wheels, including the one in your hand, head to the South? Does it only look like you are moving forward because your eyes are stuck up near your brain, far from your feet, your hands, and your heart? What about when you look in the rearview mirror?

When I stepped on life's exercise machine, the world told me to RUN, so I did. And I'm still running. My legs are burning, and my feet are ready to give out on me, but I'm still running. And I think there is something to be said about that. It would be very easy to give up, go limp, and let life pour me right over the edge.

My eyes are fighting a car's high beams. I see nothing but white now, but I know there is more there. I exist, the pedals underneath my foot exist, and the haunting apparition of the past exists. The world is beautiful and ugly, living and dying, but it is not a blank slate. The world I know is my life, and my life is a canvas. And though it has yet to be touched by paint, my canvas has begun to take form. I may not be able to see the scratch marks, but I can definitely *feel* them.

The radio is on, and the window is down as far as it will go, which is about halfway. The needle on my new I LOVE NY compass is flapping back and forth between west and southwest. It can't make up its mind where to go.

And that's just fine by me.

Acknowledgements

FIRST AND FOREMOST, I must acknowledge my chief consultant, the Lord on High, whose divine understanding withheld would have grounded this flight before it had a chance to get up in the air. Kathryn, your support and enthusiasm from the onset will never be forgotten. Ethan, cheers for humoring an earlier draft of this novel. You provided some wicked input. Aaron, thank you for letting me pick your brain at all hours of the night. Leslie, you pushed me to the finish line on this, and I can't thank you enough for that. You truly shook me from a restless slumber. I also need to give a shout out to the writing instructors and teachers who taught me the rules and then encouraged me to break them. I might split infinitives, but I always do it for poetic purposes. And to my friends who continue to sap me of my creative best, I send mad props. You make every day an adventure.

PENTIMENTO

MY DAD ALWAYS begins telephone conversations with a strange question, something in the vane of, 'Dude, where you at?' For a second I buy in to the buddy-buddy precociousness, jump ahead in my mind to a night of beers, late night dining and coffee binging with college comrades until, BANG! I jump back to reality. This is same man who made me drag garbage cans out to the curb for ten years straight. Truth be told, my dad doesn't go to bars, and he doesn't even like beer. And he cut out evening black sludge when a Boston Globe article opened up his eyes to the connection between the evening consumption of coffee and the aggravation of preexisting gastrointestinal problems. The whole process of going out involves noise, fancy footwork, and excess, and my dad can't handle that sort of shit because he's a quiet homebody with a bad leg and a hyperactive colon. And a morning person too, like I said.

He has me repeat his words just to drive home certain key points, making it altogether impossible for me to sleep through his preachy monologues, which are mercilessly delivered without the synoptic aid of scripts. And his soliloquies of sublime purpose would make any seasoned Shakespearean actor keel over in exhaustion. I mean, I could learn to deal with the memorization and the critics, but I could never accept the coercion and the long distance phone bills. I'm too poor and stubborn for that.

Some might think of all this back-and-forth banter between my father and me endearing, even 'cute', but with my father it becomes 'gaga cute', a please-change-my-diaper-I-just-pooped cute. I'm all grown up now, and I need my Sunday mornings to burn off the prior nights' indiscretions and purge the poison in uninterrupted sleep. Weekend phone protocol must be set, and then followed to the T. It's a matter of *my* survival.

My father is 'Jeopardy bright'; he has an exorbitant wealth of knowledge on the most obscure subjects. His brilliance is partly explained by his encyclopedias and watching the Discovery and History channels. This translates well when you happen to be duking it out on Final Jeopardy and are suddenly faced with Cleopatra, her vinegar-dissolved pearls, and her eagerness to prove to her subjects that she can consume a fortune in a single meal. Brilliant that he is, my father uses book smarts to take on everyone and everything. To him, everything has to be proven well beyond a reasonable doubt. He would have made a brilliant prosecutor. My Dad really likes to beat the dead horse, if you know what I mean. I should rephrase that in a form of a question.

I remember those outdoor venues back in Massachusetts, where people would stop over on mass exodus from their enslaved lives for a leg of quail and a loaf of manna. With their ragged blankets and contraband-stuffed backpacks, these self-affirmed nomads would join together in peaceful celebration, fronted by a band of Miriams that led a sing-a-long karaoke jam of eat, drink, and be merry, for *the horse and its rider he has hurled into the sea!* I, in faithful company, partook in the short-lived festivities and snarfed steamed hot dogs, chugged beers supplied by hologram carriers, jumped in on the occasional Hacky Sack circle, and inhaled drags from communal doobies that fell apart in my mouth.

Those days made everyone feel good about life, but that poetic perfection has long since passed. Times have changed. Oklahoma City. 9-11. Psychos now bring along their twisting homemade pipe bombs and twisted antecedent political storylines, much to the delight of the champions of anarchy and hate. Agoraphobes and sociophobes no longer require validation of their respective neuroses. Now, you can't even walk into a place with a Swiss Army knife on your belt. Everything has been ruined for us mildly law-abiding citizens.

OK, maybe not *everything*. My fading hippocampus has a habit of dumping memory contents on to the floor, and like a parent whose infant refuses to swallow a meal, I am losing patience cleaning up the same mess. Over and over I cram faces, stories, and experiences into a steadily decreasing number of file cabinet drawers. And I've found that life simplifies as your number of drawers decreases. Movies, bus rides, and life become GOOD, BAD, or OK. I keep my wordage clean, crisp, specific and relevant. They say Shakespeare used about thirty thousand words. Well, guess what? I just used seven. What a silly man, that Shakespeare.

Diminution considered, there are consequences for not holding on to memory drawer specificity. Human faces undergo cosmetic alteration, relived experiences become more bland or exciting than their originals, and the past slanders in its retelling. The cost of my laziness is excessive generality, a colorlessness that starts with memory recollection and proliferates, spreading to all hangars of life. 'It tastes like chicken.' 'Yeah, she's nice.' 'It was OK.' So on and so forth.

Anywho. I picked up "anywho" from Annie. She says it a lot. Whenever she does, her lips pucker into a little ball and her face takes on the appearance of someone sucking on a straw, struggling to get at the last bit of liquid from an invisible glass.

Good dreams look and feel real. Unfortunately, the unconsciousness has a habit of slipping hyper-fantasy into my dreams, a kind of awakening Transylvanian fang. As they go on, my dreams become more and more ridiculous, to the point of burlesque, loose cannon vaudeville, enough to remind me that I'm asleep. The impossible becomes possible, the improbable probable, and the tap-dancing bear finally shows up (and he always does), at which point I usually get out of the water and find a towel because the whole thing is much too strange to continue.

When I hit the lottery, I'm going to buy a Lincoln Town Car and have a mini-bar installed in it. And hire a driver who speaks monosyllabically.

Fortunately, you don't *need* a car in the City. It may be the only place in the world where you can have your life hand-delivered to you—for a price, of course.

The City is built and rebuilt to keep its residents locked within its borders, and that is why it is entirely possible to live in one of its tribal neighborhoods your entire life without ever leaving it.

Unlike children, adults do their homework before rubbing elbows with a complete stranger. Why? If a grown man isn't careful, he might inadvertently invite a poor lughead or a rich snob to a holiday barbecue and then have to spend an entire afternoon reaching uncomfortably for neutral topics like the weather—or the weather.

Bugs don't bother me so much, unless they brazenly introduce themselves to my bare feet, in which case I usually give a critter a two minute head start before sending it on a waterslide ride to the East River or to wherever my toilet pipe ends.

Decision making: it's a ticklish matter. One day you are sitting naked in your apartment having a one-sided bitch fest with your television, or walking around aimlessly in a closed mall, or painting a toilet bowl with what you think will be your last meal, and suddenly you decide that what you have—rather, what you *are*—simply will not suffice. Ding! Light bulb. Ah ha! Revelation. 'That's it!' you yell. 'I've had it!' Full of self-importance, you call for a monumental decision and the vow goes public. You want 'it', something new, something better. And with that the intake valve opens, the piston slides down, the engine sips a cylinder of air and gasoline, the piston shoots up and compresses the mixture (which shortly thereafter meets the spark of a plug and explodes), the piston drops and the exhaust valve opens. And with the crankshaft turning, the wheels of change begin turning. You are *moving*, being proactive, diligently searching and seeking 'it'.

Lofty dreams, New Year's resolutions, proclamations from the gutter—any of this ring a bell? Uh-huh. Don't we all have our days of indestructibility when we think that lying down on a set of railroad tracks will stop a war? You grab a week's supply of angel dust and a copy of *Born on the Fourth of July*, and three hours later you are marching the streets of Washington, waving your *Sunset Scenes from the Pacific* calendar on a pike, singing 'Kumbaya' all the way to the Reflecting Pool.

I'm as clueless as the next guy surviving on Easy Mac and Ritalin. I'm living my early twenties half sober, half complacent. I am ordinary, all but extraordinary.

My father's undying take on nose versus mouth: 'It's better for the lungs.' He may have been right, but no proctologist or any other doctor in the world ever had to smell biological exhaust like what poured out of the back of the Whitman's wagon. My father's argument became moot when Death began tapping its familiar beat on the door.

Our height markings continued to climb to the ceiling (crayon, marker, colored pencil), and we graduated out of the treating of Halloween and into its tricking, finding creative uses for pumpkins and jumbo eggs and, in the process, making those bone-headed troublemakers from *Animal House* look like a bunch of Julia Child wannabes. We dubbed sneaking out of houses, flattening pennies on the railroad tracks, and breaking beer bottles with baseball tosses their own sciences.

As to the three of us and our cookie-cutter behavior, my father found it slightly unsettling. I didn't mind 'The Game', as my father put it. It wasn't as if I were forced to do everything that Paul and Julian did. I wasn't trapped in an endless game of Simon Says or stuck on the line of a foosball squad. Paul and Julian were my best friends, and we were just kids, and kids always copy each other to fit in. 'I know you are, but what am I?' is what kids do to survive being kids.

But we succumbed to rising levels of testosterone, left our Big Wheels and Dyno Riders to rot in cellars and garages, and attempted to pick up girls with dope four-wheel rides. The three of us now look at the world in very different ways. We have changed with time. We *are* changing with time.

For two years I lived in the sky courtesy of NYU, peering out of my carved-out Mesa Verde bedroom window, counting the cotton balls soaking up the liquid blue sky and wondering whether my studies could wait another couple of hours. I felt like a worker ant bed on a hill, pressing on without knowing who and where the queen was.

I should be taking advantage of this and enjoying it. I should be sucking it up, fighting the hangover, playing in fruitless Strawberry Fields and acting like one of those perfect prairie kids from the movies my grandfather used to watch.

I search in my pocket for my cell. Technology is a bloody curse. I spend half the day walking around with this hunk of plastic fastened to the inside of my thigh. It pokes and turns and rubs and sticks out like a little pet trying to escape the bed sheet thrown over its head. It is annoying, but you tolerate it because its practicality far outweighs its inconvenience. Like that guy who gets to tag because he buys everyone drinks at the bar.

When I first laid eyes on Ronnie, all wrapped up like a mummy and such, I almost fainted. I expected the worst to happen to me—cops, the full weight of the law, freelance hit men bought off with the lunch money that Ronald had mugged away from other students. I sat down and readied for a counterstrike of Soviet nuclear magnitude, putting my head down on my desk and squeezing its metal legs until my hands drained of McCarthy blood.

And there is another reason to be thankful that my parents didn't choose to be Catholics. Had the grim reaper decided to pay a visit to a Catholic 158 Apple Lane on that damp September day, I would have been absolutely screwed, as the state of my salvation surely would have been up in the air at the time.

We have always wanted the freedom to move. We dream of mind-boggling feats like time-travel and teleportation, two superpowers that I've coveted since I was old enough to realize that I had been shortchanged on motoring skills. We pine for what our superheroes have. We live vicariously through plastic-sheathed, fifty-cent comic books and low-budget science fiction movies. Be these powers obtainable or not, they are the root from which we humans derive our dreams and validate our reasons to dream. They give us imaginary wings to soar above our own imprisoned realities.

If I were a politician (and Heaven forbid that to happen), I'd build my platform on a program to develop lightning-fast time portal travel as quickly as possible. It would be a hard position to take, I know. There are all sorts of crazies out there trying to slow down the world, most of them Old Guard Republicans or oil monarchs, who quietly conspire to hinder supersonic travel development. Just when you think it is time for General Motors and Ford to begin rolling out vehicles with thousand-miles-per-second speedometers, some disheveled scientist with half his teeth missing arrives in Washington, testifies his bought-out ass before Congress, and with little effort convinces legislators that such technological advances are dangerous because "the integrity of the universal time continuum could be compromised, creating consequences of the most catastrophic kind."

My AFS quirk is a strict adherence to the systematic analysis of facts. Think until you can think no more. Think until the answer arrives. *Think.* Ironically, I have found that it is emotion and not logic that usually fuels my final moments of deliberation, which are inevitably tied to the moment of action. The more I think over a decision, the more I find myself drawn to unproven emotional hunches and repelled by the hard cold facts which I had once cherished as the only truths in a world cluttered with fictional garbage. I've come to understand that real life is a variegating mixture of thought and feeling, and as much as I want to believe it to be the contrary, I know that real life isn't an algorithmic formula.

Life on the bottom of the intellectual chain sounds all refreshingly simple, but I've discovered that ultra-pragmatism lends itself to reductionist views on issues that have no simple answers. I mean, I loved my parents, but what did they know about Ronald and the Axis of Evil? Very little, obviously. You'd think that time would have changed this. But a minute passes, and the flight attendant ignores you on her last trip down the aisle with the drink cart, and there you go—the decision to not quench your thirst is made for you.

Don't worry, such is life, not a problem, don't sweat it, they tell me. "The wisest man knows when it's best to say and do nothing," and I wet my tongue and think, *Go ahead and say nothing, do nothing, exalt the intellectualization of non-action, and live your life in the lens of an electron microscope.* Total crap. These stoic idiots don't have the first flying-fuck clue. Their words and actions are sloth. I hear craven post-justification. I hear self-damnation. Deadly Sinner shit. Pope St. Gregory the Great, St. John Cassian, Dante, and C.S. Lewis hear the same thing. We call them "sinners" because they "sin" against the nature of humanity. They take the obligations that bind them to humanity—namely, choice and mobility—and sever them. Disregarding choice and movement as legitimate functions of the human temple *is* a sin.

I think of the faraway places that I've never visited but have flagged in my mind for future investigation. I imagine myself an ocean separated, in an unknown land filled with terrestrial wonder and supernatural mystery.

The sky is empty, the living green thick and endless. Nude body stretches for miles, transforming a ruddy inland stretch into a white sandbar. Standing patiently in line, I await my moment to touch 'it', and inherit a divine blessing, and—Oh shit, what is Ted doing here? Seriously, is this guy stalking me? Look at him! He's wearing that bloody suit of his! Well, at least he's clothed. Speaking of clothes—

Either way, I could change them, restore order. I still have that fluorescent vial of pheromone I bought on St. Mark's Place. The hideous crone told me to wear it around my neck to ward off evil spirits, but I know an occultist's aphrodisiac when I see one.

More people press through the door, conversely pressing out oxygen and spatial comfort. One drink has turned into another, and another, and another. They disappear as though my stomach owned them before I stepped foot into this place. Glory glory, I keep the pace steady. I never break out of the drinking box quickly. I'm a tortoise strategist with a hare's natural skill. I'm a drinking PhD. I drink slowly and consistently and savor the process of inexpensive intoxication.

Julian talks us into a departing lemon drop. A shot down the hatch, and we skedaddle, dumping out on to the sidewalk with a wonderful burn in our throats.

People come and go like farts in the wind. They arrive from nowhere, make a stink, and then pass away, dispersed by the cleansing filter of time. The emissions that I partied with in NYU dorms or on the beaches of Key West have disappeared into oblivion, and I could give a shit about most of them. There are disposable as diapers. I fling and forget them.

I suppose you don't need a gym to get in shape. You could just adopt a Rocky Balboa exercise regime: run the stairs of federal buildings and the like. But I think you have to pay to run in a marathon, and homeless people don't have the money for that sort of thing. And I can't see paying for a view from a bridge anyway. It just doesn't make any sense. I'm sure registration for a marathon costs a lot more than a ticket to the Empire State Building's observatory deck.

Styrofoam trays of sundried tomatoes, snow peas, pole beans, garlic cloves, and herbs of parsley, oregano and rosemary, all individually shrink-wrapped with clear plastic and branded with a white barcode sticker. Spared from the rains, the floodwaters. Dry, not wet. Firm, not soft. Vegetables of noble birth, deserving of noble burial. The regality of it wants me to drop to my knees and kiss the floor, slurp up the one-part-bleach-to-four-parts-water.

The only person I've known to spend more time in a supermarket is my mother. For hours my mother used to push around a cart with her cookie tin of coupons wedged in its baby seat, and vocally math out the number of UPC symbols she still needed before she could mail away for that Betty Crocker recipe book. When my nagging grew intolerable, she'd dangle a gummy worm in the air, and I'd jump up and snag it like a fish with a taste for acrobatic showmanship. She always knew how to shut me up.

They found a loophole in the Chinese Exclusion Act and all the other legislation that Congress had passed to curb immigration and alleviate the tensions created by the influx of inexpensive foreign labor into the States: money.

Political analysts claim that it was Jeb who eked out Florida for his brother George, but I believe that it was the retirement home unions that saw beyond Gore's 'lockbox' fluff, hit the voting booths early and often with Texas Justice on the mind, and made a bumbling Yale graduate the leader of the free world. I can only imagine what would have happened had the insomniacs joined my father and the retirees. Germany, circa 1942.

I remember the morning of my Driver's License road test, when I awoke just before six o'clock in the morning and began practicing in my head lefts and rights, stops and parallel parking maneuvers. It seemed a silly thing to do at the time, not knowing what my course would be in advance and all, but now that I think about, that might have been the most productive morning of my entire life. I ended up passing that test with flying colors. That afternoon I could have jumped the instructor's blue Honda on top of a moving trailer truck, glided to a full stop, dropped into a one-and-a-half somersault twist, and stuck the landing between two parked SUVs. You'd think that I would have taken something away from that experience, but I can't justify making a radical lifestyle change simply because I had one morning success story.

They talk about how Corporate America is wiping the struggling man pursuing life, liberty, and the pursuit of happiness from the face of The Declaration of Independence. They tell me to be careful about sending in my cable bill check because I might send it to the wrong address. They say it's because companies can't figure out when they are merging, acquiring, breaking up, getting back together, renaming themselves, spinning off, filing for bankruptcy, emerging or liquidating—simply because they are too busy counting pennies on their stock prices.

BVG